THE HIVE

Richard W. Black

THE HIVE

DOUBLE DRAGON

Prologue

The moonlight cast a gentle blue hue across the forest giving the land a fairytale appearance. The woodland creatures went about their nocturnal activities as if nothing were different; the world was as it had always been. There was peace. It was an illusion.

Above the tree line sat the menacing peak of the Hive reaching into the night sky. It stood 50 stories above the highest treetop like a sinister forbidden mountain none would dared climb. Even in the dark of night much was happening around it. Waspoids fluttered about in a buzz of activity. These wasp-like, six-legged creatures with torsos of various colors and humanoid-type faces were more than giant insects. They operated hover vehicles that entered and exited openings in the outer walls, carried tools and weapons, nature and science in apparent harmony. Advanced beings with a purpose, build the Hive.

Entering the Hive past brown Waspoid armed guards, there was even more taking place within the brightly lit honeycombed interior. Waspoid workers distinguished by their tan bodies were busy at their tasks; building, unloading, moving. The colony was a never-ending place of work, order and responsibility.

Deep under the multi-layered structure was a room of subdued light. On a large slab lay the Oracle, set apart from the other Waspoids by her smaller wings and light blue body. The wings could not support her weight were she to attempt to fly. But she did not, would not. Her curse was to be completely dependent on the Hive as the Hive must rely on her to survive. From the shadows, the tan worker Waspoids fluttered out and back as they saw to her needs.

The General entered flanked by his aides and floated across to her, he and those under his command were brown in color. Out of reverence, they removed their weapons before entering. Though the General was comfortable in her presence, his aides were not and kept back out of awe and fear.

His tone was respectful but firm, his speech a cross between buzzing and the spoken word to human ears. "Oracle, I am told that you do not eat. You must maintain your strength. Please take nourishment. I beg you."

"For what purpose, General?" moaned the Oracle. "I have seen the creature again. It was most unpleasant. Numbered are the days of the Hive. We are doomed on this cursed world."

The General winced at the defeat he heard in her voice and regretted immediately having brought his aides. They were too young and too impressionable to understand that this revered one had periods of contentment but mostly wallowed in the bad she saw in her visions.

"Perhaps we shall yet defeat it?" he responded hopefully.

But the Oracle merely laughed a mirthless laugh.

"That is the soldier speaking," she said. "It is your task to fight for the Hive. But I was not birthed as you. I can only do the task that is mine to perform."

"The Queen does not share your interpretation of the visions. If she is correct, we will need your skills to build the power of the Hive. I implore you again; take nourishment for the sake of the Hive."

"I shall try, General."

The General bowed and retreated from the room, his duty fulfilled.

Movement in the darkness caught her attention. Something had just entered her chamber. It had come from outside, far, far away. The Oracle was not alone as a shadowy figure lurked, watched, waited. It was human.

The creature strained to make out the features of the insect's face from where he thought himself concealed but the room was too dark and the shadows too long. His eyes, the only part of him visible in the dim light were filled with fear.

Abruptly, the Oracle shuttered causing the workers to fly away the then fluttered back to her to resume their tasks as though nothing had happened.

"Leave me," she commanded them harshly.

Obediently, they complied and she was alone, almost.

She scanned the room with more than just her eyes, for not just her wings were limited but also her physical sight. It was that sense, the ability to see with her mind that located his presence, it was indeed human. Her gaze rested on a shadowy spot where she could make out his silhouette. The intruder was not a danger to her, not as yet.

"I know you are there though these frail eyes cannot quite see you," she said to the shadows. "I can feel you, Liberator."

The human stepped from the darkness just enough that his face was visible.

The Oracle fought the dread and foreboding he caused in her but instead, presented a bold attitude in the presence of the human.

"Yes, I feel your presence," she responded to the questioning eyes. "You do not belong in our world. Leave before our Queen tastes your blood. Stay in your world. There is safety for you there."

She knew, sensed that, for the present, this creature feared her, feared the Hive. As long as that fear remained there was hope. She had one weapon.

"You have no power to liberate," she buzzed.

The human cautiously approached the Waspoid and his close proximity to her sent a sense of terror through her being. Her natural reaction was the flap her wings. For a normal Waspoid it would have prompted escape or attack. But for the Oracle and her feeble wings it meant only that the flutter created a chirping sound that caused the human beast to recoil.

Chirp, chirp, chirp...

Chapter 1

Chirp, chirp, chirp...

Wham, Barney Berry woke from his nightmare and swatted the alarm.

"The Oracle," he whispered. She was new to his nightmares. A bug with a human face. This time he saw the creature so closely that he saw her features. She was so real, so very real that he thought he was watching a real person...a real being. When would they end? In fact, the dreams were becoming worse. That face...

Chirp, chirp, chirp...

Crap! He had hit the snooze alarm. Whap, this time he switched it off.

How he hated that monster. Through slit eyes, he tried to focus on the numbers. He knew already what they said; 6:40.

Melissa McDay, the lump beside him, did not move.

"Hey," he whispered but not too softly. Still, the lump remained. He considered touching her, his hand hovered over her shoulder. His brain reminded him of the last time he touched his wife and his cold hands against her warm skin brought such a reprimand, and no lovemaking, which was the original intent. Instead, his hand fell to her side just close enough to feel her silky negligee.

It was probably best. Love was drifting away from them and he was clueless on how to bring it back. 6:41, he needed to get moving before he was late for work.

He struggled out of bed, shuffled to the bathroom, glanced at the pathetic figure in the mirror then plopped down on the toilet. He no longer peed like a man in his own apartment. It was easier to do his business from the sitting position than it was to listen to his wife complain about the urine stains on the side of the bowl. He did not know where his backbone was living these days but it was not at 123 High Park Terrance that was for sure. However, he refused to admit that it was considerably easier to urinate sitting down in the mornings and there were times when he actually caught an extra wink of sleep. Then he found himself in the shower and the hot water soothing his bruised ego and warming his cold body.

The razor did its usual nasty job on his face as he fought for that smooth skin with the overly-priced instrument of torture and its three blades. All the while he wondered how those models with the chiseled good looks managed to pull the thing across their faces without scraping off skin. Anyway, it was a good morning, no cuts or nicks but there were patches that were less than smooth.

In the bedroom on the way to the walk-in closet, he noticed the lump was gone and hoped for a cup of coffee waiting for him in the kitchen. Breakfast was out of the question but coffee was a possibility. He picked out a dark blue suit from a rack of dark blue suits, selected a shirt and tie, slipped on polished shoes then made for the kitchen and coffee.

In the hallway, Barney wondered why he set himself up for disappointment. The odds were that he would have to make the coffee or purchase an overpriced cup of not-so-great brew from the corner coffee shop on his way to work.

Yep, Melissa sat at the counter in her bathrobe with her silky long blonde hair, beautiful features and gorgeous body but with an empty coffeemaker beside her and an empty cup in hand.

He managed to catch himself before he commented on how she could have made the coffee while he was in the bathroom but decided today was not the day for a fight. Instead, he made the coffee and flipped on his electronic tablet while he waited.

Unfortunately, he made his first mistake of the day by clicking on the link to the job website where his resume was posted. The list of new want ads popped up and he scrolled down it.

Melissa sighed loudly.

Barney continued to review the ads while he unconsciously poured coffee into two cups.

Melissa sighed, again, louder.

He sipped the coffee and savored the taste. He made a fine cup of coffee and resented that she was adding flavored creamer and sweetener...

Crap! He goofed by looking over at her as he assumed that she would be doctoring his magnificent brew. She was not. Nope, she was glaring at him.

"We're not going through another job crisis, are we?" she chided him.

The want ads, he forgot how they riled her up in the mornings. He should have waiting to look at them in the subway. He started to sigh and caught himself. What he could not do was stop his idiotic mouth from saying what was on his mind.

"I hate my job," he said.

"Everyone hates their job, Barney. It's the American way."

"You don't. You love selling those six-figured properties and making those big commissions."

"You're just jealous because this year I might make more money than you."

"I hate my life. I feel worthless."

Oh, that was a poor choice of words.

"I'm part of that life," she snapped. "Do you hate me?"

He wanted to say no. That was what he was supposed to say.

"I had another nightmare..."

"So every time you have a nightmare, I must endure another flurry of job searching? We need your income to reach our financial goals. The condo we're looking at will run us over a million. Then we'll have to decorate it. Vacation will be here before you know it."

"Is that all life is to you?" he demanded. Okay, if she wanted a fight, he would give her a fight. "Bigger house, make more money, buy more stuff, go to the right parties?"

"I'm sick and tired of these bad dreams. I keep telling you, it's because you eat M&Ms or some other unhealthy junk before going to bed. Just stop doing it and the dreams will go away," she retorted.

"M&Ms? Listen, the nightmares are so real that I think I'm actually there, in person. Last night..."

"Tell me you don't talk to anyone else about these dreams?" Melissa interrupted. "Please tell me that. Phobias and psychoanalysts are no longer in fashion."

That was the way Melissa McDay fought. She never responded to criticism of her but forced him to constantly defend himself.

"No. I didn't... I don't..." That always frustrated Barney. And she always caused him to make the cardinal sin of couple's fighting, the personal attack. "And I certainly didn't mean to inconvenience your life."

It did not help that his tone was dripping in sarcasm.

"What's that supposed to mean?"

"Nothing. I'm just tired." Barney retreated. The only thing left to do was surrender.

"Sometimes I wonder just how much you love me," she snapped.

The problem was that, very often, Melissa did not accept surrender and refused to take prisoners. She wanted total victory.

"What?"

He spilled coffee over his hand and the counter. She waited until he had the paper towel to clean it up.

"Love, Barney. You know, that expression of affection two people show each other."

"Wow! This is...unexpected."

"Why? Why would it be unexpected? You know, I can't remember you ever telling me that you loved me."

"And, you've told me you love me?"

Barney learned long ago that a man should never get caught in a discussion with a woman about love. It was a no-win proposition. Yep, he certainly learned long ago, he just never learned to apply what he had learned.

"I most certainly have!"

"How?"

"I show you, that's how."

"Show me? How have you shown me that you love me?" Barney demanded.

Oops, he forgot the litany of reasons she always threw back at him when they got into the love argument.

"Are you forgetting that my father's connections gave you your job? I've always tried to motivate you." Melissa ticked them off like a list chiseled in stone. "Pushed you to succeed. Wanted you to be the best employee Baxter Life ever hired. Turned this drab apartment into a fashionable home."

She glanced at the tablet with distain and he knew the end and his complete defeat were on the horizon.

"How do you show your love for me?" her demanding voice echoed in his head.

Barney sighed, unable to answer, and switched from the want ads to the sports websites like any real man would do in the morning. She smiled, the argument won.

"I have to attend a closing for the Breadon apartment then mother and I are going shopping," she announced using her triumphant tone.

"Shopping?" he wanted to say with a great deal of indignant righteousness but did not. He had lost the right with his surrender.

Chapter 2

The tunnel interior flashed past the car that bounced and bumped its way to the next stop. Barney Berry rode in it like a sardine among the other commuters packed into the subway car. Then he shuffled along with the mob up out of the earth and onto an equally crowded sidewalk where he could see the monument to the insurance industry rising high above the other structures. So long as he was moving with the flow, he could hunker down to his own personal self-pity party but, eventually, he had to fight his way against the stream until he made it safely to the entrance of his workplace, the Baxter Life Building.

It was the building that profits built, tall and imposing over the city as it was in the business where it ruled with absolute power and might.

The tall and massive structure housed the company that a fear of the future and poor financial planning had created; Baxter Life Insurance Company was its official name. Everyone within and without of the company called it Baxter Life. Years of profiting from people who used insurance as a means to assure an inheritance for their family meant the company could construct a mammoth stone and steel structure that reached high above the city skyline and blotted out the sky. There was no more impressive building in the city. Below, thousands of employees dressed in the garb that befitted their jobs streamed in. Those attempting to ascend to the higher floors were appropriately dressed in dark suits for men and bland, shapeless versions of the suit for the women. Employees with less lofty aspirations wore clothing suitable to their place in the pecking order. At an exclusive car park entrance to the side, limousines deposited the lords and ladies who ruled from the top floors. Above, a helicopter landed on the heliport to deposit the queen at her hive.

The building's shadow loomed over Barney from the point where he left the subway entrance all the way to the front doors.

Inside the building was symmetry, choreographed activity that all had a purpose, profit. Each worker bound for his or her space, the place where they would create commerce, was a necessary link in the well-organized harmonious community. A hive, a planned and organized chaotic dance.

It was nearly eight o'clock so the lobby was filled with Barney's fellow workers all trying to arrive at their desks at the same time, the hour they were required to begin their tasks. One of the ironies of the corporate life was that no one had ever considered staggering employee work hours to trim commuting time. Which was why Barney was in a line of people crowding into elevators then, finally packed among them in the box, lifted up. On the 10th floor, he wiggled his way out onto his section of the hive, an open space of office cubicles already buzzing with activity.

"Hello hell," he muttered and trudged through the maze to his old familiar workspace.

Barney glanced at the clock. Flush mounted into the light gray wall, it blended in, a natural part of the business environment. Mostly, it was his adversary, advancing like a snail, in no hurry, going no place. He sighed. The thing controlled his life, dicing it up into little increments. Even when he was not at the office, it dominated every aspect of his existence. Tick, tock, the minute hand slid gradually to two minutes shy of the hour. He blinked. Nothing changed. The slow methodical arch of the sweep second hand started another round. Again, he sighed and dragged his poor self to that familiar three-and-a-half walled area human resources called his office. An L-shaped desk consumed one-and-a-half walls, a file cabinet rested in the corner, a chair for visitors and his worn swivel chair made up the furnishings, all a shade of gray.

A mountain of reports sat in his inbox. They contained lines and lines of data, meaningless to all except a trained eye. And Barney had eyes trained to cipher the meaning of the symbols, breaking them down into words and numbers. He slid into the chair, switched on his computer and pulled the first report from the stack. Thunk, it lay in front of him. The computer blinked on and he signed in with his latest password while praying that it had not expired. Every six weeks he had to think of a new one that met the criteria of the sadist nerds in IT then he had to remember what is was. Thankfully, the password worked, the day had begun.

He took the 12" metal ruler from his desk drawer he used to assist his experienced eyes in following the symbols across the page and laid it on the first line to be considered.

Then he looked up to the computer screen sitting 24" away. The information matched. He placed a check mark on the paper and pressed a key on his keyboard. On the screen the next cell was highlighted. Barney sighed.

His workspace in gray section was confined to five-foot high gray cubicle walls which matched the bland gray of his furniture. The carpet was a gray Berber weave and clear mats strategically placed in high traffic areas and under chairs protected it from wear. Gray section was designed by researchers who would never work in such a plain environment.

There was a light blue section, tan section and a faded, muted yellow section on the 10th floor.

Chatter, a low level of human voices, phones and general activity drifted over his short walls in a never-ending, mind-numbing stream.

With his mind in a kind of neutral, Barney slogged through the report. When he finished it, he placed it in his outbox and dared glance at his mortal enemy. The clock said that he had worked for over two hours. Coffee time.

Barney grabbed his coffee mug, the one he bought in the Caribbean with the birds and palm trees on the side. He liked it because it was larger than a regular mug so he could indulge his taste for coffee and it reminded him of his life before Melissa. The Caribbean vacation was the last he took as a free man. It was supposed to be his last big splurge before he gave his notice and started to live a real life of adventure. Two months later he met Melissa. One year later they had somehow managed to get married. The year from meeting her to marriage was a blur, if not a complete incomprehensible puzzle.

It started innocently enough.

The party was dull, no, really, really boring. The apartment was so large that it was not difficult to slip away from the other guests so he did. The music drifted to where Barney sat in the kitchen along with a myriad of assorted conversations. He nursed a drink and wondered why he was still there. Over the rim he spotted the most beautiful woman he had ever seen through the back entrance acting very strange. She was on the floor behind a large potted fern and had a drink of some type that appeared to be a slushy which she sipped with a straw. Occasionally, she glanced back down the hallway into the main room. She had blonde hair, gorgeous eyes and a killer figure. Not model skinny but what was once known as an hourglass figure. She oozed sensual sexuality.

He approached her. He was slightly hammered. That was the only way he would have ever done so since he thought that this woman was way out of his league.

"You look like you're hiding," he slurred slightly as he dropped beside her.

"Perceptive," she replied, her tone suggested that she was bored and uninterested in him.

But then, he was under the influence of his beverage and beyond being inhibited.

He glanced down the hallway where the party was still going strong.

"Why don't you leave?"

She signed. "You want to know the truth?"

"Nope," he interrupted her. "Lie to me."

"What?"

"Lie to me." He took a long drink. "I am a cost accountant. You couldn't make up a more tedious job leading to a dreary life if you tried. I could use some excitement in an otherwise very boring life."

He raised his glass, "So lie to me and make your story worthwhile or I will kill myself."

She stared at him for a minute then burst out laughing. It was a beautiful laugh. He could have sat there on the floor and listened to it all night.

Finally, she offered her hand, "Melissa McDay."

He took it. That soft, smooth hand came with a gentle whiff of a perfume. "Barney Berry," he managed as he drank in the aroma of her scent.

Like a fool, he kept the hand longer than he should have then his eyes followed hers and he realized that he still had it. He did not want to release it. Embarrassed, he eventually let her have it back.

Then she asked him what he did.

Before he could stop himself, he poured out every detail of the most boring job imaginable and she laughed. He told her about his dream of living on the edge as an artist but saw immediately that it did not impress her. What did make an impression on her was his advancement potential at Baxter Life. Insurance companies ruled the city; their executives were part of the exclusive upper-class society of formal parties, theater tickets and exclusive events frequented by the stars of music, entertainment and politics. He would later discover that she lusted after inclusion into that world.

They slipped out of the party and had coffee at one of those trendy places that served it well into the night.

Melissa was so beautiful, poised and personable that Barney could not help falling in love with her. She was exciting and a little bit dangerous with her lust for life and determination to accomplish all she wanted to achieve.

He was so infatuated that he once again set aside his career plans.

Barney intended to quit working at Baxter Life, draw cartoons and animated features fulltime and market them on the Internet. He had saved enough money that, if he lived frugally, he had three years to succeed in making a living with his art. However, when he felt the negative vibes from her, he quietly shelved them. He could not, would not lose the chance to be with this woman for the want of the career as an artist. Anyway, he reasoned, he could always come back to that idea once Melissa got to know him and discovered where his heart lay.

He could not have been more wrong.

Melissa's ambitions became Barney's curse. That excitement and lust for life meant that every weekend there was something to do and Barney was expected to do them with her. Parties of all types, exhibitions at art galleries, fundraisers for politicians and the list went on. She set her sights on penetrating the society of the insurance executives and their spouses. In this city, that was the highest social level for which a person could aspire. It was their money, really. Artists were searching for patrons to sponsor them, politicians for donors to give to their campaigns and everyone else just wanted to tap into the wealth.

As Melissa saw it, Barney was two promotions from executive status and then just one promotion from the top floor. It was a five-year plan.

The first time he heard the timeframe, Barney was heartsick.

He worked fifty hours minimum a week, his weekends were consumed with Melissa's endless events which left him very little time for his hobby. Hobby? That was all his drawings had become, a hobby. And a guilty pleasure. How many nights did he face the glares of his wife when he slipped into his office to draw and not to work for Baxter Life?

When they moved into the grossly overly-priced apartment condo, Melissa proudly showed him the spare room and the reason why she had selected it. Well, other than its fashionable address. The room was to become his office where he could work nights. That way, he could bring his work home where they could be together. While he worked on his Baxter Life career, she networked. What a team, she declared. Although, she was terribly disappointed when he moved a drawing desk into the office.

And Barney was too much in love with her to deny her anything within his power. He could not know how little power he really had to give her what she wanted.

So here he was, at the job.

Spinning his chair around, Barney was about to spring for the break room when Jeffrey St. Clair was in his face and invading his workspace.

"Happy Monday, Barney, my boy," pronounced Jeffrey with that annoying grin and clueless expression. The guy could be falling off the roof of the twenty-story Baxter Life building and find joy in the trip down to the pavement.

Baxter Life was Jeffery St. Clair's first job out of college. He had the social pedigree and proper Ivy League degree to slide into a sweet position at a prestigious company with a very nice salary. He bought into the sales pitch by the human resource manager of Baxter Life that advancement for someone as talented as Jeffery would be rapid. But there were dozens like Jeffery at Baxter Life. The company collected them, used them but promotions were rare. There were simply not enough executive positions for all of them. It was the ruthless, driven and determined ones who advanced. The rest found they were trapped in unfulfilling jobs they could not quit because of the money. They would spend the rest of their lives making Baxter Life very profitable all the while dying slowly.

Barney shot young Jeffery a bored stare. "Monday? That explains why I feel like I'm going to hurl my cookies."

But perky Jeffrey would have none of it. "Come on, ma'man, let's start the day on a happy note."

"This place sucks, Jeffrey," replied Barney. "We're no better than wasps in a hive, performing our menial little tasks for the good of the collective."

"Wasps in a hive? Where did that disturbing image come from?"

It was a commentary on Barney's life that Jeffrey was his only friend at Baxter Life. And friend was stretching it. Jeffrey was part of a group of guys with whom Barney once hung out. They went to lunch, drinks after work and did the occasional guy-stuff together on weekends. Melissa had put an end to that. Jeffrey was the only one willing to make an effort to stay connected with Barney. And not that Barney blamed the other men. After a few dozen times when he had to beg off from stopping at the sports bar for Monday night football or pool at O'Shay's, well, they just gave up on him. And what could Barney Berry say; my wife has another social trajectory for me?

"No, seriously, where did you get that metaphor?" persisted Jeffrey.

"Melissa. Every time I so much as bring up the possibility of changing jobs, she goes ballistic."

He headed for the break room with Jeffrey right with him.

"Why would you want to? We're part of the most profitable insurance company in the world," said Jeffrey. "And to show their appreciation, they pay us above-average salaries. We are the envy of the industry."

And great coffee, thought Barney. They were in the Baxter Life 10th floor break room with its industrial quality coffee makers. There was the machine that had pre-measured servings of some of the best coffee in the world including Roasted Arabian Dark. Then there was the large quantity one, push the button and it automatically brewed up a pot for meetings and groups. What frustrated Barney to no end was how people could take the last of the pot and not bother to brew another one. The pot scorched and had to be washed out or the coffee tasted burned. Consequently, even though the

24

pot contained brewed the best coffee, he routinely made the single serving.

"Money isn't everything," replied Barney as he inserted the little container for one serving into the machine. "You can't buy happiness."

He watched the black delight pouring into his mug and considered correcting that statement but thought better of it and put another serving container in the machine. His Caribbean mug held two delicious servings.

"Oh, please," snorted Jeffrey. "You just haven't tried hard enough."

Jeffrey did not drink coffee. He was selecting a beverage from the well-stocked refrigerator Baxter Life provided. He was still young enough to think that, if he took care of his body, he would have perfect health the rest of his life.

He twisted the top off of a bottle of orange juice, "I have to tell you, I'm on her side. How many guys can boast of being married to such a gorgeous woman and one of the best real estate agents in the city? I mean, Treble and Associates get all the top clients in the city."

"It's not as wonderful as you might think," muttered Barney.

"You're kidding, right?" Jeffrey's eyes lit up at the thought of Melissa McDay. And rightly so. Jeffrey was the kind of guy who could be manipulated by any pretty woman who so much as looked in his direction. He was on the lookout for the perfect trophy wife who might help advance his career and social life. "She's successful, beautiful and has the most fantastic body..."

"Don't you think it's tacky to notice the body of another man's wife?" asked Barney to which Jeffrey blushed. The innocence of youth combined with its foolishness could make for uncomfortable situations.

Barney regrettably spoke without thinking. It was the problem of having so few friends and no one to whom he could confide. So he said, "She's not even committed enough to our marriage to take my name."

"Big hairy deal! It's in vogue now for women to keep their last names. Especially when they're on an upward career path."

That part was true. Melissa worked for Treble and Associates when they met and already had a reputation and client base. Name recognition was everything so she did not want to give that up. At the time it seemed logical. Now, he considered it just another part of Melissa's plan to control and manipulate his life.

Barney sighed, "Well, I'm not even sure I love her. I've…considered divorce…"

Whoa, Jeffrey's ears perked up on that one. Like most men who have no concept of their true appeal to attractive women, he mentally considered his chances of dating an eligible Melissa McDay. However, he kept his concerned friend face firmly in place.

"That would be blatantly stupid," he said, instead of what he wanted to say. "Anyway, don't confuse love with fulfilling a much needed male bodily function. Realize that you are one lucky man just to have sex with the woman."

26

Barney frowned as they strolled back to his workspace and he sipped his brew. He was so in love with Melissa when they first met. She had seemed so perfect that he could not have imagined his life without her. Beautiful, sexy, charming and... "What?" Jeffrey had said something which penetrated his thoughts.

"I hear Zelda the Witch Queen and Old Man Unitus are announcing the new Department Manager this week," Jeffrey repeated. "Heard anything about your chances?"

"I don't know," replied Barney. "I thought I had a good interview but you never know about those things. You hear anything?"

The department manager position was the next step in Melissa's career path plans for Barney. It would boost him up two levels from his current job. Typically it went to a district manager but Barney's cost accountant position was at the same pay scale as a district manager so his wife theorized that he could make a case for receiving the promotion. She encouraged Barney, that is to say, made him apply for it. To his surprise, he was placed on the list of candidates and made it to the second interview stage with Vice-President Preston Unitus and then President Zelda Hampton.

Rumors were the common annoyance in any company. It seemed that people cannot keep their mouths closed about anything, even those in possession of privileged information meant to be kept confidential. Therefore, rumors always contained part of the truth in them. The rumors had it that Barney was one of two leading candidates and that the other was Clive Feinstein.

Sadistically cruel, that was Clive Feinstein.

While others advanced through hard work and effort, Clive had a different career plan. Life was all about the game of politics and the one who played the best game won. No facet of life was free of political intrigue and a large company was nothing but a game of politics.

In high school he learned the fundamentals of playing the game to get good grades. He was labeled a teacher's pet. In college he perfected it into an art and even slept with a female professor to keep his grade point average. Clive graduated in the top ten percent of his class even though he rarely cracked a book. Seduction proved one form but there was also blackmail, bribery and just plain charm.

He chose Baxter Life, Baxter Life did not choose him. With his impeccable college transcripts, he was highly sought after by a number of companies. His strategy for advancement was to always dress well, attend any meeting possible but always avoid being assigned tasks. He delegated but always took credit for the work of others and never let the rules interfere with successfully accomplishing a job. Cheat when necessary but always cover up was the key. He took the sales route; there was less actual work and more personal interaction. Clive had sold himself all his life so he was well trained in the art. It was so easy to convince people to purchase insurance products they did not need and manipulate them afterwards with upgrades for which they did not ask and often did not even know they had received. His sales numbers always appeared great but if anyone had bothered to dig deep into them, they would have found them average.

For his efforts, he was made a district manager. But he wanted more, higher, better. As any good corporate climber knew, it was imperative to keep an ear to the ground. In other words, pay attention to rumors and use those who spread them to shape it to one's advantage.

While Barney Berry worked hard at this job for his chance at promotion, Clive worked equally hard at manipulation and deception. He had planned his next ascension carefully and timing was essential.

Barney was just another rung Clive would use to climb the corporate ladder. The cost accountant was far more skilled in so many ways but he lacked the political killing instincts of Clive. That would be his undoing and Clive's means of moving one step closer to the top floor. And Clive had no intention of stopping there or at Zelda's seat. His aspirations were very far reaching.

Clive stepped from his office wearing best suit with a new shirt and tie. For there was one thing that Clive Feinstein knew and that was how to dress and look like an executive. His suit fit perfectly, his fingernails manicured, his hair coiffed and combed and his shaved face was baby skin smooth. He liked to think that, in another world, he would be a president of a nation or, better, a king. His nose in the air, he marched into the dull grayness of the gray section and past Jeffery and Barney. Walking directly into Barney's cubicle with an armload of computer generated reports, he promptly dropped them on Barney's desk, not his inbox, as though to give the impression that they were more important than anything on which the cost accountant was working.

"Hey!? What gives?" demanded Barney as Clive passed him on the way out of his miserable little cubicle.

"Sorry, old buddy, but Her Majesty wants this month to be our best," said Clive with a deadpanned expression. Nevertheless, inside he was relishing the moment.

Truthfully, these were the moments Clive looked forward to at the beginning of every day. He so loved to deliver misery to his fellow coworkers. And doing it to Barney Berry was especially pleasurable.

Technically, the two men were on the same level and therefore Clive did not have the authority to give Barney orders. But rule number one of the game of politics was that power was perception. If someone was perceived to have the power and authority, people tended to believe that they actually did possess it. Rule number two, the moment a politician was perceived to no longer have power, that same politician lost the authority behind the power.

Barney snatched up the top of the first report.

"These aren't right. I'm not going to sign-off on claims unless someone matches them to the policies," he said firmly.

He tried to hand the report back to Clive but the other man was not about to take it.

Clive just shrugged, "Fine. Just make sure your name appears on the hold tickets."

Then he waited smugly with his impeccable businessman look of authority.

Meanwhile, Barney knew he was trapped. If he placed his name on the hold tickets, the reports would become his responsibility. The great danger of corporate bureaucracy, and everyone knew it, was to put one's name on anything because then the person became the owner of its success or failure. And in the insurance industry, nothing was more perilous than insurance claims. Insurance companies existed to make money not pay out claims. Claims were considered expenses and a profitable company minimized expenses.

Clive grinned for the first time, the victor taking his victory lap.

"I thought as much," he said as he rubbed the salt into the wound. "That's your problem, Berry. You're afraid to step out and take the big risks."

"This is grunt work. That's all I've done since I moved into this department," Barney complained as he threw the report onto his desk. "An intern could be doing this job."

"No intern can be trained to work the magic you work. You have the knack for maximizing cash flow and reducing expenses. It's your gift."

Barney Berry was also a very talented programmer. Like many who work with computers on a daily basis, he was self-taught in the operation of software systems. Within the limits of his computer access, he was able to write simple programs that performed repetitive tasks. His position usually came with three assistants but with Barney's skills, he was able to perform the work of four and therefore the extra people were unnecessary.

"I need to quit. Find a better job."

Clive sneered, "Yeah, right. And give up that big paycheck? Not likely. Anyway you're no adventurer."

"I am too an..." Barney was suddenly struck by what he had unconsciously read on the heading on the report. He grabbed the report again. "It's your territory. You've given me reports from your territory. Why don't you process your own claims?"

Clive patted him on the back before he walked away, "It's the law of the office food chain. Zelda the Horrible makes demands on me, I make them on you. In business, turds always roll down hill."

"What if I roll the turd pile further on down?" Barney called after him.

Clive turned around, walking backward, "Nice try. Unfortunately for you, you're at the bottom of this particular turd rolling hill."

With that, Clive strolled back to his office suppressing a smirk. Since the first time that he had given Berry work, the man had never challenged Clive's authority to do so. On that day, if Barney had tossed the printouts into the trash, Clive would have been helpless to do anything else but to fish them back out and do his own work. But Berry had not and, at that moment, he belonged to Clive. The first rule of politics.

"Slime bag!" Barney muttered as he slumped down in his chair and glanced up at the clock. Five hours and thirteen minutes more in this horrible day. "How does he get away with it?"

"Because you let him bully you. He's not the department manager yet...," Jeffrey said. "Tell him you're not going to do his stinking job again."

32

Barney buried his face in his hands. "This can't be my life. I'm an insect trapped on flypaper."

"What is it that you want, then?" asked Jeffery, though Barney wished he would just go away and leave him to his misery.

"I don't know. Just not this life. I need change."

"Yeah, right," laughed Jeffrey. "The day you change is the day the Baxter Life Building implodes in a ball of fire. Ha! Good old Barney Berry changing. That will be the day."

Jeffrey bounded off to annoy someone else.

"I can change," Barney moaned.

But he did not believe it. If nothing else, Jeffrey was right. He shook his head cradled in his hands.

Then the chatter of the room suddenly stopped. It was as though everyone on the entire floor had suddenly stopped talking and left. "Don't look up, don't look up," his brain screamed. There was movement behind him and Barney did look as he twirled around...

Blurs and swirls, he was moving.

The Queen Waspoid sat perched on a dais; her bright red color distinguished her from the rest of her royal worker Waspoids buzzing around her. They were building her nest under her watchful eyes.

Barney swallowed back the fear. This was real, too real. His senses told him that he was actually in the queen's chamber in the Hive that he had approached so often in his dreams. There were sounds and smells of which he was unfamiliar. Logic said that he was crazy but he chose to listen to his senses. He allowed just his eyes to roam and they found nothing but darkness surrounding him.

He was hidden by it and went unnoticed by the insects.

He studied the Waspoid Queen. Then the Queen turned and he realized that he knew that face. He tried not to but had to look closer. Oh yes, that face was all too familiar.

He fought to contain his gasp. Zelda Hampton, the queen of the insect creatures was the spitting image of Baxter Life president Zelda Hampton. She was speaking to the commanding insert from previous dreams Barney knew was called the General. When that ugly thing saluted and pivoted around, Barney recognized those facial features as well. Barney held his breathe; it was Preston Unitus, Vice-President of Operations and his boss.

No! He forced his eyes closed.

Unfortunately, when he opened them, he was still in the dreadful place.

But then, the bright yellow eyes of the Queen found him. Suddenly, her tongue shot out at Barney and he screamed…

Barney glanced around.

How…? He was in a toilet stall. He had no idea how he had come to be in the restroom and hoped it was the men's room.

Flushing out of habit and to pretend he actually had need of the toilet, he eased out. He was alone. He washed his face and tried to compose himself.

The nightmares seemed so real but previously he was always asleep when they happened. This was the first time he had gone to the scary world during the day. And how did he get in the toilet?

The cool water did little to relieve the anxiety he felt.

Barney emerged from the restroom patting his face with a wet cloth to find the employees of Baxter Life gathering in a large open area on the 8th floor used for company-wide meetings and parties. Somehow, he had dropped two floors and missed the announcement of the meeting. He wondered what the meeting was about.

He slipped in among a group and pretended that he had been present all along as Zelda Hampton was rambling on about the last quarter and the next quarter and generally saying nothing of importance. The company president was good at that.

He allowed his eyes to wander around at the bored faces of those gathered. Suddenly, his eyes were trapped by a pair of eyes that he recognized, though from where he did not know. They locked on him and he could not shake them. He tried looking away then back but the eyes still had him. Shifting positions, he glances around the head of someone in front of him only to meet those eyes again.

Then he recognized them from his nightmares. He fought the panic, they belonged to the Oracle. He went from Zelda to Preston and back to the new set of eyes, a woman's eyes. The images of his dreams filled his mind. The Queen, the General and now the Oracle, the three insect demons had real human counterparts.

So that was the meaning of the dreams, he thought. It was nothing more than an allegory for his crap-infested life in this human hive. It was confirmation that the dreams were just that, dreams. The revelation should have reassured him but it did not.

The eyes were still staring at him and the woman to whom they belonged was moving to where she could better see him through the employees pretending to listen to Zelda. She was dressed in 60s-style back to nature hippie clothing with long straggly, unkempt hair. The raggedy woman looked so out of place among the well-dressed associates of Baxter Life. The whole look made Barney very uneasy.

Zelda was still rambling, "Ladies and Gentlemen, I'll keep this short and sweet since I know you all want to get back to work. After all, we must continue this company's record of profitability so I can take another extravagant vacation."

She smiled at her joke and a few employees laughed feebly.

Too late for that, thought Barney as he tried to force the weird hippie woman from his mind.

Then Zelda Hampton launched into her favorite subject; extolling the power and might of Baxter Life. There was no bigger company in the industry, no larger employer. The insurance giant trampled regularly under its oversized feet the competition. Sheer volume allowed the company to offer plans and rates against which it was difficult to compete. She loved to remind her employees of the strength of the corporation to discourage them from jumping ship to other companies and discourage them to seek higher wages since they knew they were the highest paid in the industry. She liked to think that she could trust the loyalty of her workforce because they had nowhere else to go.

Meanwhile, the strange woman in question continued to stare and Barney had to force his focus on Zelda when he had a sinking feeling that he knew what the meeting was all about. There had been no calls; neither Zelda nor Preston had contacted him to tell them about their decision.

"As you are all aware," she was saying, "we have performed an extensive internal search for a new department manager and believe we have found one."

In an instant, the dreams were forgotten. This is it, thought Barney. The big announcement he had waited for. The reason for all the long hours of late and endless reports carefully checked. He braced for his name to be mentioned all the while knowing he would not hear it.

As he feared, Zelda motioned to Clive and there was a subdued groan from those gathered.

"Mr. Clive Feinstein has impressed us as the best suited and most qualified for the position. It gives me great pleasure to announce his appointment as Department Manager."

Applause with less than complete enthusiasm followed as Zelda shook Clive's hand. Barney joined the others in mechanically clapping his hands together despite the sick feeling in the pit of his stomach and the small taste of bile in his throat.

Then the meeting broke up. A few people offered Clive their congratulations but most drifted back to work. Zelda mingled with the stragglers to allow those who wanted to suck up to her the opportunity to do so.

Barney wanted to get out of there. However, the creepy woman with the piercing eyes was hovering at the exit to the elevators cutting him off from a clean getaway. He turned toward the stairs and almost ran into Preston.

Preston Unitus came from an old money New England family where pedigree meant everything so long as the family wealth had not faded. To protect their status when the money dried up, many young men with family trees traced back to the original colonies were forced to work either in law firms or in industries once frowned upon. He found himself among them. Young Preston failed the bar exam three times, could not master basic accounting and was inept at a variety of other skills required by corporate America. Then he discovered that he could sell anything. It happened quite by accident when he sold a piece of property in Florida owned by the family since the days after the Civil War to pay the debt left by a father who died a drunken gambler. The property in Key West was one of the few remaining assets the old man had not lost by gambling or sold off to pay for his gambling debts. Preston sold it for twice its market value and that began his career in real estate which eventually led him into selling insurance. Unlike real estate, insurance did not require a tangible commodity to sell. A company basically created the products they were marketing out of thin air. Along the way to the top floor, he learned that the good soldier, the loyal warrior received the promotions and rewards, not the one who bravely fought in the midst of battle.

Once upon a time, Preston thought Barney Berry would make a good protégée. That was one means to amassing power in corporate America. A general gathered around him young officers who did his bidding and occasionally fell on their swords for their commander. To his disappointment, Barney proved not to possess the killer instinct deep in his belly that an executive needed to rise above the great unwashed who did their bidding. To be a good warrior was to be a killer.

"You are understandably disappointed," Preston said to Barney.

"Color me angry, Mr. Unitus," replied Barney. "I was promised quick advancement when I joined the company."

It was one of life's ironies that Barney had not cared before when he was passed over for promotion. Back when he had decided that he did not want to be part of the corporate monster, it did not bother him when others less skilled were given those positions. Now, all that he could think of was that Melissa would be very disappointed.

"You told me...," but Preston cut him off. The vice-president was not about to allow any of the fault to fall on him.

"You are one of our best cost accountants, Barney," he said. "I personally brought you into this department because I thought you had the skills to go a long way. But you've shown little enthusiasm for your work. People notice such things."

"I'm hardly challenged..."

Preston had to resist the impulse to slap the younger man. Grow a pair, he wanted to say. However this soldier had to be coddled, not because he was worth the effort but because he might be useful at another time. In war, the first who charged into a breach usually died or were wounded. A good general always needed someone expendable to make that charge into the breach. Therefore, Preston would make an effort to keep Barney Berry in the company for the day when he would need cannon fodder.

So the vice-president said, "Feinstein has proven the ability to increase profits in his division."

"But he's a butt kisser who plays office politics," whined Barney.

"He aggressively pushes the company's agenda. Meets the right people. Says the right things. Look, Barney, your work is admirable but we need team players. Soldiers ready to storm the beach for the good of Baxter Life."

He slapped Barney on the shoulder and gave him a confident smile.

"I envision a day when Zelda can stand here and announce your promotion. Dig in and show us what you're made of," he lied as though it were completely the truth. With his years of experience, it was as natural as breathing.

Preston stepped back to defer to Zelda as she made her dramatic approach. Her face was plastered with her condescending smile and her arrogance shined through. She had no desire to pacify the cost accountant's ego. Her desire was to be worshipped; either in fear or love, it mattered not to her which form it took. She would extend the carrot to this minion but she knew she also had a stick to swat him if need be.

The strange sixties-style woman was on Zelda's heels.

"Mr. Berry," crooned Zelda, "I want to thank you personally for putting yourself forward. The

40

shame is that we could only choose one department head."

Barney could not help allowing his attitude to show, "It is a disappointment. I thought we had a very good interview."

Zelda's plastered-on expression did not change. "Yes, well, you failed to measure up to the Nikita test."

That was the last thing that Barney expected. He could only stare and barely managed to say, "The...? I'm sorry, the what test?"

With a practiced condescension, Zelda responded, "Ms. Nikita, our Intuitionist. The newest management tool, Mr. Berry. An Intuitionist allows us to break through the mental and emotional walls employees tend to construct and see the real person."

Nikita was in Barney's face before he realized she had moved. She scanned him from head to toe. He thought she even sniffed him.

"Your vibes are negative, Mr. Barney," Nikita said and spoke as if she were on a hallucinatory drug. Her voice was devoid of emotion or passion. Her face was passive. "Your spirit does not reside in this world."

"We need our mid-level managers to keep their spirits in this world. The world of Baxter Life," said Zelda, as though she had completely understood what the weird woman had meant.

I have gone to whacko city, thought Barney. Some woman from the wrong century decided my fate, that was crazy. "My spirit? How would you know? We've never met..."

41

He had not told a single person at Baxter Life about his dreams but he had the sickening feeling that this woman knew all about them. Even though that was impossible. He hoped.

"...have we?" he asked Nikita.

The Intuitionist moved slowly in exaggerated gestures and Barney could not believe that anyone would take her serious. He looked from Zelda to Preston thinking that they would eventually crack a smile but everything about them suggested that they believed every word the disturbed woman said.

Nikita was still speaking in her singsong voice. "Oh, we have encountered each other. I have touched your spirit and it floats on the wind in search of that other world."

"We can't have department managers with spirits that float on the wind," said a very serious Zelda. "It's not good for the company's bottom line. I'm sure you can understand."

Then Zelda and Preston moved on before a completely stunned Barney could respond. All the long hours he had worked and the carefully covered details only to be denied a promotion because his spirit was said to be in another world? What kind of demented existence was he living? They were dreams, he wanted to scream after the departing executives. But he wisely restrained the impulse.

"It is not real, this other world. Beware, for you are in danger of making it such," Nikita said and leaned closer staring directly into his eyes. Then she nodded. "A floating spirit. Not good. Not good at all."

Then, he was alone.

With what was left of his dignity, Barney walked up the two flights and found his desk exactly where it should have been. The disappointment continued.

Mechanically, the cost accountant went through each of the pages of every report on his desk but his mind was not on his work. The clock on the wall eventually released him from the torture yet he had no desire to go home. He had no idea what he was going to tell Melissa when she asked about the promotion, and eventually she would. So he sat in his cubicle and listened to the happy voices of his fellow employees leaving because they had lives outside of this monstrous building.

He sat back in thought as the 10th floor gradually fell into silence.

The dreams, they were responsible for all his troubles, he concluded. He had to find a way to be rid of them then he could reclaim his life.

Finally, he dragged his dejected, hopeless body from the monstrous hive and sat in a subway car surrounded by the few joyous sounds of homebound commuters also taking the late trains.

Suddenly, the lights of the car flickered and it lurched to the side. Brakes screeched…

Chapter 3

Two screeching children in tattered clothing at play raced past Barney without acknowledging his presence and entered the camp. His puzzled gaze followed them. Where was he?

As if in a trance, he walked into the camp; a collection of tents, RVs in need of repair and shanties. The camp's inhabitants were lethargic, slowly performing their tasks or sitting like statues around small fires. An old man pulled a tattered blanket over his shoulders and hunkered down against the chill. A woman fed pieces of bread to a child in her lap. It was poverty unknown to him.

An unseen ghost, Barney moved among them and suffered from the pain of the squalid conditions and despair he saw.

A mother with a crying baby had her head back and eyes closed in exhaustion. A limp bottle hung just out of the baby's reach. Barney tried to lift the bottle but discovered that his hand merely passed through it. That was a small relief signifying that he was, in fact, dreaming this nightmare.

"What is this place?" he breathed in disbelief. He had always heard about poverty but like most people in his economic situation, he had never witnessed it personally.

Two teenagers tumbled past as they fought over a can of food. One teen won by beating down the other, snatched up the can then delivered a vicious kick to the other youth before he raced off.

The emotion overwhelmed Barney. His attempt to help the injured teen on the ground was a repeat of the bottle with his hands passing through the youth. Then the boy scrambled to his feet, tears streaming down his cheeks and hopelessness in his eyes, he limped away. Barney wanted to cry but found that he was so struck by what he saw that he could not. That created a new sensation of pain within his spirit that threatened to double him over. Turning in a complete circle, his eyes found misery and desolation wherever he looked.

He could take no more and ran into the woods.

He was about to wonder why the foliage was real while the inhabitants of the camp were not when, smack, a branch hit him in the face...

Barney jerked his head and looked around.

He was at his drawing table in his apartment office, pencil in his hand. For a moment he felt relieved at the familiarity of his surroundings. Then he glanced down. He had sketched a picture of the camp with all its squalor. The sense of relief quickly vanished.

Melissa popped her head in, saw him and entered.

"There you are," she said but the smile immediately changed to an angry frown at the sight of the drawing.

"You frustrate me," she complained and Barney knew a rant was about to begin. "You absolutely frustrate me."

Barney sighed, "Okay. What have I done this time?"

"Don't take that tone with me." She folded her arms over her chest and motioned with her head to the drawing. "That! I talk and I talk and I talk about applying yourself to your career. And what do I find you doing? You're drawing, again!"

"They're an expression of my life."

He realized what he had sketched and immediately tried to conceal it. A useless gesture as she had already seen the drawing.

And like a parent scolding a child, Melissa sighed in exasperation with her eyes looking to the ceiling although not moving her head. "You should be bringing work home from the office and concentrating on your career."

It was an old battle.

As a youth, Barney dreamed of being a cartoonist. He was not bad at it, or so he thought. He considered a career in the wild west of the Internet with his own comic strip and scratching out a living doing what he loved. Then life intruded on his dream. The summer before art school, he worked as a fact-checker for Washington Insurance. His first paycheck was more money than he had ever made at one time. He decided to put off his art studies for a year. After running the numbers he knew he could make enough money to pay for a degree in art school. But those paychecks were so big that the temptation to spend some of it on other things was too great. The money bought things and a lifestyle that required more money to finance and art classes were pushed further back. When Baxter Life came along with a nicer salary and benefit package for the skilled cost accountant, he jumped at the chance. Eventually, he came back to drawing but as a hobby. It proved an escape from the stresses of his life. Then Baxter Life became unbearable and he decided money and a comfortable life were overrated. He scaled back his life and socked away all the extra cash he could. He was ready to pursue his old dream when he had enough to support him for at least three years. That goal was in sight. After he met Melissa, it became the impossible dream once again. She wanted more not less so drawing was regulated back into a hobby. When he drew, he imagined what might have been but never was. Except that Melissa could not tolerate anything which did not fit into her goal for their lives as a couple.

"Why can't you understand? I have no passion for Baxter Life," Barney pleaded. "I am passionate about my art."

She was hardly interested in being the wife of a starving artist. So Melissa turned on her condescending voice, "I understand you're not focusing on what's important."

"And that would be my tedious little job?"

Barney wanted to fight for what was important to him. Stupid. Because he knew he could not win over her trump card and tonight she was in no mood to allow him the slightest belief that he could win this argument.

Wham, she played it. "You and me, our lives together, that's important. We're building something special, Barney. Can't you see your career is part of that? That is what's important."

"I want more," he said weakly.

"Then work for it," she replied softly. Oh yes, she knew she had won. Later that night she would punctuate the victory with sex. It would be a reminder of who was in charge as she pleasured him with a talent for making him explode with carnal delight. She would be the aggressor, the leader and he would be the slave to her passion, reaching for her climax by using him. For now, she was the gracious victor. "I want more for us, too. That's why I dress in the latest fashion, sell over-priced real estate and that's why we network."

"I hate networking," he pouted. He had switched to his little boy persona. Mother had scolded him and he accepted her wisdom even though he did not want to.

Melissa stroked his head, moved a stray strand of hair aside, her voice kindly informative, "Networking is how you advance in society. And why we need to upgrade our condo."

"Upgrade?" That knocked Barney from the submissive little boy. He wanted to shift into combative Barney, the guy who still thought he had control of his life. "I like it here."

But Melissa was not about to surrender control. The palm of her hand rested on the side of his face forcing him to look into her loving, compassionate and all-knowing eyes.

"No, you just don't like change," she said gently. "But upwardly mobile people change. They buy bigger and better and they dress in style."

"This might not be a good time to think about changing," Barney said unconsciously. Then he regretted because he was about to take sex off the table for the night. However, he had no choice but to finish the bad news. "Things are a little shaky at Baxter."

Mean Melissa was suddenly there with a stern, "What do you mean? What happened?"

Reluctantly, Barney took a deep breath and said, "Zelda gave the department manager's job to Clive…"

Yup, she did not allow him to finish but exploded. "Feinstein!? Clive Feinstein? She gave your job to creepy Clive!"

"I don't understand how such suck-ups get promoted."

"By sucking up," she retorted. "When will you learn how the game is played?"

"How about never?"

"You just refuse any change, don't you?"

Disgusted, Melissa stomped out.

He heard her muttering all the way down the hallway and into the living room. He could only imagine that she would call her mother and the two of them would exhaustively discuss Barney Berry's failings before they worked out a new plan for him to advance his career. Maybe this one would concede the need to change jobs.

He looked back at the drawing of the camp. After a moment, he crumbled it into a ball and tossed it at the wastebasket.

Barney thought that, given his status in the doghouse, sex was not off the table.

He was so wrong. He went to bed early with the intention of watching the sports highlights while Melissa chattered away with her mother. The sound of activity came from the bathroom but he was distracted by the story of another professional football player suspended for drug use. There was a time when he would immediately check his fantasy football league to see how the suspension would affect the other teams. Alas, that was another time and another Barney. Melissa had badgered him about his constant preoccupation with sports and he finally gave up the league because he was tired of trying to hide from her the amount of time he spent with his team.

Then he realized that his wife was in the doorway in an entirely new negligee. Really? She seductively strolled over to the foot of the bed and crawled toward him. He knew what was coming next and he was right as she pulled his pajama bottoms down to his ankles. He gasped with pleasure, the league and any sports long forgotten. For an hour, she dominated him with demands and reciprocated with pleasure.

In the subdued light and with the scent of their lovemaking still in the air, Barney and Melissa laid wrapped in each other's arms.

"You really have the gift," she purred.

And it was true. One of his great joys in their marriage, maybe the only one, was to please his wife sexually. When she cried out in delight, he felt like a man. It was the one time that he thought he had complete control over her.

"Which reminds me, Mother and I bought a new table and chairs today" she announced casually as if they were talking about a related subject.

"More furniture?" Well, there went the feeling of manhood. He had just rocked her world and her next thought was about shopping. Not only that but shopping she had already done as opposed to future shopping. "You bought more furniture? Why?"

"To entertain in style, Melissa replied in a tone that suggested that it should have been logical to him.

"Again, why?"

"To suck up," she said with a grin.

50

Barney rolled his eyes and somehow, with her head on his chest, she knew that he had.

Raising up her head, she forced him to look her in the eyes, "And what is wrong with sucking up? You admitted earlier that Clive was just promoted for doing it. I don't see why you cannot grasp the concept."

Then she was out of the bed and headed for the bathroom to begin her nightly routine before going to sleep.

"I just want for one moment to feel like my life matters," he called after her. That was the type of line better said when there was distance between them.

"Then do what's necessary to get promoted," her voice came from the other room. "Move up the corporate ladder. Then you can really make an impact."

He could not help the sarcasm dripping from his voice, "An impact? At Baxter Life? How? By selling better insurance?"

She leaned back into the bedroom, "Helping people achieve their financial goals. Making their lives richer and more rewarding through investment products that build their futures."

"You sound like our stupid commercials."

"I sound like someone who wants you to succeed. For your sake and for mine. For our sakes. I'm feeling very unappreciated." Then she was back in the bathroom.

He imagined her applying the cream to her face, the lotion to her hands and the other assorted tasks necessary to keeping a beautiful woman beautiful. Or so Melissa thought necessary.

"What would I do without you?" he muttered as he slid down under the covers.

He rolled over, his back to the bathroom door, and tried to fall asleep before she re-emerged. The same old feelings of depression and anxiety flooded over him. He was helplessly trapped in a life, in a job and, how could he think such a thing but yes, in a marriage he did not want. Was there no escape, his spirit cried out? Suddenly he curled up in the bed and grabbed his stomach. His head swirled.

"No," he breathed a prayer barely audible. He knew what would come next but had no idea how to fight it. "No..."

Chapter 4

Barney stood disoriented in the shadows of the darkened tunnels.

"Now what?" he murmured. "Now where am I?"

He ducked back deeper to study the situation. In the distant was what sounded to him like human noises. With trepidation, he eased along the wall but took care to stay as much as possible in the darkness. Touching the tunnel wall, he realized it had a fabricated quality to it, some type of synthetic material. Then he reached the end and peered around the corner.

Humans, barely clad in tattered clothing, struggled against some heavy equipment. The mere skeletons of humanity moved with a lethargic lack of energy in an effort to dig deeper and construct the synthetic walls he had felt as they went.

Buzz, Barney quickly hid.

"This is just a dream," he whispered. He tried to control his breathing, his back pressed up against the fabricated wall. "This is just a dream."

A wasp-like humanoid creature floated past him. From his brown color Barney knew the insect to be part of the military. The Waspoid joined other soldier insects guarding the humans as they worked.

A human worker on a piece of drilling equipment was having difficulty keeping it in place. The impact of the drill continually pushed him back causing the drill to disengage from the rock he was attempting to punch through. It was apparent that the human did not have sufficient energy to do the job due to a lack of nourishment.

One of the Waspoid guards shouted at him with his speech heavily laden with a buzz, "Faster, human slime."

But the human was unable to comply. From where he was observing, Barney could see that the man was at the end of his strength and sought compassion from the guard. He would not receive it.

Zap, the Waspoid lashed out with an electronic whip across the back. The human screamed. His companions winced but continued to perform their tasks. The fatigued worker still could not manage to hold the drill firmly in place.

Zap, zap, the whip struck again and again. Though it was not easy to read the expression on the insect's face, Barney felt the guard's pleasure in tormenting the human worker.

The man tumbled to the ground, unable to stand.

Zap, the electronic whip lashed out one last time and the human collapsed completely.

The Waspoid motioned to two other humans. "To disposal," he buzzed gruffly.

The worker on the ground shrieked but was too weak to resist and his pleas for mercy were ignored. The other workers hooked their arms under his armpits and drug him away followed by the Waspoid soldier. They passed Barney's hiding place.

He waited for a moment then trailed after them.

The workers hauled their companion through several tunnels with the insect soldier right behind them. Then they entered a room.

Barney crept to the doorway and glanced inside. A worker who appeared in better condition than those toiling away in the tunnel, though just barely, waited by a large machine. The workers carried the helpless one to it. The man controlling the machine muttered instructions of some kind to the others. Grabbing the hapless man by the hands and feet and ignoring his exhausted pleas, the two workers tossed him weeping into a chute where he slid into the machine. A flick of a switch and the muffled cries stopped. The machine did its job.

Barney pulled back and tried to merge with the wall as the workers and the Waspoid watcher emerged then disappeared back down the tunnel. He returned his attention to the room.

The machine operator took a clear plastic-like jug from a crate and positioned it over a large faucet protruding from the churning machine. He opened the tap and a liquid substance filled the container.

Barney was forced away from the doorway again as the man walked out and into another room across the tunnel with the container. Barney took several quick steps and pressed against the opposite wall just in time as the human came back without the plastic jar and returned to the room with the machine.

Slipping into the other room, he found that it was a storage room with rows of shelves containing hundreds of the plastic containers. Looking at one of the jars, he drew back in horror. An eye and a fingertip floated among the liquid. He fought to keep from vomiting. They all contained various pieces of body parts swimming around in a cloudy liquid.

A commotion in the tunnel caused Barney to hurry further into the storage room. Through the shelves he watched as the machine operator placed another jar on a shelf. Then a door opened behind him in the opposite direction and a Waspoid worker entered. He took a jar from the shelf and retreated back through the door.

His options were limited. He did not want to go back the way he had come. The door used by the Waspoid seemed his only means of leaving this horrific room. Putting his ear to the door, he heard buzzing; machines perhaps. With a slight push the door cracked open and he looked through it. The noise was not from machines but Waspoids of all types as he was beginning to recognize them by their colored chests. Soldiers with brown torsos, workers with their tan bodies and the red ones he had seen in the queen's chamber.

Then Barney realized what they were doing. The insect horde was consuming the contents of the jars. His mind tried to process what his eyes were seeing. Humans were food for these creatures. The bile gathered in his throat and he twirled around to flee only to remember where he was, facing the rows and rows of jars representing humans reduced to a substance the insects could eat.

He could not suppress the horror any longer. Whether it was audible or in his mind, he did not know but he screamed...

Barney awoke on the floor of his bedroom.

As rapidly as possible, he crawled to the bathroom on all fours just in time to vomit into the toilet. It was vile and disgusting. Ooh, carrots, he shouldn't have had carrots for dinner.

"Note to self," he whispered, "chew better."

Sitting back on the floor and leaning against the bathtub, it took all he could muster to expunge the images from his mind. Grabbing a towel, he wiped his mouth. He tried hard not to dwell on what he had witnessed because it might bring on more vomiting. Instead, he wept, the tears streamed down his cheeks and some of the saltiness crept into his mouth.

"I just want it to stop," he cried softly and pressed his face into the towel. "Please make it stop."

Later, he managed to wash out his mouth and stumble back into bed where the lump snored beside him.

The next morning Melissa sat in the dining room scrolling the fashion news on her electronic tablet. Barney staggered into the kitchen, surprised to find the coffee made. He poured a cup, continued on to the dining room and practically fell into a chair, groggy.

After a sip he managed, "Morning."

Melissa looked up from the tablet, her face passive, she lacked any genuine concern.

"Are you feeling okay? I thought I heard you making strange sounds last night," she asked casually. "It sounded like vomiting."

Barney was incredulous, "You heard me? Yet you didn't bother to get up and find out what was wrong?"

She rolled her eyes, "When you came back to bed I thought you were fine." Then she went back to her tablet.

"I had a nightmare last night that made me sick to my stomach," he responded angrily.

Melissa tried not to let her feelings show. She thought she had married a man. She loved Barney, yes she did, but this was getting out of hand.

When she met him, he had an adventurous, almost dangerous quality to him. The beast out of the cage with a passion. Sure it was for a bunch of silly drawings but she thought she could harness that quality. He was handsome, physically fit and a monster in bed but this nightmare thing was getting old. He should be the leader in this marriage, taking them to the next social level. At the rate they were going, she would soon out earn him. What woman should make more money than her husband? She wanted to slap him across the face to shake him out of this funk and tell him to man-up.

Instead, she said, "The Blackwells are having another charity event. I need to see if Mother or Daddy can get us an invite."

"Did you hear what I said?" demanded Barney. "I had a terrible nightmare last night. That's why I threw up."

She sighed and looked at him with a disinterested frown.

Barney shot out of his chair, almost broke the coffee cup putting it on the counter and stomped from the kitchen. The bathroom door slammed.

Shaking her head, Melissa tried to return to her fashion news but now she was aggravated. Her mind drifted to the unthinkable thought. Their marriage might be over. Granted, she had placed them on a social trajectory that required both of their incomes but she was beginning to doubt that

58

Barney would be able to keep pace with his share of the financial load.

The trend for women to make it on their own was waning. Stories were appearing in women's magazines with hints that after 40 was becoming emotionally difficult for the single, unattached woman. There was a missing element of companionship and shared financial responsibility that female friends could not fill. Along with the antidotes, she knew women, friends of friends, who were struggling to maintain their social status on their income alone. Yes, it was a two-income economy, a couple's society for anyone but the filthy rich.

She could hear him getting ready for the office. When he stormed out later there was no kiss.

A completely dejected Barney sat in the subway car and ignored the women standing around him. Many men were less than gentlemen on the subway commute but he always prided himself on his chivalry by surrendering his seat. Not today.

Brooding, he flipped through the results of a search on his smart phone. They were listings of psychiatrists. It was a slippery slope what he was planning. He doubted if it was a one-and-done proposition, here is your cure that will be a hefty fee. Nope, chances were that he would require several visits and the real difficulty was in hiding the expense from Melissa. As the train rumbled to a stop at his station, he made the decision.

The psychiatrist's office was feng shui, all harmonious and peaceful. It was as though he had transported to an Asian country. Yet Barney felt anything but harmonious and peaceful. The pretty receptionist was sweet and adorable. She offered to get him something to drink then directed him to very comfortable chairs where he scanned the latest psychology magazines. He sat, filled out the endless forms then mindlessly thumbed through one of the publications. His mind was on what he would say to the doctor.

Dr. Cedric Ling had an impressive resume of education and experience from around the world but with particular emphasis in Japan and Taiwan. Barney figured he had a better shot with someone who was not constrained by the Western inability to grasp the concept of different worlds. Face it, in Western cultures there was a mindset that, if you could not feel it, smell it or hear it, it did not exist.

Finally, on the hour, the doors slid apart and Dr. Ling appeared.

The Caucasian doctor was 6'5" with blonde hair and blue eyes. In three smooth strides, he greeted Barney with an extended hand.

"Barney, it's great to meet you," he beamed.

Dumbfounded, Barney took to offered hand. "You're…you're Dr. Ling?"

"The last name does tend to throw people off." Ling motioned him into the office and Barney unconsciously walked after the doctor as he continued to talk. Barney had the feeling he had told the story many times before. "Somewhere in my family tree there seems to be a Chinese connection. I've considered searching the family genealogy but there is a certain pleasure from not knowing."

There were two overstuffed chairs waiting near some floor to ceiling windows with a scenic view although Barney noticed there was a traditional

60

recliner and he assumed that was for those who expected the standard psychiatrist experience. Even though he thought it might be less threatening to lie down and not have to face the doctor, Barney opted to sit. He did not want to appear needy. He was just here for a consultation. At least, that was the delusion he fed himself to justify the visit.

Pad and pen in hand, Dr. Ling sat across from Barney. "What can I do for you today?"

Where to start, that was Barney's problem? I want you to tell me that it is all in my head and give me a pill that will make it all go away, he thought but did not say. Instead, he started with the first dream he could remember.

He was walking through a forest, all peaceful and content. Then he emerged onto a small hill overlooking a valley. That was when he saw the hive for the first time protruding up from the trees on the far end of a vast forest. He remembered feeling a terrible fear that caused him to wake in a cold sweat. In successive dreams, he moved ever closer to the hive until there were some very intense ones where he actually went into the place. He recounted the dreams where the bug creatures took on the images of the executives of Baxter Life.

"What do you think they mean?" Dr. Ling asked when Barney finished.

He stared at the doctor who probably took the pause for Barney thinking about his answer when in truth, he wanted to leap on the psychiatrist and choke the life out of him. The question was exactly what Barney had expected but it infuriated him that, for all his credentials, Ling could not come up with a better response to all that Barney had told him.

"My life sucks and I want a new life," Barney concluded. "But my life isn't going to change anytime soon so what do you have for me other than make a change in your life?"

Dr. Ling did not blink at the angry frustration seeping from his patient. Which infuriated Barney to no end as he thought that he was just another nut-ball to the doctor with the same old dreams every other nut-ball had, just his were in a different form.

"Barney, you could change your life," said Ling softly. "You could make dramatic changes to your surroundings, to your job, to every aspect of your life…"

Barney waited. He had the sick feeling that a "but" was coming.

"…But it would do nothing to stop the dreams," Ling continued. "This is about Barney Berry and who he is inside."

"Do you have a pill for that?" Barney asked, half-jokingly, half seriously.

Ling grinned and Barney had the impression that the head-shrink had heard that one a million times. "I have pills that will make you feel all better. Some will even take you into another world altogether where you won't care about your bug world."

But before Barney could say he wanted that pill, Ling added, "None of them will solve your problem. When the medication wears off, you will be the same old Barney Berry and that is your problem. In fact, every time you land from taking the pill, it will be worse than before."

Throwing his hands up, Barney leaped from his seat and started to pace. "So what do I do? How do I change me?"

"Liberation."

"What!?" Barney spun around and glared at the other man. He had said nothing about that part of the dreams.

Ling's expression remained passive, unemotional. "You must become the Liberator…"

Angrily Barney turned away from him before he could finish. The doctor did not know, he had kept that part from the psychiatrist.

"I can do nothing for you until you are ready to become what you must to be free from this world," Ling said in the quiet of the room.

"Don't you mean free from the bug world?" asked Barney with his back to the psychiatrist.

But when the man did not reply, he twirled around and looked Ling directly in the eyes. The doctor had not misspoken.

Before he could ask, the head doctor said, "I cannot tell you exactly how to liberate yourself from the life you detest. Only you can determine that." He smiled mischievously, "With a few more sessions, of course."

The visit to Dr. Ling had done little to change his disposition. His life still sucked big time. He hated the suggestion by the psychiatrist that he had to find the key to his own.

The elevator dumped him on the 10th floor and he shuffled his way through the hive to his cubicle without so much as a glance at his enemy on the wall mocking him. His desk was covered with reports and he nearly bumped into Christine, that messenger of ill will who constantly brought him piles of new drudgeries to slog through.

The young woman grinned, clueless as to how her job made him miserable, and went on to deliver her foul reports to other poor wretched analysts in other little impersonal workspaces.

Barney fell into his chair and his head dropped into his arms folded on the desktop.

"How I hate my job," he moaned.

Smack, somewhere a stack of papers hits the floor…

Chapter 5

Ka-boom! The earth exploded around Barney, tossed him to the ground and showered him with dirt. He spit out a pebble and pulled himself back onto his feet.

"Run!! It's a collector," screamed the woman who passed him at a dead run.

He looked around, disoriented.

Noticing that he had not followed, she returned, her face in his. "Run, you idiot," she said calmly but firmly.

Barney was stunned. The woman was Melissa; he was looking into the face of his wife. Only she could not be Melissa. This woman had short cropped black hair, khakis, a big weapon and a forceful attitude. None of which belonged to his wife, would ever belong to his wife.

"Melissa?"

"Katelyn," she responded then grabbed his arm and forced him to follow her.

Wham, the ground blew into pieces before he could ask who Katelyn was. Wham, wham, chunks of the earth was flying everywhere and she lost her grip on him as people scurried everywhere around them in a panic.

In the distance a craft of some kind hovered just above the surface. A beam of light shot out and captured a man. He fought against it but to no avail as the beam carried him into the craft.

His mind swam in the chaos. Melissa, Katelyn, whoever was calling back to him, "Come on, run or it will get you."

He watched the craft as it trapped another in its beam. That was enough. He turned and ran after the woman. Behind him people cried in terror.

They hurried through the foliage for what seemed like a long time but it was probably no more than a few minutes when they emerged at a partially hidden cave opening where others fled. He and the woman were part of a stream of people making their way inside.

Katelyn stopped in the opening and looked back. Curiosity trumped self-preservation and he joined her. From their secure location, they watched the craft scoop more humans up with its beam until the sounds of terrified people and the craft faded away.

"Bastards," Katelyn muttered. "How did they find us here?"

"Where is here? And, how did I get here?" Barney asked trying to see into the darkness of the cave.

Katelyn examined him curiously.

"Are you all right?" she asked. Did you hit your head?"

Barney cupped his face in his hands and moaned, "How can these dreams keep getting more and more real? What am I doing to cause this to happen?"

Katelyn was partially amused and serious at the same time. "If you're sleeping, this is a nightmare, not a dream."

"You got that right." He touched the wall of the cave. "A minute ago I was sitting at my desk. The next thing I know, I'm running from some spacecraft. I can't figure out how."

"Desk…?" Katelyn almost laughed then realized that he was serious. "Soldier, people have not sat at desks for years. We need to get you to a doctor. You must have hit your head or something. Then we need to find a weapon and equipment for you. You seem to have lost yours."

"Not only do I have a desk and a job that sucks but you're…"

…Melissa, my wife, he wanted to say. However, her puzzled stare kept him from it. He knew that she did not recognize him. Wait, she called him soldier? He glanced at his clothes. He wore a khaki shirt and pants with green combat boots. There was a holstered pistol around his waist.

"I don't need a doctor. I need answers," he responded. "Where am I and how did I get wherever I am?"

She pointed out across the trees. "You came from a refugee camp just over that ridge. You are now in an Armed Resistance League stronghold." She touched his forehead and he grimaced. She showed him the blood from his wound. "And you do need medical attention. Let's go."

They walked past khaki-clad guards concealed on both sides of the entrance behind nasty looking heavy weapons. Further back, other soldiers sat at the ready armed to the teeth with automatic weapons and a variety of explosive devices.

"You have the stronghold part right," he mumbled under this breath.

Reluctantly, he trailed after her as they moved deeper into the cave. It was filled with more fighters as well as those in civilian clothing. She was moving at a fast pace and he had to hurry to keep up without running over other people.

"Look, Melissa, I don't need a doctor. I just need to understand what's happening, what's happened to you and who those people in the spacecraft were."

"You're kidding, right? And why are you calling me Melissa? My name is Katelyn Sumner, Lieutenant, Armed Resistance League. And those bugs in the hovers are definitely not people."

"Bugs," he whispered. "Waspoids."

She laughed. "He begins to return to the real world."

Suddenly she stopped and he almost ran her over, his mind focused on one thing. Time to wake up.

"Fine," the lieutenant was saying, "if you don't want medical attention, let's go find some food."

"Ouch!" Pinching himself did not work, he was still asleep. He glanced around. Katelyn was gone.

"Soldier."

She had gone into an offshoot of the cave where there was a line. He sniffed the air, food.

He felt the hunger pangs in his stomach. Well, if there was food then he figured he might as well indulge the reality of the dream. He joined part of the line of those in khakis shuffling along. Katelyn picked up a plastic tray and plastic spoon so he followed suit so he did the same. They shuffled past a group of stations where kitchen personnel ladled mashed substances on plastic trays. The only difference in the appearance of each pile that was unceremoniously plopped on Barney's tray was the color; white, green, brown and a sickening yellow that Katelyn bragged on as dessert. Barney gulped back his initial response. Dessert? He was handed a cup of a black substance he thought he heard the person pouring it refer to as coffee. He sniffed the liquid, coffee it was not. He knew coffee and this bore little resemblance to it.

On the other side of the tunnel was a line of those in civilian clothing. Their fare seemed no different from what Barney could see of it but when he asked why there were two lines, Katelyn lowered her voice and her demeanor changed. The sizes of the servings and content were not the same, she explained. The resistance fighters felt the need to feed those refugees who made their way into the cave stronghold but rationed out the provisions they had. The rations were thinned and reduced to stretch them as much as possible.

Focusing on the civilians, Barney noted how raggedy these people looked.

Then he realized that Katelyn was gone and hurried to locate his companion and guide. He found the lieutenant sitting in another tunnel on the floor of the cave, her back against the wall, and already digging into her food. She was eating like a person coming off a diet.

"Great stuff, isn't it?" she smiled. "This is the best meal I've had in days."

Well, thought Barney, that accounted for how she could pass the pureed substances under her nose and spoon it into her mouth without flinching. With the first spoonful, Barney grimaced at the taste of the mashed concoctions, yuck. It was terrible. The white crud was close to tasteless and odorless so basically eatable but begged the question of why consume it. The green puddle stunk and the brown slime almost made him gag. As for the yellow dessert, it was definitely not anything he would ever call dessert. A quick glance around told him that the other soldiers scattered about were of the same opinion as Meli – Katelyn. From what he gathered as the lieutenant chattered away in between bites, these were men and women who did not often eat enough to satisfy their hunger. The fighters would not waste what was on their plastic trays. Therefore, he tried to choke down as much as he could. There was no telling when he would leave this dream sequence and his belly was growling. The stomach pains were new. This entire dream was very different from the previous ones.

"What?" he asked.

Apparently, the resistance fighter was speaking to him.

"Your name?" she repeated her question.

"Oh. I'm Barney Berry, Cost Accountant," he said and offered his hand. It did not occur to him that he had identified himself with the job title he hated. It was a reflex.

Katelyn stared at him a moment then, chuckled. "Yeah, right. Maybe in another life." Then she eyed him suspiciously. "Or are you from the cities? They say some semblances of the old ways still exist there."

He gave up on the food, tried the coffee again but that did not improve as it cooled.

"And this Armed Resistance League? What is that? Some kind of militia group or something?"

70

"Are you...?" She motioned to his tray. He glanced down at it and shrugged then handed it to her.

She dove into it with gusto. A second helping of rations was a treat for her. With her mouth full of the white mess she said, "Ha! You're one of those who bought into the president's propaganda. He's trying to keep recruits away by telling everyone we're fanatics attempting to overthrow the government."

"Is there no army? No military?"

Katelyn continued to shovel food into her mouth while she replied, "The president neutered the army long ago. What's left guards the cities but eventually they will fall apart. Their equipment is old and falling apart. If the Bugs want, they can swat them away with no problem. We're the last hope for mankind. We've hidden away the last of the heavy weapons and much ammunition as we could get our hands on. If we don't defeat the Bugs, humans are doomed on this planet."

Barney leaned back and let his eyes wander around at the soldiers gathered. Those who finished their food dwelled over the black spit that was called coffee. It reminded him of coworkers in the office who milked their breaks, not wanting to return to the unpleasantness that was their jobs. In another part of the tunnel, the refugees congregated apart from the resistance soldiers as though fearful to mingle with them. His mind drifted off to his problem while he cradled the black sludge in both hands and pretended to savor it while Katelyn cleaned his tray of every drop of the rations.

What he did not see were the eyes glaring at him from the other side of the cave. Clive Feinstein was tucked in among the group of the refugees eating. Except, Clive was not eating, the crap on the tray he was handed stunk and the taste made him want to vomit. But when he sat down to contemplate his situation; he saw Barney and a woman that looked like a black-haired version of his wife. What were those two up to? Keeping his head at an angle where to Barney and his wife could not see him, his brain worked feverishly to come up with an explanation about what was going on. His passive expression masked the confusion and fear he felt as his eyes continually scanned the area.

The morning it started was at the office the day of the announcement of the new promotion. He was walking back to his office when he abruptly appeared in the office of the president of the country. It was all an intense dream but quite enjoyable. He was pampered by a bunch of political lackeys who seemed to both fear and worship him. It may have been a dream but he loved it. He should have more dreams that real and that pleasurable. Over the next few days, there were more such dream events and he started to relish them. As the president, he partied with beautiful women, consumed great food and drank a ton of alcohol then had sex with the woman or women of his choice. What a life he was having in his dream world. And the best part of the dreams was that it felt so real. It was as if the dreams were really happening. However, just as he was beginning to relish them, he slipped into the dream state and in a limousine that was part of a convoy full of his lackeys. Before he could discover why, the line of cars was attacked by a flying spacecraft of some kind.

The limousine was hit by a laser beam and overturned. Clive struggled from the wreckage only to be forced to flee from the continued attack. This dream was officially no fun at all. The political hacks he had around him had spoken of some bug-like menace but he did not actually listen to them. Yeah, yeah, sure, sure, it was all so boring. He now wished that he had paid a little bit of attention.

When he saw one of the guards protecting him scooped into the air by a blue light reaching down from the craft, he knew that he needed to get out of there.

Joining a group of raggedly dressed people, he managed to make it to a cave where armed soldiers of what the lackeys called the Armed Resistance-something were guarding. They obviously did not know who he was, or who his dream persona was, because they shuffled him along with the dregs of humanity among whom he found himself.

Inside the cave, Clive stayed with the smelly, dirty people. He knew that, outside of the presidential palace, he was not popular. Or rather, the president was not well perceived by the people. Someone handed him the tray of slop and he sat with those eating it. That was when he spotted Barney.

Berry was somehow part of those in uniform. How did a cost accountant, a mere analyst manage to become associated with a bunch of military types? And why had Berry's wife dyed her hair black? What part did she play in this...?

Those were just the tip of the iceberg of Clive's questions.

For starters, he was now interested in how he arrived in this crazy world? Question number two; why was Barney Berry part of a group that Clive knew hated him as the president of this world?

What he would give to hear what they were discussing.

But Clive was smart enough not to make his presence known to them. For the moment, he would bide his time and wait for this dream to end. Yep, it was probably time to stop them altogether. How was the question that rose to the top?

Meanwhile among the resistance warriors, a question occurred to Katelyn.

"What unit are you with?" she asked.

Barney was roused from his stupor. "Unit? I don't belong to any unit. This is all just one reoccurring bad dream. Eventually I'll wake up." But he turned up his nose at the smell and taste of the coffee. "You would think I could dream about tastier coffee, though."

Katelyn frowned, "Dream?"

"Um, yeah, sorry," he apologized. "I am having a dream and you are part of it. This world is one screwed up place, from what I've seen of it."

"You think this is a bad dream?" she repeated slowly. Her expression and the ton of her voice told him that she did not believe him.

It made sense to him. If he were a character in a dream, he would not believe either. What was he thinking? This entire dream series he was on had gotten profoundly strange.

The lieutenant, however, was considering the thought and her eyes fell on the tray in her hands. Cautiously, she said, "No one, no matter where they came from, would turn their nose up at food. Even the cities have rationing and hungry people are not choosy."

"Exactly," confirmed Barney. This was the first opportunity in his dream state to verbally interact with anyone other than that frightening bug oracle creature. It did feel good.

"Yeah, this is a nightmare," Katelyn nodded and Barney had hope. Perhaps speaking about it to someone other than Melissa and Dr. Ling might help end them. Then she added, "Every day I wonder what it would be like to live in the world that existed before the Bugs arrived."

"Ah, well, you might consider what it would be like to live in a new world you can create after you beat the bug things," pouted Barney. "I'll wake up and be back in my real world. Let me tell you, if your world was like mine is now, you will have as sucky a life as I have. Not a pretty sight."

Katelyn lowered her cup of coffee and stared at him to see if he was sincere. "You really believe that you don't belong here?"

"I'm saying that I am dreaming and when I wake up, you'll be gone. Melissa and one nasty crap of a life will replace you and all this..." He glanced at the empty plastic tray, "At least the food is better in the real world."

"You're from somewhere else...?"

She finished her coffee while she considered what he had said. Finally, she stood.

"Come on," she said. "I have someone you need to meet."

The cave was deeper than Barney imagined with a flurry of activity everywhere.

Commander Shattner leaned over a map on an old camp table with his officers around him. His uniform was smart, clean and in good condition, his boots worn but polished to give the impression by extension that his army was in the same condition. However, he had that haggard look in his eyes of a man forced to make difficult command decisions for too long and too often. He glanced up at Katelyn then returned to his briefing.

"Try to keep the purpose of the operation as secret as possible for as long as possible. The fewer civilians that know our plans the better. We'll move out at dusk when the hive shifts to nocturnal activities. That will give us a full night," said Shattner.

"What about the refugees?" asked a young officer. His fresh, youthful face attested to his inexperience.

The other officers winced. They knew the answer. The commander paused, choosing between what he wanted to say and what he had to say.

Finally Shattner replied, "We can't allow them to tag along. They will only slow us down and hinder this force's ability to function as a military unit."

The junior officer was about to protest. He had never heard something so callous in his entire young life but one of the more senior officers touched his arm lightly with her hand, almost like an unintentional brush. Their eyes met and the poor boyish officer understood from her gaze.

"Our priority," Shattner continued, "is to keep our forces intact and in fighting form. The elevation of the new camp will put us out of reach of all but the hover craft."

He glanced around. His officers understood their orders. They moved off to carry them out.

Shattner wheeled around on Katelyn, "Lieutenant Sumner, welcome back. And where have you been?"

His tone was official and a bit displeased. His eyes said that he was relieved to see his young officer.

"A collector ventured into our zone chasing refugees," explained Katelyn. "Bad luck, the civilians ran into us and we were caught in a firefight with the bugs."

"And unfortunately tomorrow when the hovers from the collector sweeps this area for strays, they will find our installation," he added, which was why he was ordering his force to pack up and move out at dusk.

He saw it all in his mind, the mind of a military man. The Bugs would send in long-range patrols to clean up the stragglers and they would locate the mouth of the cave in the process. A firefight would ensue and the ARL would have to fight their way out before becoming trapped in an indefensible position. Shattner wanted a fight, his fighters clamored for a decisive fight. Nevertheless, the Armed Resistance League was not strong enough to win head-to-head battle with the Waspoid General. The commander had faced the Bug officer in several skirmishes and two major battles which the humans lost. Shattner knew he could not win, yet. The humans resisting the bug invasion had just one hope, hang on as an organized army long enough for the perfect opportunity to arrive when they could take their best shot.

It was not an enviable position to be in as the leader of a resistance movement. On one hand, he had to train fighters, convince them that they had the chance of victory but keep them from any real engagement with the enemy until that time arrived.

Shattner turned his attention to the man with Lieutenant Sumner. "Who are you?" he demanded in a gruff, humorless voice. The guy was in ARL khakis but he did not recognize him nor did he look like any of his fighters.

Barney extended his hand, "Barney Berry, Cost Accountant for Baxter Life."

Confused, Shattner looked down at the hand, to Barney then to Katelyn and back to the hand. He enforced military field discipline on his troops which meant that he should have received a salute. The newcomer had no clue of any military procedures.

"You are what? What are you?"

Barney rolled his eyes and wondered how many time he would have to explain who he was. He said, "I work as a cost accountant for Baxter Life. It's an insurance co…"

But Shattner cut him off by ignoring him and turning to Katelyn, "You brought me an insurance salesman?"

"Actually," Barney responded, "my job is more of a cost analyst…"

"He claims this is all a dream," Katelyn interrupted him and Barney was getting tired of it. "He expects to wake up somewhere else."

The commander's head dropped.

It took every waking hour and some when he should be sleeping to keep his army in the field. They were poorly-armed, poorly-supplied and even more poorly-supported by the Revolutionary Congress. Those roaches voted to remove the authority of the president and his government but they did not provide for the army they had raised and sent into the field. Now that force struggled to survive and stay viable enough to fight. The ARL recruited, trained and tried to keep their weapons caches hidden. What they did not need was anything which might distract the resistance from resisting.

"Oh, Lieutenant, not you, too?" moaned Shattner. "I have enough problems on my hands without my officers propagating those fairy tales."

"He actually believes…," Katelyn started to say but her commander quickly cut her off.

He was tired of the rumors. Defeated armies look for miracles, secret weapons and magic spells to snatch victory from certain defeat. The resistance did not need any of those. It needed a will to win and a prime opportunity to strike at the heart. The commander's strategy was to give his army small victories until they could strike one fatal blow. Memories of his early naiveté were always close.

"We are dealing with flesh and blood reality. Crackpots are the last thing we need," he said before she could finish.

"I'm not a crackpot," Berry retorted. He had heard enough and was also tired of these two people talking about him as though he was not standing right there with them. "I'm Barney Berry…"

"And where do you think you are, Barney Berry, Insurance Salesman," Shattner interrupted, again.

Barney did not like the commander and Shattner did not like him. What bothered Barney the most was the sense of purpose he saw in the military man's face, in the way he carried himself. For someone drifting around in an unhappy job with an unhappy life, Barney hated anyone who could not understand.

"I'm not…," Barney started to correct the commander but then thought better of it. "Okay, fine. I have these very intense dreams, like this one, where I'm transported to a world being attacked by insects…big insects. Eventually, I wake up."

"Right….," said an unconvinced commander.

"Intelligence says the Bugs are afraid of…," the lieutenant tried to say.

But Shattner cut her off with a poignant warning finger. "Don't say it," he warned her.

Katelyn would not be deterred, however. "Not talking about it won't make it go away! You know and I know that the Bugs are worried."

"The Bugs are a bunch of giant mindless insects. Their only concern is building their hive. What we need is to find a fly swatter big-enough to squish them. Not a fairy tale story about some great liberator."

"What if the story of the Liberator is true?"

Shattner turned snidely to Barney, "Cost Accountant, do you think you're the great liberator sent to free mankind from the Bugs?"

"Excuse me?" Barney chose ignorance over truth. The Waspoid Oracle called him by the same name when he went deep into the hive. He did not believe her then and he certainly did not believe that he had what it took to be the liberator that could lead any kind of resistance group on some crusade against giant bugs.

However, he may not be this person Katelyn believed him to be but, she was also not his wife. She was better. Katelyn was a gorgeous copy of Melissa and so much more. This woman had a sense of danger about her; a khaki-clad she-soldier who was not worried about decorating an apartment or her social standing. He would like to see her in action. Well, on TV from the comfort and safety of his recliner. Nevertheless, he knew she would be formidable on the battlefield.

Once-upon-a-time, he imaged that Melissa could have been Katelyn when he thought about the night he first saw Melissa...

What was that, thought Barney? While he was daydreaming, the two resistance fighters continued to talk.

"You see, Lieutenant, he's clueless."

The man who thought he was an insurance salesman was old news to the commander. He started to pack a few items into a backpack that he had with him at all times. His mind was already on all the details of moving a large force of soldiers from one point to another.

"Hit and run on the Bugs is our best strategy, not the reliance on superstitious blather," Shattner muttered as he worked. "We chip away at their harvesters. Starve the Hive of its resources. Wait

81

until we are strong enough and they are weak enough. Then we attack the Hive. That's how we win."

"H...hive!?" asked Barney. "There is a hive?"

The two resistance soldiers were staring at him and he realized that he had made a terrible mistake. The look, especially on Shattner's face, confirmed that opinion.

"Is that supposed to be a joke?" Shattner demanded angrily.

"I want to see the hive."

Shattner gazed suspiciously at Barney. "See it?"

"I need to see it," said Barney solemnly.

How many dreams had he endured about the hive? He had lost count. Inside, outside and from all angles, he thought he had seen it from all angles. However, those were all dream dreams. This was more like real life. What he wanted was for the hive not to look at all like the hives in his dreams. That is, his other dreams.

"We're moving out. In two days, we will set up a new camp." Commander Shattner smiled and Barney was sure that he did not like the thoughts behind it. "Then we will show you your hive."

They set out just as the sun disappeared over the mountains. First it was a long slog up to reach the top of the mountain range and then they followed an old foot trail that wound around from peak to peak until almost dawn. It was slow going with some of the heavier weapons needed to protect them from the Bugs' flying crafts but they had experience at moving quickly with the burdensome loads. As the sun peaked over the horizon, they

82

pitched tents, camouflaged their position and disappeared inside the shelters to eat cold rations and sleep.

Katelyn offered to allow Barney to share her tent since he did not have any equipment of his own. Nor a sleeping bag. To compensate, she unzipped it and laid it on the floor of the tent and they used coats as coverings as they lay back-to-back beside each other for warmth. Barney was so tired that he thought he would collapse into sleep but did not. His hope of falling asleep and waking up in his own bed did not happen.

"Problems," Katelyn asked, sensing his restlessness.

"This is the longest I've stayed in a dream," he replied. "And it's a little unnerving."

They lay in silence a few moments until he recognized that she was not going to fall asleep either. For him, it was the daylight outside the tent. He suspected that she had something on her mind since, from what he knew of soldiers, she probably had the ability to fall asleep anywhere and at any time.

"Who do you think that I am?" he finally inquired softly.

He knew that the bug equivalent to a corporate intuitionist thought, or feared, that he was a threat to their existence. What might a resistance fighter think that he was? In her answer might be the solution to his dilemma on how to end these dreams.

Ironically, when he considered that he might stop the dreams it occurred to him that Katelyn Sumner would disappear. She was this real person whom he liked very much. It was a sad thought to think that she would be gone for good.

She rolled over and her mouth was close to his lips. Her voice was Melissa but nothing else resembled his wife, especially those bright eyes. She whispered and he suspected it was so that no one outside the tent would overhear. Barney knew the commander had ordered his lieutenant not to speak of this matter with anyone else and she was following orders like the good soldier she was.

"Intelligence reports started trickling in a few months ago. The Bugs have this oracle, an insect older than even the queen." Barney winced but tried to keep his expression passive. She continued without apparently noticing, "They keep her well protected. They believe she looks into the future. She foretold of a human coming to free humanity from the Bugs' control."

Barney laughed, "You can't think I'm this liberator?"

That was exactly what the Bug intuitionist suggested in his dreams, notably the really scary ones when he visited her chamber. This world was crazy to think that Barney Berry, cost accountant, might be some gung-ho action guy out to save the world. He could not even save himself from his lousy life, how could anyone think he could help them destroy a monster like the Hive?

Katelyn pursed her lips, "Apparently, Commander Shattner docs not."

"But you do?"

Katelyn gave a weak smile. Barney wanted to roar out in laughter but fought the impulse. For some reason, he wanted to impress this woman. For some reason? No, he knew why he wanted to impress her.

Instead he said, "Look, I'm just Barney Berry, Cost Accountant." Then he looked deep into her eyes, right into the innocence that actually believed. "Nothing more. And this is nothing but an intense dream. No, nightmare. This is an intense nightmare."

"You keep looking at me in this strange way. Like you think you know me."

He considered whether or not he should tell her. There they were in the tent so close to each other that he could kiss her and take her into his arms. There was the risk that she might slap the crap out of him if he did any of those two things. But he figured there was no harm. Sometime soon he would be leaving this dream for his apartment and Melissa and another day at Baxter Life.

"You are the spitting image of someone I know in real life. That is, my other life," he said. "Except…"

"Except what?"

"She has no faith whatsoever in me. And, she wouldn't be caught dead in khaki or carrying automatic weapons. The woman is really anti-guns of any kind."

Okay, he did a speed bump on telling her that she was essentially his wife with black hair and an aggressive attitude, a sexy attitude. Oh how he wanted to reach over and take her in his arms, kiss her and make love. He looked into that familiar face but it was so different. If it were not for those bug things out there that were also a part of these nasty dreams, he would like to stay with this Melissa…Katelyn…whoever she was…

"But to you," she said softly, "I'm just a character in a dream."

"You want to know something funny?" he sighed. "In my dreams as a kid, I used to be wearing nothing but a pair of underwear, tighty whities. I thought those were scary dreams, being practically naked." He smiled weakly. "They don't seem so frightening, now."

Fortunately for the camp, the sky was overcast and the sun's light was dimmed by the heavy clouds. The fatigue from the night of hiking the trail finally caught up to him and he slipped off into sleep. His breathing soon became even and rhythmic.

Beside him, Katelyn softly touched his face. He was a handsome man, one she could love, she thought.

"I believe in you," she whispered.

Chapter 6

They woke before nightfall.

Through the aches and pains of sleeping on the hard ground, Barney cursed under his breath. This was not his apartment. And that was a bad sign. First the dreams were extending in time and now, he actually went to sleep in the scary world and woke up still in it. Not good.

They ate some dried product that resembled beef jerky only without much in the way of taste and washed it down with water.

Seeing the difficulty Barney was having with it, Katelyn assured him that, once they reached their new camp, they would be back on kitchen rations like what they enjoyed in the cave. Swell, that was hardly music to his ears. He managed to finish the rations. The secret was keeping the inside of his mouth as moist as possible. Since he had no idea how long he would be in this world this time, he figured he better get as much food energy inside of him as he could.

As he assisted Katelyn in packing her gear and rolling up the tent he considered the possibility that he might be stuck in this world until he could figure out how to permanently terminate them completely. He noticed the lieutenant discreetly watching him and thought that staying in this world with her was potentially compensation for dealing with the giant insects. With her equipment in good order, she wandered off to see to her platoon. Barney sat back against a tree and watched her as she issued orders and verified that all of her fighters were ready to move out. He marveled at how amazing a woman Lieutenant Katelyn Sumner was.

As darkness descended the lead units were already out and scouting ahead.

The army hiked up and down the rough terrain all night but it was relatively out in the open. Barney worked out the kinks in his stiff bones then his feet started to hurt with new pains. Katelyn explained that the bug hover crafts did not like to venture into higher elevations because it exposed their command decks and engine compartments to attack from above. The underbellies were heavily armored but the glass windscreens for the pilots and the rear propulsion drives were easy targets for even small arms fire. Therefore, the resistance army could set up camp in a small mountain range that was quite near to the hive where they would be able to harass and harry the Bugs but would give the Bug General pause in considering a direct attack. The insects had initially erroneously built their hive in a valley surrounded by the mountains to hide its existence from the human occupants. That now proved to be its one weakness as venturing too far from it exposed Bug military and scavenger units to isolation and attack.

However, the Bugs eventually would locate the general location of the Armed Resistance League and move their laser mortars to reinforced positions within range of it then zero them in on the camp. When that happened, the ARL would have to relocate. The ARL circled the mountain range from new position to new position trying to keep one step ahead of the Bug General.

At first light, Shattner's command reached their new camp, an outcrop of rock formations facing away from the direction in which any approaching Bug hover craft would travel. It served to hide their presence. As his soldiers set up the new camp, Shattner ordered Lieutenant Sumner to mount an escort patrol to take him and the cost accountant for a tour.

The escort, Shattner and Barney dropped down a few kilometers to an open rock formation.

The patrol stayed back in the foliage while Shattner, Katelyn and Barney emerged from the woods into a small clearing and Barney could not believe his eyes. The sight beyond was that of the dome-shaped Hive lifting 50 stories above the tree line. Waspoids fluttered about entering and exiting small openings in its wall. Hover crafts came and went. They arrived just in time to watch a huge oval machine rumble from the largest of the openings on the ground level. It was over one hundred meters in length and thirty in width with eight massive wheels that crunched everything under them.

"Harvester," Katelyn said quietly.

Barney did not need to be told. He was very familiar with the work of those dreaded machines. Watching one lumber along creating its own road was awe-inspiring and terrifying all at once. He knew that the machine was headed for some location out of the valley and beyond the mountains where it would setup like a small fortress to protect the worker bugs foraging for food and materials to supply the hive. There were hundreds of harvesters in every direction from the monster.

But the harvester was not what had his attention. He had also been in every part of the Hive in his dreams but never had it seemed so real as now.

Barney swallowed hard, "Whew! That is one big wasps nest."

"Got that right," remarked Shattner.

Katelyn sighed, "Every time I come here, it seems to grow larger."

A hover craft skimmed the surface heading toward them making Barney very nervous.

"You're not afraid to be so exposed?" he asked with just a touch of apprehension in his voice.

"They know we watch them but they do very little to stop it," replied Shattner. "They have little fear of us."

"And they've lost their fair share of hover crafts trying to push back patrols from their outermost perimeter," added Katelyn.

"Why do you allow them to make that thing bigger?" His previous experience inside the Hive told Barney that it was an evil place. He could not imagine that humans would not have exterminated it by now. "Have you not tried to attack it?" he demanded tersely.

Shattner hid his reaction to the attitude of disgust he felt coming from the cost accountant behind his binoculars. Instead, he trained them on the level constructed on the top. It was not there the last time he looked at it.

"A year ago, when it was smaller, we did," he said with the binoculars covering his expression. "Cost me a hundred fighters and we didn't even make a dent. The walls were so thick they stopped everything we threw at them. Managed to punch a few holes in it but couldn't fight our way inside."

He handed the other man his binoculars.

Barney scanned the Hive with them. "You could infiltrate someone inside to look for weaknesses."

"No human has ever returned from inside the Hive," said Katelyn.

"I've been inside," Barney replied casually without thinking.

Silence, Katelyn and Shattner glanced at each other.

When Barney lowered the binoculars he realized that he might have made a mistake from the looks that Katelyn and the commander were giving him.

Then Shattner laughed at the absurdity of it, "That's impossible."

He was now certain the cost accountant was completely insane.

"It's honeycombed with tunnels like a maze" Barney's mouth continued to speak while his brain told him to shut up. Look at the disbelief in their faces, his brain shouted. But no, he went on, "It's very easy to get lost. There's about five or six more levels underground. The queen is somewhere in the last level."

Shattner looked to a smiling Katelyn and read her thoughts. She believed in the Liberator. He glared at Barney suspiciously, "What's your angle, Berry? Are you trying to barter information for something else?"

Deciding to take a relaxed approach to his stupidity, Barney shrugged, "No angle. Just trying to be helpful. In my dreams, I've found myself inside that monstrosity. I might be able to draw a map to give your people some idea of what they can expect. Maybe you can drill a hole in the side and crawl in. Plant some bombs or something."

Cautiously, Shattner summarized, "So, you're not volunteering to go back inside, just providing free information?"

"Go back! Not on your life," replied Barney quickly. "This may be one horrible dream but, I'm not foolish enough to make it even more terrifying."

That sounded very cowardly. He put the binoculars back to his eyes to hide his embarrassment and added, "I thought if I help you figure out how to destroy that thing then, maybe my dreams would stop."

Shattner studied Barney a moment as the other man pretended to scrutinize the Hive then he walked away.

Barney lowered the binoculars and turned to Katelyn, "What's his problem?"

"You're an idiot," she said bluntly, shook her head and sadly followed her commander.

Barney looked around, he was alone. He called after her, "Still think I'm the liberator?"

He chuckled at his cleaver response until he considered the dangers of being alone.

As he hurried to catch up to her, Katelyn pushed a limb out of her way and deliberately allowed it to snap back into his face. He ducked out of the way.

What happened?

Barney was bent over and looked up as a custodial worker awkwardly swung a large potted plant around nearly hitting him in the face.

"Sorry," the man apologized. "I didn't see you there."

"The story of my life," remarked Barney sadly.

He looked around. He must have just stepped off of the elevator. This place had the virtue of being new. Then he spotted the sign behind the receptionist at the end of the corridor. It read Dr. Dwight Monroe, MD.

He did not remember making an appointment with a new doctor.

The receptionist looked up as he approached the desk.

"Um, Barney Berry?"

"Yes, Mr. Berry, the doctor is ready for you."

Minutes later, Barney was sitting across from Dr. Monroe.

"When would be best for you to undergo the procedure?" asked the doctor.

"Refresh my memory," Barney replied slowly, "what procedure would that be?"

The doctor consulted the file on his desk.

"Let's see, you were referred by Dr. Cedric Ling," responded Monroe. "He thought we should do a few brain scans looking for any cerebral abnormalities. Apparently, you are having some problems and we want to rule out any physical causes."

The doctor leaned forward, patiently. "Tell me a little about what you're dealing with."

Barney relaxed. Relieved, that Dr. Ling must believe that he was having a real problem. He sat

93

back and gave the physician a capsulated account of the Hive and his experience with the Armed Resistance League.

There was a pause. The doctor made one final note on the file.

Finally, Barney asked, "So, when can we get started?"

The answer was immediately.

Monroe was current with the medical trend where doctors ran mini-clinics with just about every type of medical service. It was a one-stop office.

Barney had to peel off his clothes and put on that embarrassing backward gown then tramp from room to room where he was scanned, poked, x-rayed, pricked and a couple of tests he thought the doctor just made up to add a few more charges to the bill. A rule of thumb is to never give a doctor a carte blanche on tests yet Barney Berry was that desperate for something, if not treatable, at least medically verifiable to be wrong with him. Several hours later the humiliation was over and he was released.

Two dreary days later, Barney was escorted back into Monroe's office where the doctor had the results.

Standing in front of the lighted panel, Barney and the doctor started with the x-rays of his head and chest. He did not see a thing and that was apparently the point. Negative was a common word the physician used most often. Monroe showed him charts and numbers and they all told the doctor the same story.

"Mr. Berry, you are one very healthy man," announced Dr. Monroe at the conclusion of the presentation.

Barney was beyond disappointed and told the doctor as much.

"I'm sorry," replied the physician, "but I deal in what I can treat and you have nothing physically wrong with you."

The consultation was over. With nothing the doctor could latch onto that would allow him to run the patient through an endless loop of medical tests and treatments, he was finished with the man. He did not have the time to waste on a non-productive client. Despite the questions still rolling around in his head, Barney got the hint and left. Although not before signing the release to bill his insurance plan through Baxter Life.

Crossing the city, Barney reflected on the doctor's diagnosis that he wanted nothing more than to be wrong. Nevertheless, it was hard to argue with the results laid out in black and white, thorough results. It all fell back to Dr. Cedric Ling's admonition that the solution to ending his dreams lay in Barney's hands.

So what did he have? There were two depressing worlds; one with a wife who was slowly becoming boring to him and the other with a wildly exciting woman. Both women were, in essence, the same woman.

"That's it," he shouted. Oops, people on the subway were staring.

"That's it," he whispered to himself. Change Melissa and make her into the perfect wife for him, that was the secret.

He sat back and smiled. Next appointment, he would share his revelation with Dr. Ling. Certainly a psychiatrist would have insight into how to change a person. Obviously, the doctor had known the answer since Barney had related everything about the two women and their similarities but wanted the patient to reach the conclusion. To his credit, Barney Berry did it after just one visit. He was proud of himself.

The elation did not last. His computer blinked with an urgent email to greet him when he arrived at his desk. The message from Zelda was an hour old. The visit to Dr. Monroe's office took far longer than he had expected and, the worst part of it, he had nothing wrong which he could use to illicit sympathy for being late to his desk.

"Oh," he groaned, "this is not good. Nope, not good at all."

The ride up the elevator to the top floor was painful, filled with doubts and apprehension.

Martin led him in immediately, which was also not a good sign. Usually the gatekeeper played his part as the guardian of the throne by making those with appointments wait even if they arrived on time. Zelda Hampton's corner office had plush furniture, expensive carpet and a spectacular view of the city. The entire room screamed power office. Thick wood paneling, gold light fixtures and a bar stocked with the finest liquor and other spirits money could buy. Zelda sat behind a massive desk shuffling through papers. Behind her was a large portrait of Zelda Hampton looking dignified and presidential which she secretly thought made her look like a member of royalty if not a CEO of Baxter Life. She was the queen of this building and she had the oil portrait hanging on the wall to prove it.

Preston Unitus occupied the overstuffed couch, impassive. Nikita stood partially concealed behind a large potted plant from which she peered out. She was just the observer, not a participant.

What was he doing here? Barney was unsure of what to do when Zelda looked up briefly from her papers.

"It's about time. Come in, come in, Mr. Berry. Sit," she said bluntly.

Barney meekly walked to a chair in front of the desk and gingerly slid into it. Zelda then returned to her papers. But that was one of her weapons to remind him that he was just a lowly cost accountant and not an executive.

He snuck a glance over at Preston but the VP continued to blankly stare out the windows as though he did not have a care in the world. How Barney hated to be reminded of how much of a nonperson he was to these people. His ego told him to walk out on the executives. He imagined himself abruptly leaping from the uncomfortable chair and casually marching out. Yep, he imagined it. Yet there he sat.

After a few minutes, Zelda looked up at Barney. His chair was low to the floor and he seemed to sink into it. Consequently, she could stare down at him from a position of power. It was an executive ploy to remind anyone sitting in front of the desk that they were nothing important.

Zelda plastered on her well-practiced expression that passed for a smile, "Thank you for coming, Mr. Berry. We have a slight problem which requires your particular expertise."

That answered one of Barney's questions. He had been summoned to dump some kind of tedious job on him. He should be honored; company presidents did not normally personally give assignments to underlings. That task was usually delegated to lower level managers.

Meanwhile, Zelda slid a stack of computer printouts across the desk. Barney had to scoot forward in the chair to reach them. He sat back and examined the first couple of pages in an attempt to try to get ahead of her.

"One of our territories has had an irregularity in paying certain claims," Zelda continued in a nonchalant if not arrogant tone. "The amounts are alarmingly high. We want you to fix the problem."

Barney was instantly confused by what he read and her instructions. At first glance, the problem was clear. Someone had failed to send out payments on the claims of legitimate policies. He was not sure what they expected him to do about it. It seemed like a problem for the accounting department.

"I, uh...," he searched for the words. "You want me to authorize the checks? Um, this is the responsibility of the account manager for that territory. A standard 5-0-9 authorization, a couple of hours with this number of claims."

"No," she snapped, coming close to yelling but then managed to restrain her voice. "That would be monumentally foolish. The sums are too significant..."

Barney looked at the pages again and his eyes widened. He flipped to the past page and there was a summary. Now he understood the problem. The sums combined were beyond substantial, they were large enough to alter significantly the bottom line of a major company like Baxter Life. The hit would shake investor confidence in the company and depress the stock.

Barney looked at Zelda then at Preston. Oh yes, it would do more than that. It would cause the abrupt end to several careers starting with Zelda and Preston and probably down to the next level of executive management. His mind could not conceive of how this large number of unpaid claims could have accumulated without anyone noticing.

Barney managed only, "This would...!"

Neither Zelda nor Preston would verbalize any of what Barney was thinking.

"But how...? This amount of...?" Barney could not fathom the sums represented on the reports in his hands. The amount of money would pay for a small county.

His hands! He wanted to drop the computer reports like they were on fire, and they felt in his hands as though they were, but he resisted the impulse.

Zelda casted an accusatory glance in Preston's direction while the vice-president maintained his inexpressive face. There was a very long silence. Though he clearly did not want to speak, Preston was obligated to do so. The two executives were in this together and that required the vice-president to participate verbally.

"Apparently, the person responsible has been withholding claim adjustments for two years," he said softly and carefully. "Deferring them in some cases using language in the policies to justify the delays. In other instances, legitimate claims were incorrectly rejected but the customer appealed and has a legal right to payment.

"It came to our attention this week," added Zelda, "when a couple of policyholders filed a lawsuit. Should it turn into a class action suit, all hell will break out."

"I've been involved in a few such suits," Barney noted as he scanned and let his foolish mouth speak without his brain's permission. "The discovery process alone might reveal a pattern which could open the company up to an investigation."

Shaking his head in astonishment, he made the mistake of looking at Zelda with a disbelieving grin. She was not amused. Nor was Preston, who returned to his vigil out the windows.

"But who...?" he started to ask. Then his trained eye recognized the territory identification number. His head shot up and he glared at Zelda. However, he managed not to say, "Clive Feinstein!"

Both Zelda and Preston knew that he knew.

But there was something else about these reports that just did not seem right. He tried to focus his mind on what he was missing but Zelda was droning on and it slipped away momentarily.

She tried to appear disconnected when she said, "It has presented us with a challenge in the individual's overzealous desire to see Baxter Life prosper."

Barney could tell that the Baxter Life president did not want to openly admit the severity of the

100

situation but there was a fear behind her reserved demeanor.

You don't even want to say his name, do you, Barney wanted to demand? He wanted to say it for all in this room to hear. He just could not because he was a coward.

What came out was, "You mean he violated company policy and broke the law in order to get promoted?"

"That is a very narrow view of the problem," remarked Zelda with her presidential voice from her high place on her executive throne and looking down on him.

Forget this whole pile of cow turds, Barney thought. He was not going to have anything to do with it. They promoted Clive; let him clean up his own mess. He tried to hand the stack of reports back, sliding it over the edge of Zelda's desk, but she made no move to retrieve it. So, he dropped the papers on the desk. He was finally, once and for all, going to stand up to those who would not give him the promotion he earned, he deserved. No, alternatively they gave it to a guy who handed them a heap of horse dung as a thank you gift. Well Barney Berry had a spine and a little dignity left in him. He was not going to do their dirty job. Yes, exactly, that was what he needed to tell them.

Zelda looked down at the stack of computer reports, her face devoid of any emotion. This amateur had no idea who he was dealing with. She took out her competition on her way up the ladder, knife those in the back who were looking the wrong way and faced down the big boys in the boardroom.

One little twerp was not going to destroy a career she had worked long and hard build.

"This is a serious predicament," she said with no feeling in her voice. It was as though she were ordering an expensive meal at an upscale restaurant and Barney was nothing more than a faceless waiter. "We can't pay all these claims without the risk of sending our company into a financial tailspin. Nor can we allow Mr. Feinstein's deviations from company policy to become public."

"The clock is ticking," Preston said softly yet it startled Barney. He felt like the room shook. "The quarterly statements are due out at the end of the month. We require a unique solution."

There was a long pause, a silence that hurt Barney's ears because he knew they were not finished. He was trapped in the room until they dismissed him. It was a question of corporate games and somewhere out there was the carrot for his participation in saving their skins. They did not want to offer it unless he remained resolute. The stick would come first.

"I have convinced Ms. Hampton to give you broad powers for the project," continued Preston with an even tone. "The authority will help to expedite whatever plan you develop."

"You just promoted him to department manager," Barney snapped back. The anger seemed to burst out of him. For a moment, just one brief moment he considered pushing the executive to the point where they would have no choice but to fire him. He wanted to. It only required a bit of guts…he could not, would not.

The reports sat untouched on Zelda's desk within his easy reach. The company president made no move to take them. Preston had not moved an inch.

"Focus, Mr. Berry," said Zelda, again in that nonchalant executive voice. "To have Mr. Feinstein's actions revealed after the fact would reflect poorly on all concerned."

Yeah right, thought Barney. They were in the stick phase, whop, whop. He inwardly scowled at them. You two are just trying to implicate me in this affair so I will go along. Then he remembered the strange woman hiding behind the plants and glanced over at her. It took all his willpower to muster an offense.

"The three of you are afraid of the board-of-directors," he said with an emphasis on the word three. And he felt a little ashamed of himself because he was going after the one he perceived as the weakest of the three.

Nikita ducked quickly behind her plant and he considered the retreat a small victory. He pushed his attack.

"Maybe you should have checked on where Clive's spirit was before you promoted him," he taunted the Intuitionist.

"Let's not make this personal," Zelda said evenly. "What we want is for you to devise a strategy for quietly fixing the problem without a dramatic hit on company profits."

"You would be saving hundreds of jobs, including your own," Preston noted.

Barney wondered how he made that statement with his nose so high in the air. He wanted to laugh out loud. Sure, save hundreds of jobs and the most important was the job of Preston Unitus.

"You denied me promotion then ask me to protect the job of the man you promoted over me? Does anyone not see the absurdity of this all?" Barney retorted.

Zelda Hampton's face changed to a vicious scowl. Barney could imagine smoke coming from her ears as she growled, "I'm not asking, Mr. Berry. I am ordering you to make it happen. And, I am reminding you of the confidentiality agreement you signed as part of your salary package."

"You're threatening me?" asked Barney. What he thought was that they were coming to the end of the stick and it was not a very big one. If this was the best they had, he was going to walk out on them and not look back.

"I am doing my job as the president of Baxter Life," Zelda snapped. "That is what I'm paid to do and you will do what you are paid to do."

"There is a personal component that does affect you, Barney," said Preston quietly. "Mr. Feinstein managed to keep his name off of the paperwork."

Terror flooded over Barney as the implication of statement hit home. He snatched up the printouts and quickly scanned them. That little detail fighting inside his brain to come out suddenly exploded. His employee number leaped off of the pages and slammed him in the face. That was what was bothering him but because he was accustomed to reviewing reports with his ID number on them, it had not initially occurred to him that it should not be on these reports.

"My employee number!" he yelled in anger. "My ID number is on these...these things!"

"The computer recorded you as the account auditor for each of the claims in question," smirked the president. You are not playing with an amateur, she sneered inside. This was her revenge for his impertinence in forcing her to compel him to do her dirty work. "So you see, Mr. Berry, your professional life hangs in the balance with Baxter Life. As well, there could be the possibility of criminal charges..."

Barney was deflated. The stick hit him again and again.

"He forged my ID number on those claims," he pleaded.

Zelda sat back triumphantly, "Can you prove that claim? Our IT people would dispute the possibility of that happening."

"He, um..." Barney thought desperately to explain how it could have happened. "Clive must have used my computer to process the claims. It's the only explanation."

"Can you prove that rather implausible charge, Mr. Berry?" the Baxter Life president chided him.

Of course he could not. Barney routinely left his desk without logging out of the system despite company policy that specifically instructed employees to do so. It was such a hassle to sign back on. Everyone did it. Nevertheless, to admit as much was no defense of someone else then using his computer and, therefore, his employee number to work on the system. Barney was screwed.

"His name is not linked to the claims. Nor is anyone else. Just yours," responded Preston. For his part, Barney saw that the man took no pleasure in forcing the cost accountant to do the filthy deed.

"I'll go to the authorities anyway," Barney muttered. But they all knew that he would not.

"And hang yourself in the process," scoffed Zelda, voicing what everyone in the room knew. "I will be shocked to discover your violation of company procedures."

By not doing what they wanted, Barney would be setting himself up as the perfect scapegoat. Before he walked into the offices of the government agency responsible for overseeing the insurance industry, these three would have memos and emails questioning the improper claims to cover their butts. Clive would leap on board and might even take credit for discovering that someone had screwed around with the accounts in his territory. And the computer trail would lead right back to Barney Berry as the culprit. He would be legally hung out to sway in the wind.

He slumped down in the chair and the reports dropped into his lap. "What's in it for me?" Barney asked weakly. The carrot was still out there and he might as well force them to give it to him.

Nikita's soft, tentative voice came out from behind the plants, "Your life is linked with the collective lives in this building. They are relying upon your ability to liberate them from this beast."

There was the carrot, and not much of one at that. His reward was to save himself and his fellow employees from the consequences of these three people and that slime Clive Feinstein. If he could not solve the problem, not only would he go down with the ship but hundreds of people with whom he associated daily would lose their jobs. All their hopes and dreams would be shattered if he failed to save Baxter Life from...

His eyes went from Nikita to Preston then to wicked, despicable Zelda and finally rested on the reports lying limply in his lap. There was a slight possibility that Clive might pay a price but that was doubtful. As well, the three executives would not suffer. Barney Berry was a low-level employee hired by human resources and recently passed over as unqualified for promotion. His failure would reflect on his immediate supervisor, a midlevel manager named Nancy Glace who rarely interfered with Barney because of his ability to work unsupervised. Poor Nancy would have to be sacrificed for not micromanaging Barney.

Barney's shoulders fell in defeat. The life slipped from him. The meeting was over. He grasped the reports in both hands, stood up and shuffled toward the door. He could feel Zelda's sense of victory over an inferior and Preston's smug confidence that a subordinate would bend to his will. But just before he reached the door, he felt or heard Nikita.

"Liberator," she whispered.

Barney paused and glanced at her over his shoulder. Their eyes met and he saw fear in them. "Liberator," she mouthed soundlessly. Then he was out the door and in the large outer office.

Martin, Zelda's milquetoast administrative assistant who liked to bully others but kowtowed to the president like no other, watched him drag his broken self out. Barney saw the delight in the man's eyes and the slight grin and wanted to smack the toad. Martin was never physically in meetings but always seemed to know what occurred in them. How Barney wanted to wipe that expression off of Martin's face.

He did not. Instead, he stopped and looked back at the door.

"Liberator," Barney whispered. And he was very much afraid.

Back in the office, Zelda and Preston watched their underling leave with the feeling that they had succeeded. If Barney failed to accomplish the task to their satisfaction, they had a scapegoat they would crush. There would be a setback to the company if they had to pay out all the claims but they had skilled attorneys that could push off the charges to the bottom line for a few years spreading out the hit. Should he succeed, the two executives would make sure the incident never saw the light of day and that included silencing Barney.

"That is one sorry excuse for a man," sneered Zelda.

"You realize that you have placed the welfare of this company in his hands?" Preston said in Nikita's direction. He was mentally constructing his defense should it become necessary to throw these two women under the bus if Berry botched the job.

Meanwhile, Nikita stepped away from her plant and stared hard at the closed door.

"His spirit is the only one suited for the task," she said softly.

"But will he do what we need done," Zelda stated, as if that would make it truly happen. "Without, of course, going public on us."

The Intuitionist studied the door for a moment as though watching Barney through the wooden closure. "His soul wanders," mumbled Nikita finally. Walking over, she touched the door trying to sense Barney's spiritual energy.

Zelda laughed in contempt, "I don't give rat's rump about his fantasies. I only care about that cost accountant solving my problem."

Publicly, she would never dare question the wisdom of her Intuitionist. An executive with aspirations of rising even higher did not scoff at the corporate philosophies that were in style unless the ambitious person had a track record of success which defied them. It was a catch 22 and the business landscape was scattered with the career corpses of those who thought they had a better way and failed.

Privately, however, Zelda believed in Zelda and would do what was necessary to advance the career of her favorite person, Zelda Hampton. She hired Nikita when Wilbur Tread the CEO of Baxter Life rambled on during one of their boring luncheons about the newest trend sweeping the corporate world. He inquired of her if she knew about Intuitionists. Not wanting to appear ignorant of the latest and greatest, Zelda responded that, not only did she know about them, she was in the final stages of hiring one. Wilbur was impressed and anxious to meet her final candidate. The president of Baxter Life was on the phone to HR the moment she climbed into her limousine for the trip back across town to the Baxter Life Building. She wanted an Intuitionist hired by the end of the week or heads would roll.

Watching across the room as Nikita rubbed her hand across the surface of the door, Zelda inwardly fumed. Her problem was that the freak of a woman was right too many times. Nikita had warned that Clive Feinstein was hiding something during the interview process. The Intuitionist sensed the danger of the unpaid claims and that led to a closer audit of every department which eventually unearthed the time bomb. Zelda could not readily dismiss anything the goofball said without evidence to the contrary and when it came to the cost accountant, the president did not have it, just a bad feeling. And feelings were not grounds for her to make a decision.

"He fears his other world," Nikita mumbled on. "Does not want it. He will eventually return to us and do what is best for the collective."

"He had better or I'll neuter him like a stray dog in the pound," muttered Zelda gruffly.

What the president of Baxter Life heard was that Barney Berry was going to effectuate an outcome she wanted. Her mind shifted to other issues as she took up the next set of papers on her desk, she had moved on to the next task on her list.

However, Preston frowned, his comments directed toward Nikita, "Let's hope what is best for the...collective is best for us."

The Baxter Life vice-president did not like the look on the Intuitionist's face. The expression conveyed that the strange woman did not believe this would work out as Zelda and Preston might want. Preston determined to keep a careful eye on Berry. He was frightened. It was far too late in his career to search for another position. His fate was linked to the company, whether he liked it or not.

From her position at the door and across the room from the other two executives, Nikita shivered imperceptively. She feared for the future but was powerless to do anything about what she saw of it coming toward her.

As a child, Nikita had that aloof personality which was ammunition for the other children who did not want to be looked at as different so they attacked anyone who was as a means of deflecting attention to themselves.

Nikita's mind worked differently from other children's. She did not have to connect the dots together to reach a conclusion, she just saw the end result of problems and that was that. When she innocently told other kids how events would come about she was ridiculed as a freak, an oddball. The children missed the point that she had been right most of the time. As a teenager, she dressed differently from other girls, preferring loose clothes that allowed for free movement as opposed to the tight-fitting, very restrictive clothing of her peers. She covered her body when the fashion was to show as much as possible. Then she began announcing the beginnings and endings of relationships and when they happened or fell apart, the girls came to her for advice on different boys. But it was not like they wanted her for a friend; she was too creepy for that. They just wanted to know if a specific boy could be conquered. However, it did not make her very popular with the boys when they discovered her gift. As they saw it, they were being manipulated and did not like it. Nikita saw that she had a certain power that set her apart so she had to hide it or suffer as a social outcast.

Unfortunately, her personality traits proved impossible to hide. She might recognize the dangers in being different but she did not have what it took to be the same as those around her. Her gift proved to be a curse.

In college she earned two degrees and felt less like an oddball around the academics who saw her quirks as normal but the degrees proved useless in the real world since her appearance dissuaded any potential employer from hiring her. When a friend spilled her soul to Nikita and she was able to give her a plan for overcoming her latest emotional distress, the woman suggested that Nikita set up shop as a fortune teller. After all, everything Nikita told her came about as predicted especially when the friend followed her advice and dumped the loser who was plaguing her life. In need of cash and slim on options, Nikita rented a storefront next to the corner coffee shop and managed a nice living. She determined correctly that those who were foolish enough to pay inflated prices for coffee that was not all that good would also drop a few bucks to have their futures scoped out for them.

A normal session started with the client talking about their past and current career path as well as any relationships. It was as if Nikita could see the entire life of the person laid out as they spoke and it gave her a sense of power. She accepted that she was different than others and the more she did not speak like those around her the more her clients trusted her words.

One day, the human resource manager from Baxter Life came to her with a proposition. The woman had been a repeat client of Nikita's for a year and offered her a job with the company. All that she had to do was give the top executives her exclusive opinions on a variety of issues. Nikita was happy with her little niche and initially rejected the offer until the HR person returned with the salary and benefit package. Wow, Nikita had never imagined making that kind of money. She took the job.

She rejected the offer of an office and an administrative assistant. The company gave her a cell phone and the freedom to wander the building. Nikita become a fixture at meetings, a ghost that slipped around the edges then had a quiet word with whoever was leading the meeting afterward. As her reputation built among the top executives who profited from knowing what the people under them were thinking, her power grew and so did her temperament to stay constantly on the fringes. Being consistently right had a price to pay, fear. And the more she learned about Baxter Life, the more she feared for the company and her salary package. She had become addicted to the freedom being wealthy and the lack of restraints on her.

The curse of her gift had reared its ugly head. Her fate was tied to the success of the company and the company to her ability to change from any destructive course. She had learned the stupidity of humans on a level she had never thought possible. She could see into the future, not like a wizard with mystical powers but with a mind that calculated out the inevitable results of current actions and behaviors of the employees of Baxter Life.

Looking at the other two executives, she knew that the faithful soldier understood the danger. He had given his life to the company in anticipation that he would eventually be rewarded with a life of peace and comfort. He understood that his future was in jeopardy. The other one was different. Power and the desire for more had clouded her thinking. She was planning a future grab for more and could not conceive that anyone for whom she had contempt would be a hindrance. She sensed the cost accountant in the elevator on his way back to his workstation and wondered what she could do to restrain him in his prison. For the moment he broke free of his chains, her life as she knew it was over.

Chapter 7

Barney stepped off the elevator and glanced up at his old enemy on the wall. Three more hours until this day was over.

His cell phone rang as he reached his cubicle. Melissa's happy voice was in his ear.

"Hey, sweetie," she chirped.

Oh no, he thought. The friendly voice could only mean that she wanted something from him.

"Remember how I told you that I met Dana Miles? Well, she and Mick are having a party tonight," she sang. "They want us to come."

He dropped the reports onto his desk and slumped into his chair. Bumping into his desk caused the mouse to giggle prompting the monitor to come to life. With one hand, he typed in his password as his wife continued to speak.

"Mick is nothing but connected to the insurance world..."

Great, Barney had two dozen or more new messages, half marked urgent. People had no idea what that word meant. It would take more than an hour just to respond to them.

Blah, blah, blah... "This is a wonderful opportunity for you to network with him." Then she waited for his response. Silence.

Barney suddenly became conscious that she expected him to say something. She must have said something which required his response.

"Um...," he managed.

"Come on, Barney," she moaned. "What excuse can you make to not go with me?"

"I just had a major project dumped on me..."

"Noooo, Barney!"

"…By the president of the company."

Silence again while Melissa processed what he was telling her. Or she processed it the way that his wife could in their relationship, how it affected her.

"The president?" she eventually said and her tone was not all that disappointed. "Zelda Hampton gave you an assignment?"

"Yes and it will take a long time," he sighed as he looked at the pile of papers and contemplated the task ahead. "I was going to work late tonight to get a jump on it…"

"Of course." The excitement in her voice blasted through the phone. "This could be your chance. No, it is your chance. She gave you a project to prep you for bigger and better things to come. Oh, you have to stay late. Do whatever you have to."

Finally, she stopped for a breath.

"I'll call you before I leave the office," he said with no enthusiasm.

"Work hard, Barney," she chirped. "Do a good job for both of us. And don't let me keep you from working."

"I will…" But Barney was talking to no one. His wife had hung up on him.

He imagined her at the party telling everyone about her upwardly mobile husband working late on a special, sent down from the top floor, project. She would be the widow of business with the husband who just had to work those long hours since he was so vital to the company.

His head dropped into his folded arms on the desk. Around him the chatter of the office was shifting. People were winding down their work and preparing to leave for the day. Over the next hour the office would be transformed into night mode with a few stragglers still finishing the odd job or pressing project. He would be here a lot longer than the longest-staying diehard.

"The world is coming apart," he moaned.

Something was different.

Above the cubicle wall the sound had abruptly changed.

Barney shifted his eyes side to side without moving. No cubicle and he had an automatic pistol in his hand while lying prone behind a log next to Melissa...

Nope, that was not right. Black hair and wearing khaki this had to be Katelyn and, crap, the world of the bugs. He glanced over at her.

Katelyn had one nasty looking automatic weapon and several grenades at the ready with an intense stare at something in the forest beyond the log.

Double crap!

Carefully, she shifted his gaze.

Spread out among the foliage was Katelyn's unit, barely visible under their camouflage.

Below them, an armed patrol of brown Waspoid warriors floated down the trail herding human along. The prisoners were a haggard bunch devoid of hope. The insects carried strange weapons particular to their appendages but Barney knew from past experience that they shot a deadly laser beam.

Katelyn eased up to see over the log and that was when Barney noticed the detonator switch in her hand. His eyes trailed hers to explosives strapped to the back of some trees at both ends of the trail. When the Waspoids were inside the perimeter of the rigged trees, she pressed the trigger.

The charges exploded and ripped up the trail with shrapnel, filled the air with smoke and toppled the trees.

Khaki clad resistance fighters appeared everywhere along the trail. Small arms weapons fire tore into the Bugs. The rounds ripped apart the screeching insect bodies sending parts and red goo splattering everywhere. The shrapnel also hit some of the prisoners.

The rest of the humans scattered in the chaos. Another one was hit by a resistance fighter when she ran between him and a Bug. Others were wounded by the blue beams from the Bugs' weapons as they shot at resistance fighters and prisoners alike. A prisoner raced toward where Katelyn and Barney hid, chased by a Waspoid, and leaped over their log. The Bug followed aimed the beam weapon at the prisoner, apparently not seeing Barney and Katelyn. Barney rose to his knees and aimed but could not make his gun work. Having given away his position, the insect warrior shifted to him.

That was when Katelyn quickly fired two shots from her oversized gun. The Bug shattered into a myriad of insect pieces that pelted Barney and he was also sprayed with the red gel-like slime.

He wanted to vomit but she was shouting at him, "Take the safety off!"

She motioned impatiently to the lever on the side of her weapon then, blasted another Waspoid into oblivion before she charged down the incline with her platoon. They forced the attack on the enemy before the insect warriors could form any kind of a defense.

At the same time, Barney turned his weapon over until he found the safety.

"Oh, I get it," he said to no one in particular because, he was alone on the little rise.

The Bugs recognized their situation and were attempting to retreat. One of them headed directly at Barney.

He flicked off the safety, gripped the weapon with both hands and fired at the Waspoid. The weapon bucked in his hands. He missed his target but at least he did not kill any humans in the process. Splat, another member of the unit took out the Bug.

As the resistance unit cleaned up the last of the enemy, the weapons fire tailed off. Abruptly, silence fell over the small battlefield except for the muffled cries of the wounded, human and insect. Injured Bugs emitted a buzzing whine that caused Barney to cringe. Bam, bam, two shots finished off the insects.

Barney was taking stock of the scene when he felt red slime trickle down his face. His clothing was covered in it. Just in time, he caught the gag reflex but bile still rose to his mouth. Unfortunately, the foul taste triggered his stomach to spew its contents and he barely managed to lean over a fallen log before the vomiting began.

Katelyn slapped him on the back, "Still think you're having an intense dream?"

White-faced, Barney wiped his mouth on the sleeve without red goo.

"I will grant you, it is intense and sticky," he said as he flicked off a wad of slime from his clothing. "It's still just a dream...nightmare."

She shook her head in disgust and walked away. "Sergeant Jack, fan out and round up all the humans you can find. We'll drop them off at a refugee camp. Be quick about it. We need to be a long way from here before the Bugs send out a patrol to search for their missing unit."

The sergeant and his team went off to follow their orders.

"Corporal, pile up the Bug weapons," she instructed then turned to Barney. "You need weapons training."

He glanced down at his red-slimed clothes. "I, um, could really use a shower," he concluded.

"You should also learn how to duck when Bugs are being blown away at close range."

"Good tip. I'll try to remember that for the next time."

Within minutes, the weapons were piled together and Sergeant Jack returned with only five humans. He shrugged, "All we could find, LT."

"Okay, Sergeant," ordered Katelyn, "Let's move out."

She motioned to the corporal who tossed a grenade onto the pile of weapons then hurried to join the unit. A few seconds later, the grenade kicked of a larger explosion.

"Why did you blow up those weapons?" Barney asked. "They are a lot better technology then what you're carrying."

"Except we can't easily fire them," answered the lieutenant. "They're made for the Bugs." Before he could ask, she added, "We've tried to adapt them but we don't have the scientific resources and the feds are not about to help us. So we destroy them. At least the Bugs will have to expend a greater portion of their resources to build more of them."

The unit moved carefully through the woods with Katelyn keeping an eye on everyone to make sure they were alert and doing their jobs. Once they deposited their human charges at a refugee camp, she and the team seemed to relax. They were climbing and Barney assumed the elevation made them feel safer. That and the five survivors they had escorted were noisy.

"You look so cute in Bug goo," Katelyn abruptly said.

Barney held out his arms and red slime dripped from them. He tried wiping it off on leaves but the stuff was like slippery gum. It formed into globs that became too heavy to remain attached and finally dropped off.

"Then how about a big hug?" he grinned.

"Yeah. That's not happening. I don't love you that much," she replied then waited.

Barney did not respond. He was wondering if he really heard her correctly. Loved him, really? For a moment, he considered telling her that he loved her in return. There was the realization that he might not love Melissa back in that other world anymore but this woman he did love. Still, a relationship with Katelyn would not solve his problem. In fact, it might even make things worse. He had to change Melissa into Katelyn back in the horrid world of Baxter Life. That was his pressing problem.

"Did you hear what I said? Katelyn asked. "I do love you, Barney Berry."

"I heard...," he said but he did not want to respond further.

"Well?"

"I think you're...swell."

She glared at him angrily, "Swell? That's all, just swell."

"Swell and pretty...," he searched for the words that would not betray his thoughts. "...gorgeous, you're fantastically gorgeous."

Katelyn sighed, shook her head and walked away.

"What?" he asked. "What did I say...?" But he was speaking to himself. Katelyn's unit passed him, the disappointment for what he must have done to their lieutenant apparent on their faces.

Katelyn, Barney and her platoon strolled into camp. Barney was forced to walk past the ARL soldiers watching them still covered in the red slime.

The camp was on a mountain slope filled with crevasses that made nice shelters from air attack and the elements. At the base where the ground flattened out under camouflage nets was the kitchen and further down were the latrines. A small stream trickling out of the mountain provided cold fresh water.

Shattner met them at the overhang Katelyn had selected for her living space and pitched her tent. The commander laughed heartily at his appearance, his voice dripped in sarcasm. "The Great Liberator."

Barney kept on walking, "Blow it out your ear."

"Barney," hissed Katelyn, "that's the commander."

"Touchy," chided Shattner. "Fighting Bugs isn't as easy as you imagined, is it?"

Barney stormed back and into Shattner's face, "What's your deal, Commander? I'm not the one claiming I'm this liberator."

Shattner glanced at Katelyn, "Others are."

"Well I can't control what others say about me," snapped Barney. "I'm just trying to do what's expected of me while I'm in this crazy insane world."

But Shattner did not back down. Pushing his face back into Barney's, he sneered, "Why don't you just go back to wherever you came from?"

"I wish I could," Barney retorted. "You think so little of me, Commander, throw me out."

"I tolerate you because Lieutenant Sumner thinks you can be useful," said Shattner in a low voice. "How, I don't know. But I respect her opinion. She's earned it. You've earned nothing, as far as I'm concerned, Cost Accountant."

The reality was a little different than he was pretending it to be. Most of his command believed this slime-covered insurance salesman was someone special. Whether they believed that he was actually the Liberator, there were degrees of faith. He could not force the man out of camp without severe repercussions. With his primary concern in keeping his army intact, he would have to tolerate the man until opinion shifted.

Barney flicked a blob of red slime onto the ground at Commander Shattner's feet. At least the guy had his title right, he thought.

"I'm fighting your Bugs," Barney noted. "What more do you want from me?"

"Commitment," Shattner stated flatly.

The word hung in the air between them.

"Do you want me to put my hand on some sacred book and swear loyalty to your great armed rebellion?" sniped Barney at last.

Shattner was abruptly in his face, his eyes wild with rage. For a moment, Barney thought he was going to be killed.

"My father was a general in the Federal Army Forces," Shattner hissed at him. "Fought the Bugs back when the government let the military defend the people and before the politicians took over running the war. He died doing what he thought was right. I expect nothing less of those who serve with me."

"And I just want this dream to end and I never come back to this place. No liberator. No saving the world," said Barney. His response was cold and unemotional, absent of any conviction, commitment.

Commander Shattner shook his head, glanced at Lieutenant Sumner and walked away.

In the early days of the hive, there was a consensus that the Bugs were a danger to the human race. General Shattner was authorized to use whatever force he thought necessary to wipe them out. Captain Shattner was his father's aide and at his side during the planning of the operation; Pest Control. Those were heady days when humans could not conceive of another force on the planet that could pose a threat to their existence. The army sent against the hive was comprised of three infantry brigades, a tank brigade and a complete wing of the air force. Planning and preparations were meticulous. The battle plan fell apart before the first shot was fired.

The air force was going to pound the structure into rubble then the tanks would roll over the mountain and into the valley to lead the direct assault. As the first wave of the winged attack swept over the mountain range, the Bugs' flying craft came up to meet them with their beam weapons that took out the planes' missiles before destroying every single human aircraft. When the tanks went in, they were helpless against the air superiority of the Waspoids. Then the insect army went after the following infantry coming out of the mountains and into a fiery hell. Those that managed to retreat into the mountains were safe until they emerged on the other side. The Bugs deployed units that were waiting for them and the slaughter continued. The only survivors were the lucky ones who hid in the mountains and waited until the mopping up ended.

When his father's forward headquarters was hit in the opening hours, Captain Shattner carried the wounded general to safety only to watch him die as all escape routes were cut off.

From his concealed position, he watched the insect workers pour over the dead humans and shattered war machines. They stripped everything and carried materials and human beings alike into the hive. He saw the worker insects process the human corpses and store the contents in containers. Later, when rumors surfaced that the Bugs ate humans, he was ready to believe it.

He buried his father's body where it would never be found and made his way back to the capital.

The Hive grew and wiped out two cities on the other side of the mountains. There were then three more fruitless attacks before the appeasers took over the government and offered peace terms. At that point, the army was but a skeleton force able to defend a few of the cities and nothing more.

After stripping the valley of all its resources, the harvesters appeared. These armed and mobile vehicles branched out from the hive's valley. They afforded the Waspoids better protection against attack while their foraged for their building material and supplies.

By the last attack, Colonel Shattner realized that a direct attack was not going to succeed but the only thing the appeasers were going to accomplish was to prolong the inevitable. However, he could not defend those who purposely sent human sacrifices to the Bugs as peace offerings. He quit the federal army and joined the new resistance movement that refused to hunker down in the major cities and wait out extinction. The Armed Resistance League was dedicated to continuing to pressure the Hive until a weakness could be discovered and exploited. When the two previous commanders were killed, he inherited the job.

Opinion had gradually changed from firm opposition to ever giving in to the Bugs to a passive let-live philosophy. Shattner knew that could only lead to one inevitable result, the extinction of humanity on the planet. Spies told tales of the Bugs' plans to keep the human race alive to provide them with a food source but that was hardly a future.

With the ARL as humanity's last hope to fight back, it left the commander of the resistance as the only leader not willing to compromise with the Hive Queen. It was a heavy responsibility for one person.

Katelyn watched her commander walk away. She had witnessed the entire encounter in disbelief. Since the first moment she had heard of the Liberator, she had faith that he would emerge and lead the humans in a heroic battle to end the tyranny of the Hive. It seemed so long ago that she remembered learning in school of the heroes who built her country, the country that now lay in shambles. She imagined the Liberator as a modern day version or those people. Instead, he was this malcontent. Only, she could not shake her belief in him.

"The Liberator has the chance to save humanity here, in this world," she tried again to invoke a sense of purpose in him. "Could you possibly have a more important job in that other world you keep talking about?"

"I could save a few hundred jobs," Barney softly muttered.

"And that compares how to leading an assault team in a desperate attempt to strike down evil?"

He could not stop the reflexive chuckle. She glared at him but his mouth then added to his stupidity, "You're kidding, right? That kind of thing can get you killed. Killed very dead."

"I would rather die doing something worthwhile than live a long life without ever making a difference," Katelyn whispered.

He was not sure how to respond. The face that stared at him with such disdain was the one he saw every morning planning a day of showing houses and working to make sure a closing went through without any hitches.

She marched off leaving Barney unsure what to do.

"I wish Melissa had said that," he finally murmured before making his way over to the makeshift shower area where he scrubbed the red gunk from his khakis and body. It gave him the chance to think. Commitment, the commander said.

Commitment, that was a tough word for Barney Berry. He came from a sleepy little town called Millersburg, Indiana. It was not the end of the world but it could be seen from there. He never made any friends growing up on the edge of the quaint little rural community in the middle of corn country and he was a stranger in his own family. All he could think about as he grew up was getting out. His art was supposed to be his ticket out but he did not hold onto the dream, a lack of commitment. Then the promise from Preston Unitus that he could rule the world from the top floor of Baxter Life enticed him into the insurance industry yet, he lacked the commitment to do what was necessary to advance. Melissa came along and the top floor dream faded as his infatuation with his wife grew. The couple talked about where they would take their lives together and he felt excited for a while. Somewhere the thrill behind their love stalled. He contemplated divorce, quitting his job and wandering the world when the dreams began.

Commitment, he was convinced that his marriage was the key. And changing Melissa into a woman he could love. Repair and restore his marriage into something to which he could commit. No, recommit.

It occurred to him as he scraped a glob of red grime from his arm that the best way to make Melissa into Katelyn was to study the ARL lieutenant. Somehow, this woman had become a woman of action and passion.

Two hours later, a freshly washed Barney walked in his underwear to the tent he shared with the lieutenant. His khakis were still damp but cleaned of red bug slime as was his body.

She had gotten their rations and was dishing out the mashed substances and pouring the nasty black coffee.

He noticed that clumps of soldiers watching him pass then speaking softly to each other.

"What's the deal with all the whispered conversations?" he asked his tent mate.

Surprisingly, she responded. A good sign that, maybe, she was no longer mad at him. "It's why Commander Shattner is concerned. Many in the camp believe."

"Believe?"

She sighed and lowered her head as though ashamed of the answer, "In the Liberator."

"Maybe you're the Liberator? Ever thought about that?" Barney asked. "You could be the one who defeats the Bugs."

Katelyn laughed at the idea. "Me!? What would make you think that I could be the Liberator?"

"Well, for one thing, you're not covered in bug slime," he replied.

He sat across from her and began to eat. He had learned to swallow the pureed rations and drink the sludge. As they ate, she thought about his question.

She was nothing special, she maintained. She was just another person who refused to allow the Bugs to take over her world without a fight. It was the sentiment that kept the resistance together despite the pushback from the established government. To the average resistance fighter, the federal government was made up of nothing but professional politicians more interested in saving their own skins and enriching their lives than the needs of the governed. The fighters of the resistance were patriots, patriots of humanity.

Once again, the passion burst from her. While she spoke, he tried to imagine the same fervor in Melissa but all he heard in his mind was her voice telling him to make money, buy a bigger home and fill it with stuff.

Night fell as he sat back beside Katelyn, cupped the metal coffee mug in both hands and finished the coffee. There was immense pleasure being with her even though she still had a hint of anger he felt from her shoulder touching his. He closed his eyes and sighed contentedly…

Chapter 8

The feel of Katelyn's shoulder was gone. Barney twirled around. Where was he? Examining his hands, the metal coffee mug had disappeared. Then the face of an angry Melissa was in his. There were the noises of a large party happening around them. Melissa was stunningly dressed. She could really look spectacular when she wanted to. Her long blonde hair was brushed out and hung around her face down onto her shoulders.

"What is going on in your head?" she chastised him.

He had no idea where he was or how he had gotten here. There was a vague recollection of a party at...? He could not remember.

Deciding to act innocent, he grabbed her glass and took a quick sip. "What? What did I do?"

"You're standing here all alone staring out the window in a room with people who can advance your career," she snapped, her voice low but distinctly upset with him. "What are you thinking? Miiiingle!"

"I was going to, uh, the bathroom."

"You can't mingle in the bathroom."

"I can't mingle when I need to piss."

"Fine. You've pissed now get out there!" She hooked his arm and tried to pull him into the room.

It was a large apartment, stylish with plants everywhere and loud music playing.

"Have you ever fired a gun?" Barney asked her abruptly.

As fabulous as she was in her evening dress and accessories, she somehow did not measure up to his

131

memory of Katelyn. That sounded dumb when he really thought about it. Her skimpy dress framed her succulent body and he imagined other men envying him. Nevertheless, there was something about a hot woman in khakis with a weapon in her hands. Then there was the passion, it was missing from her eyes.

"What?" Melissa shook her head in disbelief. "Don't be stupid. Of course I haven't. Why would I?"

"I was thinking about us taking a camping trip. Or an outing at a gun range." He smiled at the thought. "Have you ever thought of wearing a khaki outfit?"

Bam, Melissa smacked his arm. Though light, her tone was demanding, she meant business. "Will you focus on tonight? Anyway, I never wear khaki. The color does nothing for my body. Now…"

She was guiding him into a gathering of people and he panicked. "I'm, uh, not feeling well. I'm going to get some fresh air."

Breaking away, he hurried away and she threw up her hands in frustration.

Barney circled around the people chatting, eating and drinking. It must be one of those informal party affairs, he thought. That was good. He would not be missed as he would be at a dinner party.

"Barney!" Some perky woman was in his face.

Dana Miles? Right, the party was at Dana and Mick Miles.

"How are you?" Dana continued. "We haven't had a chance yet to talk."

"Hold on to that thought," Barney quickly responded and made a straight line for the front door.

Dana watched him leave, confused.

In the hallway, Barney rushed to the entrance. They were in a brownstone and the Miles had an apartment on the first floor. Music and conversation followed him out. He hit the front door and felt the fresh night air...

Barney stopped and twirled around in a complete circle.

What street was this? Even in the darkness, he could tell that it was not the affluent neighborhood where the Miles lived. The streetlights were out. The sidewalks were dirty and there was litter everywhere. A small, light breeze pushed odd pieces of paper down the street.

"What now?" he whispered.

Yet, something was familiar about the street. He walked half a block, his footsteps echoing in the night. Suddenly, he recognized where he was. Looking up, he saw the familiar image of the Baxter Life Building.

The building looked in poor condition in the darkness. The front doors he entered everyday had an old and rusty look to them. Pushing against them, a creaking sound accompanied him inside.

"Impossible," he breathed.

He quietly, cautiously crossed the dark and dirty floor of the lobby to the elevator and hit the familiar button but nothing happened. Great, no electricity. The moonlight passively seeping in the windows was all that illuminated the inside of the building. "Guess I'm taking the stairs," he muttered then quickly recoiled. His voice bounced off the walls as if he had shouted. It rattled around.

When he pushed open the door to the stairwell, the squeaky hinges made him flinch. The steps were as filthy as the lobby. It was official, something was wrong with this picture. He could feel the filth with every step up to the 10th floor. It clung to his hands when he used the handrails. Slipping out of the stairwell he walked into a strange place. Dust covered everything, cubicle walls, cabinets and other furniture that as also broken and rusted. He staggered to what should have been a familiar spot, his workspace, that cubicle where he spent so much time. Inside was his chair, or what remained of it.

"I'm back in the bug world," he said very quietly to himself. As hard as it was to believe, it was true. "I'm back."

This time though, he had not fallen asleep or closed his eyes so, was this considered dreaming then? The thought frightened him. He remembered feeling the panic of being thrown into the party. Selling himself to a bunch of people about whom he could care less was too stressful to endure. What a wreck he had become. Anyway, it was no longer about falling asleep and waking up. So what was it about?

Barney looked up at the ceiling, "Are you there? Is there some cosmic god trying to tell me something? Huh? Speak up, I'm listening."

Unconsciously, he entered the walled area and slumped into his old seat. That was a mistake, it collapsed and he sprawled out on the floor in a cloud of dust.

"Ouch!"

He stayed on the floor.

"Well, what did you expect, idiot?" he whispered. "Did you think someone would magically supply you with all the answers?"

Sitting in the dark on the floor, he sighed and glanced around. The moonlight from the windows cast strange shadows.

The implications were clear, this was his world. The employees were all gone. Baxter Life was no more. This was his future if he did not stop the dreams, he reasoned. He had a life he hated back in that other world and a future which was hardly any better in this world. Was Katelyn his Melissa in the future? What had caused Melissa to become Katelyn? Had she lost her memory or would there be an event that would steal it from her? More than ever he felt the need to bring the dreams to an end.

Footsteps. Someone else was in the building.

Barney crept over to the opening of the cubicle where he could see but not be seen.

The footsteps were ascending the steps.

He waited in his hiding place.

Clive carefully emerged from the same stairwell door he had taken. What was he doing here? There were now two people he knew from his world who were in this one.

"What is going on?" Clive demanded. His voice reverberated around the floor. "What has happened to this place?"

Clive stumbled on in the direction of his office. Rather, where he once had an office.

"Is anyone here?" Clive called as he vanished into the shambles of what was once an office of cubicles.

He could go after the wretched slime ball and ask him what was going on but Barney would not trust any answer that creep gave him.

Discretion was the better part of valor, he chose instead to hurry to the stairwell door and leave the floor. Behind him, the door made a terrible noise but he did not care. He was flying down the stairs and would be gone before Clive could catch up to him. He was not sure what his adversary was doing in the world of Bugs but he was confident that it was not a good sign for him.

Back up on the 10th floor, Clive rushed back into the cubicle area in response to the loud noises.

"Who's there?" he yelled. But no one replied.

Below, Barney pushed his way out of the building and the pressure change caused the elevator doors to rattle and Clive turned…

The elevator was clean, dust free.

The doors to the elevator of the 10th floor in the Baxter Life building opened and Barney turned around in a circle. He was back again in his world and his Baxter Life Building. He saw a stern-faced Clive watching him as he stepped off cautiously from the elevator then made his way to his cubicle. The newly-promoted department manager's eyes followed him. Barney had his briefcase in hand and clean clothes. How, he had no idea.

The monster on the wall said he was very early which accounted for only a few people scattered in the cubicles. Clive's presence was another matter. Was he still here, a product of Barney's jump?

"At least everything looks normal," Barney mumbled under his breath.

A moment earlier he was racing down the dirty steps of this building going toward the lobby. Now, he found himself back on the 10th floor.

"Berry!" he heard the annoying voice of Clive calling him.

"Rats."

Slowly, Barney turned to the voice. He can see the questions raging behind Clive's eyes but he had to wonder if the other man would have the guts to ask them.

"You're here early, Clive," he said in an even tone.

"Busy day. Much to do," replied Clive.

In reality, Clive had no idea how he had arrived at the office this early. A moment ago, he was in that spooky world full of giant bugs but not in the presidential palace. Instead, he was transported to a street of dilapidated buildings that included the Baxter Life Building. Some unknown person or persons was also in the building. Then, in a flash, he was back in the real Baxter Life and wearing fresh clothing. He had no idea what was going on but he was certain that Barney Berry knew something. But just how does a man of Clive's pride ask an underling about the crazy things he had experienced?

"You're never here early," Berry was saying to him, "even when you have a lot to do."

The tone of Berry's voice infuriated Clive. Even so, he could not afford to alienate the man given his two problems; a mysterious bug world where he saw Barney Berry and his claim crisis Zelda and Preston had given to Berry to solve.

137

"I'm concerned about the claim situation," Clive noted discretely. He chose to focus on the issue relevant to the real world where he apparently was at the moment.

"Should have thought about the...claim situation... before you got the company into this mess," snapped Barney and Clive fought the impulse to ream him a new one.

"What's our status?" asked Clive instead.

"I just heard about it yesterday."

"That means you had all night to work on it" Clive insisted. He intended to keep the pressure on. Maybe that would blunt this attitude Berry was giving him. "What have you come up with?"

However, Barney was not feeling docile. He played by the rules, put in the hours and the work and yet this skunk received his promotion all the while placing the company at risk. And what was Clive doing in his nightmare, Barney's mind screamed?

Anyway, Barney kept his desire to rip Clive apart under control and his voice close to a whisper, "What were you thinking, Clive? I've dissected this thing a billion times and I can't imagine what you thought was going to happen."

"What I thought would happen," Feinstein sneered back, "was that the company's profits would increase and I would receive the promotion I deserved."

Clive arrogantly held his arms out to the side and shrugged, voila.

"Congratulations," Barney huffed cynically.

Clive puffed out his chest, as it seemed to Barney, apparently unrepentant, "I know how to

138

make things happen. You know how to clean up afterwards. I did my job. Now, do yours."

The egotism angered Barney. Although he had to asked himself if it was because of what Clive Feinstein had done or because Barney was jealous that the man had the guts to make such unethical choices without apparent struggle with the morality of it. Hundreds of jobs or more were in danger because of Clive's actions and yet the man showed no sign of remorse.

"I have the perfect solution," Barney said. "You admit publicly that you cheated honest policyholders out of their rightful money. The company pays what it owes and takes the consequences. There, problem all cleaned up."

Clive laughed. Of course he did. What else could be expected from such a degenerate person?

He leaned closer to Barney and gloated softly, "Yeah. Well, you and I know that will never happen. The old witch of the top floor and her general cannot afford the embarrassment. The board of directors would throw them out on their ears if this ever became public. And you would face some nasty legal problems."

"Zelda and Preston should nail your sorry butt to the wall."

"Ha! And risk me telling the story to The Wall Street Journal? Not a chance. So long as those two are running this company, I'm on a path to the top."

"You're a scum bag, Clive."

The insult only made Clive smile. "I know. But one day, I'll be looking down at you from on high and you'll still be a grunt. Now, fix the problem."

Pivoting around, Clive started for his office.

"I'll go public?" Barney suggested in an even tone that made Clive pause. "I'll tell the media all about it."

When Clive turned around he was grinning. "No you won't. You're the one who authorized the payment rejections. Snitch and go to jail."

"You used my computer to make it look like I did it"

"Can you prove that erroneous charge?" Clive's smug expression infuriated Barney and he so wanted to wipe it off the other man's face. "Anyway, they picked you because you're no world-beater. You're more a play it safe, take orders and follow along kind of guy. Steady, dependable Barney Berry."

Unfortunately, Barney knew the slime ball was right. The cost accountant would do nothing except his job and do it to the best of his ability. That was the sad truth about Barney Berry.

"I know what I want from this world and I'm willing to go get it," Clive continued. "You, on the other hand, are a wuss. Afraid to take even the smallest of chances. That is why I'll succeed and you'll be a nothing."

Clive started to leave again but had one final thought. "By the way. You weren't in the office last night, were you?"

The question took Barney by surprise. Again, he wondered if Clive was reading his mind. Given all that had happened to him, he was not prepared to rule out anything.

"I was at a party with my wife being very bored," Barney finally replied. Then innocently added, "Why?"

Waving him off, Clive offered a flippant response that both men knew was a lie, "Security was making inquiries about some irregularities. Managers were told to ask around."

"Couldn't have been me. I was somewhere else. Far, far away."

Clive studied the insolent man for a moment then decided not to challenge the answer that he was sure was a lie. Barney Berry was not incapable of lying, just not good at it and Clive knew a lie when he heard one. He decided not to press the issue. One crisis at a time. So, he abruptly left the other man without another word.

With a sigh, Barney continued on to his cubicle, removed the printouts from his briefcase and switched on his computer. He began studying the problem handed to him more closely. What with the jump to the other world and the party he left early, he had not yet had much of an opportunity to calculate the extent of the crisis.

Around him were the sounds of the office filling with workers. Innocent men and women walked from the elevators to their desks with no idea of the burden that he carried for their jobs. Using the back of a scrap of paper, he wrote the numbers from the reports in columns. With a hand calculator, he ran the numbers he had run in his head a dozen times and the results were the same, financial catastrophe for Baxter Life. He still could not bring himself to enter the figures on a computer spreadsheet. Doing so would make it too real.

On paper, Baxter Life was an insurance juggernaut that rumbled over any and all of the competition. No one or nothing could hope to topple the giant of the industry from without. The truth of it, as Barney knew from his scrap of paper, was that it could fall from within, implode from a wound of its own making.

Reaching for another piece of paper from his scrap pile, he made detailed notes in an effort to find a way to do exactly what Zelda and Preston wanted, or something close to it, and failed.

He decided he needed coffee so he grabbed his mug and headed for the kitchen.

Christine burst from the kitchen right into Barney's path. Shaken out of his deep thought, he was knocked off balance and fell backward where he tripped over a large potted plant then fell onto the floor.

Ouch!

Barney was embarrassed, sprawled out on the floor like a circus clown, and was going to scold little Christine when he realized he was no longer in the office. He froze.

He was in a tent, a small one, and heard rustling. The scent was familiar. Katelyn! Obviously, he was in her tent. An eye opened slowly. Across from him Katelyn was crawling from her sleeping bag while trying not to disturb him. She may wear khakis and look absolutely wonderful in them but her underwear was definitely not khaki or anything military. Wearing white silky panties and a matching sports bra, she pulled on khaki-colored socks, tired her hair back, slipped on khaki pants and her boots. Dressed, she rose up onto her knees and nudged him while she slipped on her t-shirt and shirt.

"Up and at 'em," she prodded Barney.

Barney moaned and she mistook it for the desire to continue to sleep.

"Come on," she chided. "You can't sleep away the whole day."

"Where are we going?" he groaned. As he moved, his entire body hurt. It was as though he had slept all night on the ground.

"Call it a date."

"A date? But, we're mar..."

He was going to say that they were married and, therefore, no longer dated. Yeah, sure, there were married couples who still did that kind of thing but Melissa reminded him on numerous occasions that they were grown people, not teenagers. As such, they lived as mature married people.

"I'm sorry, we're what?" Katelyn asked.

"Oh!" Barney pulled his sore body out of the sleeping bag and stretched. He felt his bones creak and crack.

"You and I..." He stopped, thinking better of letting her into his mind. "Never mind. I'm having a disjointed day. This dream seems to go on forever."

And he noticed that he was wearing nothing but his shorts.

He quickly dressed while she went out to retrieve their breakfast rations.

A few minutes later, he crawled from the tent just as she returned from the kitchen below with two bowls of a green pudding substance and coffee.

It was hardly tasty. The camp was only a few days old so the kitchen had yet to receive the supplies necessary to make the standard breakfast rations of dried meat and fruit with a warm cereal. That meant that they were still eating field rations

143

and plain tasteless coffee. It filled the stomach but hardly satisfied the taste buds.

Most of the camp was not yet awake. Commander Shattner had granted a few days of rest and his soldiers were taking advantage of it by sleeping. Actually, there was little else to do anyway until he made a new battle plan. A few scouting units would be sent out but not allowed to engage the enemy unless forced to do so.

After breakfast, Katelyn took Barney to a cave armed to the teeth.

"You need some serious small arms practice," she explained.

The cave contained a target range used to train new recruits and test fire weapons. Barney looked around at the various plywood targets in the shape of and painted as Waspoids.

"I'm not sure this is a good idea."

Katelyn chuckled, "You really need to become more comfortable with weapons."

"Why are you doing this?" Barney could not help asking.

"I believe in you."

Barney cringed.

Katelyn did not notice, or pretended not to. Instead, she smoothly squared off, her feet apart and both hands on the weapon and fired several rounds. The Waspoid target was blown apart.

"Easy as eating cake," she grinned.

"You've never really watched me eat, have you?" he quipped.

She nudged him playfully, "Shoot."

"What I wouldn't give for a piece of cake just now," muttered Barney then took deliberate aim and

144

squeezed the trigger. It kicked in his hands. He managed to hit the target but not the Waspoid figure on it. He fired again and again until he emptied the clip. No hits.

"Where did the Bugs come from?" he asked as he ejected the clip and reloaded.

She studied him, not sure if he was serious but then decided he might not actually know.

"In the beginning, they seemed to appear out of nowhere. We didn't know they had built the hive in the valley. The whole area was a federal reserve and hardly anyone came here. The few people who hiked it and disappeared were treated as missing persons. Reports were filed and search parties were sent in to find them. They vanished. By the time the government finally acted, the hive was too powerful. The Bugs pounced on any concentration of troops like a swarm."

Katelyn took a deep breath then let it out slowly and fired, every shot was a kill shot.

"Now we harass them and probe for a weak spot."

For the first time since meeting her, Barney saw the despair in her. He took better aim and fired off the second clip and came closer; one hit the Waspoid in the leg.

"The appeasers took over the federal government. One of their members rose above the swill named Poisie. Within days of taking office, President Poisie sent negotiators to meet with the Bugs."

While she was speaking, Barney inserted another clip and took aim.

"Wait," she said.

Positioning behind him, she placed her hands on his hips and kicked his legs further apart then squared his shoulders. He felt her body against his and a sensation shot up his spine. With her face close to his, he took in her scent. It was so pleasurable.

"Eyes open," she ordered, and he realized he had closed them to smell her.

He aimed and fired, hit. Emptying his clip, he had several loose groupings.

"So how did the Bugs respond?"

"The appeaser president claimed a victory for diplomacy over war," she continued with the story. "Said we could live together and share the planet. Said the lack of attacks on humans proved his strategy worked."

"I take it, he was wrong?"

To punctuate her anger, Katelyn drew her weapon and fired several rapid shots, all hits.

"Total betrayal of mankind," she spat out, her scorn spilled out with the words. "The Bugs were just building their strength. When their harvesting units appeared everywhere beyond the mountains around the valley, we knew the truth. And worst of all, the hive was growing. Finally the Bugs attacked. The government retreated instead of counterattacking. They ran away to the cities. Gave up ground, hoping the Bugs would eventually be satisfied. They weren't."

She glanced over at him, "They never will be satisfied."

Her pain was evident. He knew the look well. The camp was filled with resistance fighters with that same look of pain and resignation.

"President Poisie offered the Bugs hostages in exchange for peace. That was the beginning of a new hell. The harvesters pushed further and further but the appeaser claimed the Queen of the Bugs promised they would no longer attack the human army if they received regular shipments of hostages to work for the insects."

She went on, her eyes staring at nothing as she remembered, "The resistance army grew with every new batch of humans sent to the hive. Relatives of those chosen to be given over joined either to escape the same fate or to fight with the hope of retrieving their loved ones. Meanwhile, in the cities controlled by the federal government, fear of being deported to a harvester or the hive keeps people loyal to the president."

Barney felt slightly ashamed. All that he wanted was for the dreams to stop so that he did not have to come to this horrible world anymore. But if and when he left, they would still be here fighting the Waspoid creatures. He would like to think that he had created this world completely in his mind and that when he left it, it disappeared. So if he never returned, it would no longer exist. That is what he wanted to believe. It made his lack of enthusiasm at becoming the Liberator.

She was staring at him. He could not help but wonder if she saw through to his thoughts.

"You smell nice," he finally said to break the tension of the moment.

"It repels insects."

Of course it does, he thought.

"The Bugs demand more workers to run the harvesters and build their Hive. The president turns over thousands, hundreds of thousands who never return. The Bugs insist on more and more be sent."

Barney's brained raced to a bad place, his memories of the occasions when he jumped into the hive and shuttered at what he had seen. None of it he dared tell her.

He almost choked on the inevitable question, "Where does he find people? Volunteers?"

"Hardly," Katelyn replied. "He emptied the jails. Claimed he was giving convicts a chance to earn their parole or even pardons. No one cared, they were criminals."

Again, Katelyn squared off and emptied her clip at a Waspoid target. She was aiming for the head and put a nice clean pattern in the center right between the bug's eyes. In Barney's experience, just one would have been enough to blow apart the head of a real bug.

He allowed his gaze to drift to her face. The eyes were angry but the rest of her features were gorgeous. Oh sure, he looked at that face every day and many a night he was over her making love while she lay under him, eyes closed as she savored his touch. Melissa was not really a passionate lover. She was more mechanical. That was to say, she enjoyed the act of love but it did not drive her into a wild throe of extreme sexual pleasure. The pleasure in blowing away a target that Barney saw in Katelyn was more than he had ever seen in his wife during lovemaking.

Wait, this was his wife...?

"What kind of excuses can you make for people, even convicts, not coming back?" he asked to mask the confusion he felt about her.

148

For her part, Katelyn took his bewilderment as relating to his question. Ejecting the clip, she reloaded as she spoke, "You would be surprised at what people are willing to believe to escape an uncomfortable truth. They want to believe that Poisie is telling the truth about having their interests at heart in his decisions. He takes the meager resources that are left and hands them out to those who support him. And the recipients praise him for his generosity."

He steadied his stance and took aim. Then, woops, she was once again behind him and adjusting his position.

"Relax more," she instructed him.

Yeah, right. Relax with those pretty hands all over him and that intoxicating bug repellent perfume in his nose.

A thought occurred to him. He glanced over his shoulder into those lovely eyes. "Why not just nuke the thing and get it over with?"

She chuckled dryly, "Nuclear weapons, in fact, everything nuclear were outlawed years ago but international treaty. They dismantled all of them. The rest of the world shut their doors and their ears to our plight. We are alone and virtually defenseless. We need a miracle…"

Bang, his shot hit the bull's eye on the head of the Waspoid.

"Like a liberator with a magic wand? Wave the wand and the bad insect creatures disappear?" he asked.

His question pained her and he could see and feel it.

"This is serious, Barney."

"And I am serious. I'm just me, good old Barney Berry." He twisted around again so he could look directly into her eyes as she stood behind him. He did not want to hurt those eyes, that beautiful face. What he wanted was to make love to her. Somehow, he knew that Katelyn Sumner would dive into sex with great passion and come with the force of a bullet fired from her weapon. However, the guilt that it might somehow be an unfaithful act to Melissa pounded him.

Sighing, he added, "I can't do anything for this world. I belong in my own world."

"Where you can save it one insurance policy at a time?" she sniped angrily.

That was enough to kill the moment of sexual desire Barney felt. The look on her face was definitely familiar to him. It was the same Melissa used to display her disappointment with him. Two different worlds, two different women but the same look of derision.

"You have no idea what it's like to be a cost accountant. Boring doesn't even come close to describing it."

"Stay here, in this world," Katelyn said simply. "You could lead us to victory then take over the government."

He laughed to conceal the surprise.

Unconsciously, Barney pointed his gun and squeezed off three shots. He hit three bull's eyes but did not notice.

"If you are the Liberator, your destiny is to save this world," Katelyn said in a whispered voice.

Hardly, he thought. He had discovered through his confrontation with Clive that he could not even stand up for himself, let alone the other employees of Baxter Life or the humanity of a strange world. However, he fought the impulse to speak the words. This version of Melissa or this Katelyn, whoever she was, would not be impressed with Barney the Wimp. How he loved this woman with the black hair and the khaki uniform but his hope lie in changing the copy in the other world with whom he was married. The one in the fashionable clothing and desire to advance socially.

Katelyn declared him a marksman and the training finished. They walked from the cave into a camp completely awake.

"Well, that was interesting, to say the least," he remarked.

Katelyn chuckled, "Everyone should have a hobby."

"I have to tell you that I don't know many women whose idea of fun is using heavy ordinance to waste cardboard targets." He joked and nudged her. Inside he signed. He made love to a naked Melissa yet he felt more of a sexual sensation with that one little touch then an hour of full-blown sex.

"Obviously, you don't frequent the right places."

They field stripped and cleaned their weapons sitting crossed-legged in front of their tent. Barney was enjoying the moment when a thought occurred to him. He hefted the assembled handgun and grinned. Katelyn noticed it but did not ask what brought it on.

She then transformed into Lieutenant Sumner and they were out on patrol. Her unit was charged with reconnoitering the far edge of the forest for

151

signs of the Waspoids incursions. Commander Shattner wanted to see if the Bugs had found the new ARL camp yet.

Barney went along, safely ensconced in the center of the platoon although he had a new confidence with the weapon at his side and the automatic rifle in his hands.

"How did you become part of the Resistance?" he asked as they walked along. There was no evidence that the Bugs had started searching for the resistance so the fighters relaxed a bit so talking softly was tolerated among those not on point. The question was not as innocent as it appeared. In Barney's mind, the key to stopping the dreams was Melissa and understanding how he could change her from that self-absorbed person to this woman who would give her life to good a cause. So he was fishing for how to effectuate the change.

According to Katelyn Sumner, she had an idyllic childhood despite the arrival of the Waspoid Hive. Her little town, the name Barney recognized as Melissa's birthplace, was like many others not touched by the war with the Bugs. The insects were attacking cities near their harvesters. The people in the small communities considered the war the problem of the larger urban centers that drew the attention of the Hive's occupants. That proved more a prayer than reality.

Then, one day the Bugs came to the town. It was a peaceful start to the morning. Katelyn was headed to her job at the coffee shop when her whole world exploded. There were explosions everywhere. People were being shot and hover craft swooped in from all over the place with their beam weapons tearing up buildings and bodies. For the life of her, Katelyn had no idea how she survived.

The collection followed the attack. From her hiding place, she watched individuals caught up in the beams of the hover craft and others herded into carriers that landed in the center of the town square next to the ruined monument honoring the fallen heroes from the town who had died in foreign battles. She saw two of her female friends forced inside along with a boy who had once asked her out on a date.

Eventually, there was quiet. As night fell, she snuck home but her house no longer existed and her parents were gone.

She ran and spent a cold night in the woods, shivering and scared by every sound in the darkness, and there were many. Eventually she found a refugee camp. She would still be in one of those camps had not an old veteran of two wars taught her how to shoot an old handgun he kept from his military days. He claimed that every human needed to know how to use weapons. She almost blew off his foot the first time she tried to fire it but gradually became skilled.

Recruiters for the Resistance came through the camp and funneled her to one of their units.

Her first firefight was a blur of chaos and fear. The first Bug she killed blew into little pieces when she emptied an entire clip of an automatic rifle into him. Nevertheless, combat eventually slowed down and she learned to remain calm under battle conditions.

She worked her way up to a squad leader. The promotion to lieutenant was recent.

The patrol reached the outer most point of their area and circled around to return to the camp. As a rule, a unit never walked the same route twice so they were moving down a different trail.

"Do you ever miss being a real woman?" asked Barney. "You know, dressing in the latest fashion, makeup and such?"

"Real woman?" Katelyn thought for a few minutes, the pause was so long that Barney thought she had forgotten the question. Finally, "That doesn't even sound appealing. Why would I want a life that boring? Why would anyone?"

Barney could only shrug sheepishly.

She snorted, "What, go back to making coffee. A brewista?"

Oops, Katelyn saw the expression on his face and realized she had hit a nerve. Good, she thought. He needed a kick in the butt if he was going to embrace his destiny.

"How does a cost accountant trapped in a life he hates travel to this world?" she asked.

How indeed?

It started as a normal dream. It was after one of those weeks when Barney was really feeling the pain of the corporate life. Pressure to put out the work was intense at Baxter Life and Melissa had their social calendar packed with events. Hours of tedious assignments, endless reports and deadlines. Once he left the office, there were boring parties and the opening of an art exhibit. The realization hit home. This was his life and there was no change in sight. Nauseated, Barney rushed to the restroom and vomited. What followed was like an out-of-body experience. In a flash, he was in a large domed

154

room watching wasp-like creatures. They were…using people, feeding them to larvae. He drifted through each experience like a ghost.

Then the dreams kind of became real. His first physical contact with anyone in this different world was the day he met Katelyn.

The lieutenant regarded him for a moment. "I don't get how you can think that you are making this world up in your mind now." She touched him, poking his arm, "How can you think that you are dreaming me?"

"You're like this person I know in my…in the other world," he said cautiously.

She blinked. "Is she pretty?"

They were at the camp and passing the camouflaged outer defensive positions. Barney mentally patted himself on the back for recognizing them among the foliage.

"She likes dressing in expensive clothes and decorating her home," he replied. "Her idea of fun is going to parties. To tell you the truth, I had more fun wasting Bug targets than I've had at any of her fancy affairs."

She was beside him, their shoulders touching, transformed into Katelyn again, the lieutenant set aside now that they were back in the safety of the camp.

For the first time since they had met, he heard that seductive voice Melissa used when she wanted sex. "Maybe you can find out what else I'm good at?"

It was the first time she had brought up the idea of sex. Lord have mercy, yes he wanted her. He had wanted her for a long time but the struggle with faithfulness to his wife had prevented him for making a move on her. Well, if it could be said that Barney Berry had moves, which was debatable. Anyway, he had to be honest.

"I have to explain something." He spoke slowly, carefully. "That other woman... We're married. But..."

She did not allow him to finish but exploded right there with her unit watching and the entire camp around them. "Married!? You're married? You're married and didn't think to mention it before?"

The platoon moved on and left them to their public privacy. Or rather, they pretended to do so. What Katelyn's soldiers did was to blend in with others around them so they could watch. There was not a lot of entertainment in the camp and no one was going to miss Lieutenant Sumner in a heated discussion with the Liberator.

Meanwhile, Barney was trying to explain, "Technically, I'm not sure we're married in this world..."

She did not see the logic in his argument. "What do you take me for, a whore? Not married in this world. You're married!"

"There's something else you need to know about her..."

Again, she cut him off as her anger built. "Oh, yeah? Like she'll understand if you make love to another woman in a pretend world? After all, that's not really sex."

"No, it's not like that. You see..."

"Oh ho! I see it all," she glared at him. "You think you're making up this world so you can cheat on your wife without guilt."

Barney's head fell. This world was not so different from his other world. In that world, he had fights with the woman that he once loved and wanted to love again. And now... He looked at Katelyn; there was no doubt that he loved the woman soldier in khaki.

"If you only knew," he said softly. "Our marriage is confusing."

With this man, that was a word she understood. She felt sorry for him. There was no way that she could comprehend the struggles happening inside of him if any of what he was telling her was true.

"Do you love her?"

I love you and I want to love her like I love you, Barney wanted to say. Instead, he managed, "I don't even know if I like me. How can I claim to love someone else?"

His eyes drifted around and he noticed the entire camp was watching them.

"I'm going to the tent," he muttered and walked off.

Night fell and Katelyn found Barney sitting alone by the embers of what was a small fire. After dark all fires were reduced to smoldering coals. She sat across from him in the little heat the dying fire provided.

"Tell me about her," she prompted him in a quiet voice.

Barney stirred the coals with a stick. When he spoke, it poured out of him quickly.

They met at a party. They were both bored and seeking an escape. There were a few dates. He had no idea that she was the slightest bit interested in him beyond those occasions and three nights that ended in sex. Marriage was a big surprise. She came up with the whole wedding idea. Barney did not have much of a say about it or that she had somehow started to live with him. She talked him into running off to Vegas. The woman was so pretty, sexy, with a personality that attracted people that he could not help loving her. Along with her physical qualities, she was safe, predictable, just like his job. He advanced at Baxter Life and their marriage advanced. With her, his life was manageable. That was before predictable became boring and boring changed to tedious. It was a revelation that his marriage joined his defunct career at Baxter Life and his floundering hobby as an artist.

"But then I met you," Barney concluded, looking across the flames at her. "You're dangerous, exciting and scary. A wonderful scary. And you look exactly…"

She cut him off.

"I'm not a thief," she said quickly. "I don't steal men from other women. And I'm definitely not a fantasy life prostitute."

"I didn't mean…" He hated fighting with her. It was like being with Melissa, fighting with Melissa. "Look, I don't fully understand the rules to this jumping between worlds."

"Excuses."

"What?"

"You make excuses. It seems like everything in that other world is someone else's fault. You don't want to take risks so, you make excuses for why you can't change. You want my advice, tell your other woman how you feel. Take a chance. She may surprise you."

He turned so that she could not see his face for fear that she might read his mind. "I need to go."

"Back to your old world?"

Barney gave her a weak smile. "I have no control over that." He sighed, "I just think it would be best if…"

He left her to finish the thought. They sat in silence for a long time. There was something between them now that had not been there before when they were friends and occasional teases. Everything had changed and not for the best.

The camp slowly drifted into a collective sleep.

Eventually, Barney walked off and found a place on the edge of camp under a tree. He sat back against the trunk and shivered in the cold. At one point, his head dropped to his chest as exhaustion from the emotional stress took over his body.

Chapter 9

The park seemed so lonely. Barney found that he was sitting on a bench under a light. He listened, the quiet was scary. He eased off of his seat and slid into the bushes where he felt more secure. Avoiding the foot police, he made his way to sidewalks where he blended in with the bar hoppers still out looking for another drink and a good time.

Once he had his bearings, he walked to the street of his apartment building.

He quietly eased into the apartment. It was very still, only one lamp in the living room was on. He thought he was safe, Melissa must be in bed. He did not see her sitting in the semi-darkened room until he was almost to the hallway headed back to the bedrooms when she cleared her throat.

"Where have you been?" Melissa demanded in a calm, cool voice. He jumped a mile. "I called your cell, the office."

He had never thought to check his phone for missed calls when he found himself back in his real world. Pulling it from his pocket, he saw five calls and five messages as well as quiet a number of e-mails.

"You know...I...I..."

She waited.

Hang on, he thought. What right did she have to check up on him like a little boy? He had some moral ground to stand on, here.

"You were checking up on me?" He tried to sound as indignant as possible.

"You are good old Barney, remember? You've had the same routine since I've known you. When you didn't come home I was afraid you had been mugged. I was concerned about you."

She raced into his arms and sobbed on his shoulder. He was taken completely by surprise. She sobbed on about how worried she had been. She called everyone they knew hunting for him.

"I was out with a friend," he explained.

Then it all went bad, very bad. She took in air in between her sniffles. But then she sniffed. There was a new scent in the air. Her expression changed from concern to anger to rage.

"Who is she, Barney Berry!?"

Barney was taken aback. "What are you talking about?"

She pushed him away and he saw that he was in big trouble.

"You've been with another woman," she said, just a bit lower than a shout. "Don't try to deny it. I can smell her scent, her perfume."

Without thinking, Barney blurted out, "She is...a friend from the...office. We were just talking..."

Wham, the hand came out of nowhere and across his cheek.

"Ouch!" That really hurt.

Now she was shouting, "You're a lousy liar." She sniffed him a second time. "You can't get a woman's perfume all over you from just a casual conversation. Have you slept with her? You slept with her!"

Desperately, Barney tried to figure out how he could have gotten Katelyn's scent on his clothing. Oh no, he had slept in her tent. But he sure could not tell his wife that was how he had gotten the scent of another woman all over him. There was no way that she would believe a woman in a dream left the smell on him. He was defenseless.

She beat his chest, "You betrayed me! After all that I've done for you. We were planning our lives together!"

That was the point when Barney snapped. First Katelyn had scolded him and now Melissa was accusing him of something that he had not done. He did not care how the perfume had made its way onto his clothing. He was mad.

"You," he shot back, "you are planning our lives, my life. I have no say in any of it."

The apartment was so quiet that her arms moving against her side could be heard. Her eyes teared up and she was momentarily speechless.

Had Barney been better at domestic combat, he would have jumped in and kept her on the defensive. Sadly for him, he was not and she found her voice and filled the void.

"Why didn't you tell me you wanted a different life?" demanded Melissa indignantly. "You're a user, Barney Berry. You take from people until you've used them up then move on to the next whore in line! Isn't that right? That's all women are to you, whores."

"She is not...!" He stopped for breath and to calm his spirit. Barney had in his mind the image of Katelyn in khakis. He was defending that woman against the same woman dressed in Gucci and Chanel or whatever.

He continued only with a softer tone, "I did tell you. I told you I was bored to tears. I told you my

162

job was sucking the very life out of me. I told you everything."

"And this was your solution to the problem? Sleeping with another woman?"

"We didn't...!" He tried to remain composed. "It's complicated. What is best is to talk about this tomorrow when our heads are clearer."

Barney was tired. Jumping between worlds was beginning to take a physical toll on him. He was sleeping very little in either world. He started to walk toward the bedroom.

"Oh no you don't!" Melissa pushed past him and cut off the bedroom. "You're not staying here tonight! I will not be in the same house with you."

"Where do you expect me to go?"

"Go back to your lover."

"If only I knew how," muttered Barney and just a bit too loudly.

Humph, she twirled around and marched to the bedroom. The door slammed shut.

Barney did not move. He had no idea what to do or where to go. He had no friends. At least none of his own. Melissa had so structured his life that the old buddies stopped calling him to come over for the big game or poker or any number of things he used to do with them.

Melissa swung open the bedroom door and he had the slight ray of hope.

"Just tell me why?" she sniffled. "You were on the verge of having everything a man could want. All you had to do was reach out and take it. Every chance this world could offer you was yours. So, why?"

"I hate this world! I hate me! I hate me and this hideous monster you call my life," he said, remarkably even and controlled.

"I'm...I was in that life, Barney." He thought she was going to slam the door in his face but she did not. "What's to become of us?" she whispered.

"How is there an us, Melissa?" He remained surprisingly calm considering the turmoil building inside of him. "I'm a man searching for a life. And do you help me? No. You kick me while I'm down. How is that a life together?"

It was his turn to walk out and he headed for the front door.

"Barney..." He stopped with his hand on the doorknob to listen to her, give her one last chance to apologize. As he saw it, he had done nothing wrong. "Where are you going?"

"What's it to you? You're throwing me out, remember?"

With that, he left.

Wandering the streets, Barney bought a coffee from an all-night diner and drifted. He really had no place to go.

Lamenting his marriage failure, he considered it comical that he thought the secret to ending his nightmare life was to change his wife. What was it, he wondered, that kept causing he trials?

Eventually, he figured, he would be forced to check into a hotel or sleep on the bus stop bench where he was sitting with the empty Styrofoam coffee cup. The cup hit the ground as he buried his face in his hands and fought the urge to cry. A depression was setting in. Then an all too familiar wave of overwhelming despair swarmed over him.

Whoosh, a large delivery truck drove past and the wind and blew dirt into his eyes.

Chapter 10

Whoosh. Barney ducked down instinctively as a hover craft whisked over the treetops.

"Oh no," he moaned. "No need for that hotel room."

He scanned his surroundings. He did not like what he was thinking. Things were starting to register. He was not happy about what he believed was happening. That almost made him chuckle. Not happy...?

How was it possible? He was not the first man to hate his life. So how could that be the catalyst to sending him into this nightmare world? Could it be that it was not his wife who had to change? That was a terrifying thought.

He watched the hover craft disappear into the distance. He was in what he had learned was no-man's-land. In one direction was the Hive and the other led to the ARL camp. He turned toward the camp.

Barney walked out of the woods and into the camouflaged tents of the Armed Resistance League camp. None of the guards challenged him as they would anyone else. He ignored Commander Shattner standing stoically in front of his tent. He could imagine the discussions that had circulated the resistance fighters since his unexpected disappearance after the quarrel with Katelyn.

He found the lieutenant sitting in front of her tent using the light of a small lantern to field strip and clean her weapons. She did not look up from her work when Barney sat down sheepishly beside her. The ever-present pot of coffee warmed on a stone carefully placed in the embers of a former fire for just that purpose. He took a spare cup and poured a small amount into it.

"Thought you were going back to that other world," she finally said, her attention still on the weapon.

"I did." He sipped the coffee. It was terrible but tasted great. He stared into the cup and wondered how that could be. "My wife thought we had slept together. She threw me out. I tried to tell her. She just wouldn't listen. Then, bang, I'm right back here."

That caused her to look over at him. "I'm so sorry. I didn't..." But she did not know how to finish.

"It's not your fault." He sighed, "Why can't I stand up for myself? What's wrong with me?"

He nursed the coffee and she pretended to adjust the gun.

"I hate that world and yet I can't change anything in it. I just go along with my wife's plans for me, my company's demands on me and, thanks to my life; the worst of it is that I hurt people."

She waited sensing that he was not finished speaking and he loved her for it. He longed to have this kind of relationship with Melissa.

"I think I know why I jump." He paused and waited until she would look at him. He wanted her to know that he was serious. She had an automatic rifle in hand and was cleaning the firing mechanism. She looked up. "Discontentment."

"Discontentment?" She thought about it for a moment and tried to make sense of the idea. She lived in a world under the constant threat of killer bugs. Contentment was not a word most would use to describe their lives. She really did not have a frame of reference, not for a long time. "I don't follow you."

"When Melissa threw me out…"

"Melissa, the…wife?" She almost could not add "wife" but did manage.

He could only nod and continue, "I had this tremendous feeling of despair. It made me sick to my stomach. It dawned on me that I've felt that feeling before."

She held the automatic rifle with the barrel pointed in the air and pulled the trigger, click. She nodded in appreciation of the sound. He waited. She was thinking and he did not want to break into those thoughts but let her come to her own conclusion.

"You think you do this jump thing because you're unhappy in your other world?" she asked, a hint of disbelief escaped with the question.

"More than unhappy. Beyond despair. It's the moments when I can see no hope, no end to the tedium in my life that I jump." He grabbed a twig, snapped off small pieces and flicked them into the coals and they flamed briefly then merged with the coals. "The same thing happens in reverse while in this world. When I gain enough hatred for the Bugs, I pop back to that other world."

"Here is a thought," she said as she slapped home an ammunition clip into the weapon as though to punctuate her thought. "Maybe you really belong here. That other world could be the bad dream."

"There's more."

"There always is."

168

"When I find that I am more contented in that other world then in this world I also go back to that other world," he said. "I have to believe that world is my real home."

She swallowed hard, "Then I am...?" However, she could not finish the sentence.

They both knew what she was thinking. If this world was all in his demented imagination then, she was nothing more than his imagination as well.

"You are one messed up guy, Barney Berry, Cost Accountant," she whispered finally.

They sipped the last of the coffee. He watched as she stripped and reassembled another weapon. After an hour or so, he stood.

"I think I will see if the quartermaster will issue me a tent," he said. "I could really use some sleep."

He waited for the briefest of seconds but she did not offer to share her tent. So he went in search of a tent.

Morning came too quickly. The camp was awake before the sun. The camp kitchen was running and they had managed a few treats for those fortunate enough to get there early. Barney was among them and eating dried fruit, hard bread and coffee for breakfast when he saw Katelyn walking toward Shattner's tent. The commander was holding a briefing at his field table. Barney included himself with the command staff even though he had not been invited. Shattner did not dare ask him to leave; he was the Liberator in the minds of a large portion of the commander's soldiers. Katelyn ignored Barney. They were in a new relationship neither yet understood.

Commander Shattner was planning a major attack but needed intel. Patrols were to look for specific information on Bug military movements. Therefore, they were not to engage the enemy unless there were no other options available.

Barney geared-up and attached himself to the rear of Katelyn's platoon. She glared back at him but she also could not refuse to allow him along. He hung back with the team trailing the patrol guarding the rear. Unlike most operations, this one was loose. They were out for intelligence, not seek and destroy. They moved with a quick quiet. Look, study and return to camp.

Simon was a new young recruit on his first mission. He was the sort who gravitated to the resistance, idealistic and full of the desire to help humans battle the insect monsters. Life was still an adventure for him. He also was a bit star-struck by the Liberator.

Barney struck up a hushed conversation with him as they made their way through the thick section of the woods. He liked the kid. Simon was the type of person an army needed; too young to know real fear but old enough to be an adult. His family had been collected by a harvester while the government stood by and did nothing. He and a bunch of his friends, children really, had managed to escape. Now that he was old enough, he thought it time to join the Armed Resistance League. The youth was fresh from training.

It happened so quickly and unexpectantly that Barney was taken completely by surprise.

The soldier on point held up a fist. The unit froze then slowly each member dropped down into a concealed posture without disturbing the foliage and waited. The patrol had walked right up on a group of worker Bugs busily collecting building materials. When one of the tan bodied workers spotted movement, he communicated to the brown torso Waspoid soldier standing guard for them. The warrior insect scanned the undergrowth. He must have spotted something because he turned his beam weapon on the general area where the human patrol was hiding and fired a burst. The Bug hit nothing but leaves and branches.

The skilled resistance fighters knew to remain frozen in place without moving any part of their bodies.

However, Simon panicked. He had never been under fire before. Instinct told him to return fire. Rising up, he sprayed the Bug with his entire clip. Boom, the creature exploded into red slime and brown insect parts.

The worker Bugs retreated. Their concern was in salvaging the building material they had gathered. But the soldier Bugs were there to protect and fight so that is what they did. Blue beams filled the air. Simon took a burst in the shoulder, spun around and fell back.

The firefight lasted only a few minutes as Katelyn ordered a retreat. Barney popped off a couple of shots before rushing to Simon's side and helping to carry him out of harm's way. It did not take the disciplined platoon long to disengage with the enemy and pull back out of danger with Simon's wounded body in tow.

The young fighter died a few minutes later with Katelyn and Barney hovering over him.

Once they were sure that the Bugs were not trailing them, they buried Simon's body and camouflaged his grave to prevent animals or the Waspoids from digging it up.

The march back to the ARL camp was solemn. The chatter was gone. Lieutenant Sumner and her noncommissioned officers mostly communicated with hand signals.

Commander Shattner was there to meet the platoon when they arrived. He spoke briefly with his officer then let Katelyn go to her tent.

Barney watched her crawl inside.

"There is nothing you can say," Shattner said to him, as though he had read Barney's mind. "The first KIA is always the hardest for an officer."

"Simon was her first?" That came as a surprise to Barney.

"Simon?" Shattner nodded. "That was his name, then."

Before Barney could scold the commander for not knowing the name of one of his soldiers, Shattner walked way, his mind elsewhere. He could feel the somber mood of the camp as he drifted aimlessly to his tent.

As the camp settled in for the night, Barney tried to sleep but the grief he felt for Katelyn and the brief connection he had made with Simon would not allow it. He did not want this suffering, this world of death and destruction. He hated the Bugs, especially the Queen and her General. Yes, it was all the fault of those evil insects that he now grieved for the woman he loved. He draped his arm over his eyes and suffered for her.

172

Then the cramps in his stomach started and he tried to fight them. This was not what he wanted. He hated this world but not as much as that other world. As the pain ripped through his body, his soul was in complete confusion. His spirit was torn between two worlds.

He screamed, "Noooo..."

Then he blinked and blinked again.

The elevator stopped and the doors opened. Barney leaned back against the wall. He felt very bad. This was a first. He brought pain back from the other world. After a few deep breathes, he took stock of his situation. He was in the elevator of his apartment building.

He stepped out into the familiar hallway, walked to the end where he stopped in front of the door to his apartment. He loved Katelyn. He had lost his love for Melissa but he loved the version of her that he had discovered in that world of hell. Hell? For the first time, he actually fought to remain in the land of the Bugs. She was pulling him there, or rather keeping him there.

Pushing open the door, he removed an envelope taped to it. He did not need the note to know what had happened.

"How long was I gone?" he wondered out loud.

The apartment was completely empty.

He walked through every room and, with the exception of his office and all his art supplies, she had removed everything. That must have taken some time. He checked his phone for the date. Two days!? Melissa had cleared out their entire apartment in two days. Technically, it was his apartment. After they were married, she moved in all her belongings, removed all his old furniture and completely redecorated every room except for his office. Somehow, they had never gotten around to adding her name to the lease since her plans for their life together included a new and bigger place. Officially and legally, the apartment itself was Barney's and his responsibility.

"I guess she figured the furniture was hers," he muttered as he walked around the empty spaces. He hated that stuff, all fluffy with tons of pillows everywhere.

He looked to the ceiling and shouted, "Why were there so many pillows!?"

Eventually, he turned his attention to the envelope and removed a single piece of paper. It was a formal letter from a very expensive law firm, judging by the letterhead.

It read, "This is to inform you of the intent to begin divorce proceedings by Melissa McDay."

Obviously, she was working on the premise that possession is nine-tenths of the law. That is, ownership is easier to maintain if one has possession and difficult to claim if one does not.

He was in the empty bedroom with the view of the city where they had made love. He remembered the feel of her skin, her many scents and the fire in her eyes. No! In his mind though, he imagined Katelyn and not Melissa in the bed that once dominated the room. It was the resistance fighter whose touch he remembered and whose marvelous body he once held.

Returning to the only furnished room in the apartment, he slumped at his desk. The reports were laid out where he had left them after the last time he had worked on the problem, an excuse not to go to bed with Melissa. They mocked him and the remnants of his life. His marriage was over and with it his social life as his soon-to-be former wife had alienated him from his past friends and his current acquaintances were part of her social circle. All that remained for him was his career; his boring, tedious, pitiful job. If he could not create a solution to the crisis that was acceptable to Zelda and Preston, he was certain that they would not only take his job away from him, they would make it all but impossible to find a new job.

He shuffled the papers around but had absolutely no interest in working on them. He did not want to be in this world. Knowing that he could stop it, instead he built on the feelings of helplessness and discontentment.

Letting the emotion build, he slid to the floor and tears developed in his eyes. As his stomach churned, he did not fight against it. Not this time. He was jumping voluntarily. His head tilted back in pain, his mouth opened, he screamed to the ceiling. "I hate my life!"

Chapter 11

A heavy truck rumbled past. Barney spun around. The office was gone. He was outside, not in the empty apartment.

"It worked!"

He looked up at the night sky.

"I can control them," he said to the stars. "I can jump at will!"

Contentment, that was the secret. All that he had to do to stop jumping from world to world was find contentment in whichever world he wanted to remain. Oh, but which world?

Oooh! That thought brought down his joyous mood.

"Relax," he whispered to himself. "Relax or you will cause yourself to jump."

He took several deep breaths. Staying in Katelyn's world was what he wanted right now. Anyway, how would he determine in which world he wanted? Neither world appealed to him at the moment. They only reason he could tolerate the Waspoid world was Katelyn. There had to be a solution...

Perhaps there was a third world? He laughed and in the quiet of the night, it sounded loud. Someone close to him tensed and he realized he was no longer alone. How did that happen?

"Halt," cried a voice from the darkness.

Army Private Morgan had been sitting in his uncomfortable foxhole muttering to himself about what a pain army life was for those in the ranks. Initially, he joined the Federal Army Forces because they did not worry about being chosen for collection. But like anyone who began to take the advantages of a position for granted, he started to complain about what he did not like.

The army was well paid and clothed, and the military installations were comfortable with plenty of rations, including alcohol. Outside of the politicians who ran the government, no one lived better. It was those very same politicians who provided the fine accommodations for the military. Not because they respected those who served but to assure the loyalty of the military. A grumbling military could revolt. A military that was content tended to protect the status quo.

Then this loud guy appeared out of the night. He gave the soldier the chance to leave that hole but also gave him the opportunity to exert his authority. The Federation Army soldiers just loved to lord their authority over the common people. It was one of their few perks. It was the principle of the turd rolling down the hill.

"You got a problem, Happy Man?" Morgan demanded of Barney Berry with his weapon leveled at Barney's chest to punctuate his dominance over the poor slob.

"I'm sorry?" The ARL fighters told Barney about their contempt for the Federal Army Forces soldiers but this was his first encounter with them.

"Your ID card, where is it?"

Barney was momentarily confused. Instinctively, he patted his pockets and looked around to get an idea of where he was. A moment ago he was walking down a road all alone. Somehow, while he was thinking, he had wandered into a group of people who had arrived at a Federal

Army checkpoint. The people lined up behind him all had a laminated card in their hands. That must be what the soldier was demanding.

Forget the fact that he did not have an identification card; Barney had an immediate dislike for the gun-toting bully. Mentally, he considered his options. The chances of being shot were minimal. As he understood it, the federal government needed bodies to fill their quota of victims sent to the Bugs. So, it was highly likely that the worse Barney could receive from this toy soldier was to be held for collection. Well, if that were the case, he could just jump back to the empty apartment or Baxter Live. Granted, those were two depressing choices but far better than being handed over to the Waspoids.

"ID card?" Barney shook his head, a hint of his contemptuous attitude showing. "Yeah, I'm not finding it."

Without turning, Morgan yelled over his shoulder, "Sergeant Willard."

Sergeant Willard had pulled his sorry self from his foxhole a few paces back when he saw the approaching line of civilians. The hole was not the most comfortable place to spend a night but the alternatives were less pleasant. His philosophy was to perform his duty to the best of his ability, show his loyalty to the federal government and enjoy the off-duty perks to being part of the Federal Army Forces. He was a hardened, gruff old vet experienced in military procedures. The conflict with the Bugs suited him just fine, even if the politicians had surrendered, because it gave the army unusual powers and he reveled in using his authority. Strutting up to Barney, he glared in the man's face but spoke to Morgan.

"What'cha got here, Morgan?"

"This guy's trying to be funny," said Morgan. "Doesn't want to show his ID."

"Okay, pal, what's the deal?" demanded the Sergeant. "Where's your card?"

The epiphany Barney had after jumping worlds gave him a strange sense of invincibility. Perhaps a dangerous sense of invincibility, he conceded to himself. Nevertheless, he had no fear of these two brutish soldiers.

He smiled at Willard and continued to pat his clothing, "Um, Sergeant, I have no idea. I'm sure it's around somewhere." Looking down, he realized he was in the Khaki green of the resistance, though without any weapons.

Willard wanted to punch the insolent fool but hesitated. A voice inside his head warned him. Civilians feared the army but this one did not. As well, he was dressed in ARL clothing which meant that he had spent some time with them or was a resistance spy. Either way, this was too brazen of behavior to be taken lightly. The guy had to know that one false move could put him in a military brig. From there, he would find their name on a selection list for the harvesters, that was a certainty. So why did this guy not appear scared in the least? Yep, every sense in his body told him to be very wary of Barney.

"Great, a comic," spouted a clueless Morgan. The private did not have the sense to know danger when it looked him straight in the eyes. "That's all we need tonight."

The Sergeant glanced up and down the group of people waiting behind the funny man to have their IDs out to check. "Any of you know Mister Comic, here?"

The group shuffled uncomfortably. That was better, a little fear. It boosted his confidence somewhat.

"Someone needs to speak up," he ordered. "I'll send you all to a collection center if I have to."

He scowled at the collection of raggedy figures. Most of them would not be able to avoid selection should a collection team happen to round them up. Nevertheless, he had no orders to detain anyone with proper identification but they did not know that.

"You, old man, who is Mister Funny?" Willard demanded of some poor soul in the wrong place at the wrong time.

The old man cleared his throat, reluctant to speak. He had witnessed something that he did not want to admit. However, he was too afraid to lie.

"He's...the Liberator...," the man stammered. All he wanted to do was move on.

Rumor had it that the Armed Resistance fighters were camped in the hills. Refugees were trickling into the hills headed to the valley on the other side. So long as the ARL stayed in the area, the Bugs would not make any forays into the valley beyond the area the resistance occupied. Part of the whispered talk was that the Liberator had appeared among the ARL forces. Those who believed the tales of how this human would drive out the Waspoids and destroy the hive were encouraged that the end to the human nightmare was in sight.

180

The man being challenged by the two Federal soldiers had appeared in front of the refugees. He was not there and then he was, walking along and yelling at the sky as though he commanded the stars. The old man had seen it with his own eyes. And he was terrified.

"Sarge, it..."

"Shut up, Morgan!" snapped Willard. Then he turned on the old man as he fought the fear. In his mind, he tried to think of a scenario where his superiors did not court marital him and send him off to a collection point. Barely, he kept his voice even and his tone firm, "You're crazy, old man. The Liberator is a myth, a story."

"They say the Liberator can come and go as he pleases," replied the old man meekly. "Walks through walls..."

"You're talking about jumpers," Willard growled. "The president says they don't exist." The sergeant raised his hand to strike the old fool.

"I can only tell you what I saw," whispered the old man shaking in fear. He was certain that he was about to die. He glanced over at the stranger who had caused his imminent death and pleaded with his eyes and in his mind. If this was the Liberator, he would save him. "One minute he wasn't with us and the next he was..."

Instead of striking him, Willard grabbed the old man, "Don't lie to me, you old fart. I want the truth!"

"Might I speak," said Barney softly but his voice echoed in the stillness of the night.

Everyone stopped. No one dared move.

Morgan swallowed hard. The look on his sergeant's face was troubling. It suddenly occurred to him that he and Sergeant Willard might be in big trouble and he tried not to look at the guy who would not show his ID.

"Sarge, they say the Bugs can't kill the Liberator," the private whispered. "No one can."

It was a revelation to Barney. Actually, everything said about the Liberator, regardless of how little, was new to him. The resistance soldiers, and that included Katelyn, gave him few details about this liberating person. In the ARL camp he was so revered that they all assumed he knew exactly who he was and what he could accomplish. Or rather, the Liberator knew. And since Barney was the Liberator, he knew.

"Shut up," Sergeant Willard yelled at Morgan.

"But even the Bugs are afraid of him…"

"I said…"

The old man's soft voice pierced through Willard's booming one, "The legend says anyone who tries to kill the Liberator will die."

The sergeant lost control. Unconsciously, he drew his sidearm and chambered a round. For a long moment he stared at the old man then at Barney.

In response, Barney smiled. It was time for him to take command of the situation.

"I wouldn't kill you, Sergeant," he said with a touch of levity. Then he let the words hang out there in the darkness. Finally, he added, "I like you."

Willard put on his bravest face, "I could waste you and no one would care."

Barney's eyes hardened and his tone was unflinching. He had just about all he was going to take from this bully idiot of a brute. Time to play hardball.

"Go ahead, Sergeant. If you think you can, go right ahead," he said softly.

The Federal Army Sergeant was visibly shaken, struggling with what to do. The tension that filled the air made it difficult for him to breath. His brain swirled. He did not want to believe in the Liberator. Life with the Bugs was terrifying for humanity but those who collaborated with the government had comfortable lives so long as they cooperated with federal government policies. But should the Bugs be chased away, those in the government and those who helped them could be made to pay. If this funny guy was the Liberator, then there was nothing the soldier could do. However, if he was not and Willard turned him over to his commander, the sergeant could be punished for believing that the Liberator existed.

Finally, Barney held up an empty hand and smiled lightly. "Ah, here's my ID. I'll grant you, it's not a flattering picture." But then his voice turned as hard as stone. "Do you need more proof of who I am?"

Think you cannot kill me, Barney thought as he glared at the soldier, then what will you do to stop me?

Shaken by the eyes, the soldier made his choice.

"You can go." Willard waved Barney on. Then he waved everyone on impatiently, afraid. "Go, get out of here, all of you."

183

Shocked, the group of civilians wasted no time in hurrying away. They would tell their tale this night and many more to come. Rumors of the Liberator would grow.

But as Sergeant Willard stood with Private Morgan and watched the group walk down the road before fading into the distance, he did not care.

The youthful stupidity of Morgan was on full display, "Now what, Sarge? Do we report this?"

Willard panicked in his mind. The civilians could talk all they wanted, it would be impossible for his superiors to learn that the Liberator passed through his checkpoint. The problem was this rookie soldier with the big mouth. He still had the weapon in his hand and a round in the chamber. For a second, he considered what he would do. Morgan was an idiot and would eventually say the wrong thing to the wrong person. They could both be sent to a harvester.

Bam, the gun shot broke the calm of the night. Private Morgan never knew he had been killed. There was a small hole between his eyes and a massive one in the back. His body fell backward and kicked up dust when hitting the ground. Sergeant Willard dove for his hole, retrieved his automatic weapon and fired into the darkness down the road from where the civilians and the funny guy had come, then pulled the pin on a grenade and tossed it.

The explosion hurried the reinforcements from the outpost. The company laid down a torrent of fire until Willard ordered a ceasefire. He sent a squad down the road to check for bodies. None were found.

The sergeant blamed it on the rebels. No one would dispute his report and the only witness to the incident was the lone casualty.

In the darkness ahead, Calvin and Hobbes were at the alert.

The sound of small arms fire and grenades erupted in the direction of a Federal Army Forces security point. The resistance fighters hated the Feds. They were constantly setting up checkpoints to harass any civilians who might seek refuge with the ARL. The outpost several meters away had been established soon after the ARL had relocated. These small federal encampments also alerted the Bugs to the locations of the resistance camps.

The two fighters covered the road with their weapons. It had once been a major highway through the hills that sheltered the ARL camp. It was in disrepair. For days, people had used it to make for a small valley on the other side of the hills. It made their jobs harder. No one wanted to mistakenly shoot a civilian. Waiting to discover if those who approached were friends or foes was nerve-racking.

Barney sauntered out of the darkness.

When the shooting started, the civilians had scattered into the woods and were no doubt hiding until first light when they would make their way through the Armed Resistance lines then up and over the mountain to the safety of the valley beyond.

"Halt or I'll shoot!" Calvin called out. "Password!?"

"I have no clue," Barney replied nonchalantly, now completely alone.

"What?"

185

Calvin was confused. He had never received such a response.

Barney raised both hands and walked toward the fighters. "Sorry, boys, but I have no idea what the password could possibly be. Give me a hint."

Hobbes leveled his rifle, "What are you doing here if you don't know the password?"

"We can shoot you and no one would blame us," said Calvin.

"I'd blame you," joked Barney. It was a strange feeling, stranger than any he had experienced. He was not afraid. For the first time in his life, he felt free. "I'd blame you a lot. And I would be pretty unhappy, too."

His weapon still raised, Calvin called back to the darkness, "Lieutenant, up!"

Katelyn appeared and smiled at the sight of Barney. "We've got to stop meeting like this."

"I'll stop if you'll stop," replied Barney. It was good to see her smiling again. Then he frowned. "They have you on guard duty, now?"

He did not recognize the two fighters as part of her platoon. Was Shattner punishing her? It did not seem the commander's style.

She did not respond and he knew. She was still shaken from the death of young Simon. She probably was punishing herself by volunteering to command the night sentries. He had his work cut out for him. The moment had come to change this world. But he loved Katelyn. He wanted Katelyn. He was determined to figure out how to take her back with him. But first, there was the Hive and that nasty Queen with which to deal.

They walk together toward the camp.

"You look like crap," she joked.

"And you look wonderful. Khaki is your color," he replied and meant it.

She pretended to ignore the compliment. There was a hidden meaning she did not understand. "You took a big chance coming up on our pickets in the middle of the night."

Barney snorted, "Not as chancy as going through a Federal Army Forces military checkpoint without an ID card."

"No! You didn't?"

Katelyn knew, everyone knew, the Federal soldiers used every excuse to funnel people into the harvesters. Lack of the official ID card was the most common. As it was against the law to be without one, there was no need for a trial. The offender was automatically whisked off to a collection point.

"I seem to have the touch. Unfortunately, I jumped into a group of people who were headed for the checkpoint. They apparently witnessed my abrupt appearance. They all seem to think they saw the Liberator appear."

Her heart leapt. He had changed since the last time they were together. When she finally emerged from her tent after dealing with Simon's death, Barney had disappeared. No one knew where he had gone. She and the other resistance fighters were becoming accustomed to it. Commander Shattner was annoyed by it. He thought the cost accountant was trying to make his case for being the Liberator regardless of what he claimed or disclaimed. Katelyn wanted to believe that this new Barney had finally accepted the truth.

She brushed up against him, "Okay, I give up. Why are you in such a good mood?"

"Am I?"

"Yes. Look at you. You have this goofy grin and the air of a cat that just caught a mouse."

Barney glanced around. They were entering the camp and the customary stares were following them. They passed where his tent was still set up and continued on to her tent. Commander Shattner was inspecting a crate of weapons. There was a secret arms factory the government kept to arm its troops. On occasion, the resistance sent units undercover to ambush the shipments. He looked up at Barney and Katelyn and frowned.

"I can control my jumps," whispered Barney.

Katelyn understood the implications. Deep in her heart, she had begun to believe that he was telling the truth about living in another world. Unfortunately, it served as the only explanation of his bizarre behavior, strange comings and goings and his lack of knowledge of this world. It was not the response she wanted. In her heart, she knew that he had not accepted his role in this world... This world? She was beginning to think like him, more proof of his claims. Anyway, if he could control the jumps, he could leave at any time and potentially never return.

"How?" The word almost caught in her throat. She did not want to ask. What she wanted to say was, please be our liberator. Please be my liberator. But she did not.

"I released all my negative emotions and, bang, I'm here." Oh how excited he was to say it out loud. It seemed to make the whole concept more real.

"When I'm here and feel really depressed, whoosh, I'm at Baxter Life."

"What, like Peter Pan and thinking happy thoughts?"

Huh, he had not thought of it in those terms.

"Yeah, sure, something like that. If I can find contentment at Baxter Life, I should be able to stop the jumps."

There it was, the dreaded thought she did not want to think.

"And leave this world?" she asked quietly. "Do you really want to?"

Do you really want to leave me, she meant.

"Isn't that what I've been saying since the day we met? What could possibly keep me in this dreadful place?"

For his part, Barney wished that he had phrased it a little better. She was looking at him with those soft eyes that twinkled in the light of the campfires and her dark hair was tickled by the night breeze. He should tell her that he loved her. He opened his mouth…

"How about the job of the Liberator." She stated.

"Not interested."

He said it so flippantly that the tone even offended him. Those twinkling eyes were hurt and he regretted being the cause of that pain.

"You say you want a change in your life. Here, now, this is a job worth doing." She looked around the camp, "Liberating humanity, these people from the Bugs is a noble cause."

They were at her tent. He wanted to crawl inside where they could have more privacy. Or rather, where he did not have to look at those who made up the resistance.

His head dropped. He could not bear for her to see his eyes, look into his soul. "It's not the change I want."

"How about us?" she asked. "What happens to us, here, without the Liberator?"

Without another word, she pushed back the flap on her tent and disappeared inside and let the flap fall. Barney looked around helplessly. She had not invited him to follow.

Two day's walk from the hills where the Armed Resistance League camped, across the mountains and into the adjacent valley was what remained of a city, one of the first hit by the Hive when the Waspoids stated to expand beyond the mountain range which protected them for so long. In those early days, the government took a military stand against the advance of the insects. There was a battle in which the government troops were defeated and were forced to retreat. The Bugs took what it wanted from the city to build the hive higher and bigger then left the ruins.

The gangsters moved in soon after. Lawless ones, they saw the opportunity to take advantage of the lack of a governing authority in the remains of the city. Under the rubble of the buildings, they made clubs and other places of pleasure.

The government was too preoccupied with stemming the Waspoid incursions to notice the gangsters and their operations. The insects, on the other hand, thought they had victims for their slave units as they had discovered a taste for the liquefied remains when their usefulness came to an end. The insect General led a force into the city in search of humans. It proved an expensive mistake.

The gangsters were heavily armed and not so easily beaten as the Federal troops. Desperate people with no place to go fight with a fury the insect warriors could not match. From fortified positions in the rubble, the gangsters fought for every inch of ground and the Waspoid General soon pulled his forces back. For what they had to gain, the price was too high. After that, the Hive left the city alone with the exception of an occasional foray to remind the gangsters that they were not forgotten and to test their defenses for weaknesses.

It had been a week since his return and Katelyn had finally softened a bit toward Barney. Her platoon was granted leave and they made the trek to the city. Barney tagged along.

On the trip to the city, Katelyn explained that the ARL gave fighters valuables picked up on the battlefield to pay for their leaves. The gangsters accepted just about anything as payment. They had an extensive black market business that profited from whatever the resistance soldier brought them.

There were strict rules. Anyone who came to eat, drink and have a good time was guaranteed protection and allowed to indulge. Troublemakers got the boot or just disappeared if they challenged or insulted the gangsters. There were rumors that those who offended their hosts were sold to the Hive as just another profit center for the gangsters.

The platoon settled into their comfortable rooms in the basement of what had once been the city hall with luxuries long forgotten then went in search of entertainment. The club was constructed in the upper room that at on long ago days served as a ballroom for official city government parties and other functions.

Thunderous music greeted Katelyn and Barney. They had to shout to be heard over the noise. Everywhere were those dancing, drinking and enjoying themselves. The resistance fighters dove into having a good time. Katelyn also waded into the revelry while Barney watched from the safety of the edge of the party. He did not quite feel like one of them and the Liberator was treated with a certain reverence which made his participation awkward, to say the least. Therefore, he sipped the first decent drink he had enjoyed since jumping into the Bug world and observed.

The woman out on the dance floor balancing a drink while moving to the beat looked like Melissa, her voice was the same and only the khakis and hair color were different on the exterior. It was the inner person where the differences were found and Barney loved that person. Again, he marveled at the absurdity. He had to jump into a scary, terrifying world to find the woman he loved in the woman he had married. He could not imagine Melissa reveling with common type people who could do nothing to advance her career or social aspirations. She would be aghast at the thought of going to a common, everyday club where anyone could get in and beer and nachos were preferred over mixed drinks and sushi appetizers.

He savored the drink and thought about that whole concept one more time.

The Queen of the Waspoids was Zelda Hampton's counterpart and the Bug General was this world's version of Preston Unitus and the Oracle its version of that strange Nikita the Intuitionist. None of them appeared to know that they had human equivalents in another world. On the other hand, Clive Feinstein jumped into this world at least once. From what Barney had witnessed in the ruins of Baxter Life, Clive knew he was Clive from that other real world. Therefore his counterpart in this world and Clive had to exist simultaneously. Barney reasoned that, if he could figure out how to help Katelyn jump to the real world with him, she should be able to exist at the same time with Melissa.

Barney knew he wanted to return to the world of Baxter Life and never come back here but he wanted Katelyn with him. How, that was the problem. Until he solved the problem, he had to continue to come to the giant insect infested world.

The thought of a life with Katelyn pleased him and a smile slipped out. From the dance floor, Katelyn saw it and beamed. He could not remember the last time he had enjoyed an evening out with his wife. Only, this woman was not his wife.

"What's with you?" she asked when she returned to the table where he sat.

It was hard for Barney to suppress the happiness he was experiencing. "This lust for life I see in you, it's so refreshing. Drinking beer and eating hotdogs. So different from…"

It was the wrong thing to say and he realized it in an instant.

Her eyes flashed in anger and her voice went cold, "That other woman?"

Barney frowned and wished he could take it back.

"This is what happens when everyday could be your last," an irritated Katelyn went on. "You have the tendency to live every moment to its fullest."

Dropping his head in embarrassment, he closed his eyes and sighed. What was it about Barney Berry that he had to ruin a great time? Too late, he felt the sickening sensation in the pit of his stomach.

What had he done!?

Katelyn nearly fell off of her chair. Around her, the club patrons continued to party. No one had noticed. In the blink of an eye, Barney had disappeared.

She took a quick drink of beer and considered the implications.

Chapter 12

Darkness had fallen. Barney was alone, that much he knew without raising his head. The quiet was deafening.

His head was down, his forehead resting on crossed arms. He did not want to but he finally looked up. As expected, he was in his cubicle on the 10th floor of the Baxter Life building and surrounded by those ever-present reports that plagued his every moment in this world.

"How long will you resist this world?" he jumped at the unexpected voice of Nikita ask.

After a moment to calm down, he glanced out of the opening of the cubicle. He spotted Nikita at the windows with her back to him gazing out at the lights of the city.

During the planning of the installation of the cubicle maze, a brilliant contract consultant had recommended that none of the working spaces be open to the exterior windows. Those precious spaces were reserved for a walkway with a scattering of backless benches where employees could sit and contemplate. Perhaps even take their breaks or eat lunch. The benches were rarely used and the windows mostly ignored.

He walked over to where she stood beside one of the useless benches.

"What is it you think you know?" he asked.

The reject from the hippie generation did not look at him. He speculated that she was high on drugs. Granted, it was a stereotype but it fit her.

"The world where your spirit roams is of your own making," was her cryptic response.

195

Barney wondered, was this the Oracle speaking to him from the Bug world or a stoned-out woman from another time lost in the wrong age?

"You're telling me that I'm creating a fantasy world I hate?" he demanded. The woman had a way of irritating him with the lack of emotion in her voice. Did the woman have any passion in her? "That's ridiculous," he added.

"Nevertheless," she continued as though she did not hear the anger in his voice. "You should not desire to become a sacrifice for them." She glanced at him, "For her."

In a burst of anger, Barney almost responded but at the last second surmised that it would give legitimacy to what she said and remained quiet.

"Do not throw your life away in an attempt to give it meaning," she said. "It is a fabrication of your own mind; do not try to save it."

Barney regarded her for a minute. What did this woman know? How deep into his mind could she see? Was she in contact with her counterpart, the Bug Oracle, and now trying to chase him from that other world before he was ready to leave?

"I'm not alone," he said cautiously. "There are others who go with me."

"Foolish man. They are drawn in by your discontented spirit. So long as you drift on the wind, so shall they. Prisoners of your world, only you can release them. Find peace here before you can no longer escape."

"I have learned to control it," Barney said, just a little too quickly. Then he regretted it but he could not beep from saying, "I can keep from going back anytime I choose."

He winced. He had not meant to tell anyone other than Katelyn.

Nikita stared at him for a good long while. Finally, she said, "Then use your power to remain in this world. Take on your task and save this company."

"I hate my life in this world." His resentment flared, "I hate this company."

"Nothing in that other world is real. In your heart you know I am right. Baxter Life is the reality. This company is your lifeblood. It supports you, feeds you, makes your life possible. Without it," her voice momentarily dripped with emotion, "you are nothing."

"But to protect the company, I have to..."

"So long as this company exists, your destiny is linked to it. Accept what must be. Accept your role in this life and grow the collective along with the rest of us."

"So long as the company exists...," he repeated slowly, thoughtfully.

When he looked back, Nikita had her back to him and was walking to the elevators. The bell and closed doors suggested that she was gone.

The thought that his life was connected to the life of this company was horrible. Baxter Life had existed for generations, tracing its beginnings of the country. Nevertheless, he knew the Intuitionist was right. The company could destroy him and any chance of finding a decent job if Zelda and Preston wanted to do so. What kind of a life would he bring Katelyn to if the wrath of Baxter Life came down on him? That exciting, energetic and desirable woman could not live in a dull and mirthless existence where the two of them scratched out a living with minimum wage jobs.

Below him though, the windows in the night, human figures moved about consumed with their lives. He felt a detachment from them.

"There must be another way," he whispered.

The reports were calling him back, demanding that he solve the problem to everyone's satisfaction but his own.

Suddenly his hand reached out to the window to brace him from the sensation that tried to double him over. The pain was...

The hallway was well appointed. It led to the office of a powerful person. Barney twirled around. He knew the Baxter Life Building and this hallway was not in it.

Was Barney in a government office? Horrified, he considered that he might be in the State's Insurance Regulators office. Had he gone completely mad and decided to report Baxter Life for ethics violations? The world hates whistle blowers worse than the criminals on whom they inform.

Footsteps, he ducked behind a large clock.

A pretty woman in formal office attire strutted by without noticing him. She reached the doors at the end of the corridor, knocked then entered.

"Mr. President...," he heard her say before the door was closed.

President? He was relieved. Yes, it made perfect sense. He did not, could not solve the problem of Baxter Life without compromising his entire soul. Therefore, his only hope was to solve the problem of the Hive. Then he could stay in this world with Katelyn. The thought pleased him and he knew that to be happy in this world was to stay in it.

Nodding to himself, he considered how to approach the president of…? Well, it did not matter that he had no name for the bug world. He was the Liberator and that gave him a certain power. If the president gave him grief, Barney only needed to jump away to safety.

He marched to the door and threw it open.

"Mr. President," Barney announced boldly. Then he stopped dead.

Clive Feinstein sat in the executive chair with the secretary straddling him. His hands were exploring the fruits of her body and they were moments away from a sexual encounter.

The poor woman jumped and screamed at Barney's intrusion but Clive merely grinned, as though he had been expecting the other man all along.

"Barney Berry," Clive crooned like a fox with the chicken firmly cornered.

Whop, he pushed the woman off and smacked her on her butt. "That will be all, Miss Niger."

Miss Niger straightened her clothing, summoned up what dignity she had left and hurried out.

A coy Clive took a smoldering cigar from the ashtray and sucked life back into it. "I have been expecting you."

He drew in the smoke then blew it out into the air, "So, Barney Berry, how did you manage to evade my security personnel and what may I do for you?"

Two more puffs and he added, "How pitiful you look in this world."

"How did you get here?" demanded Barney.

Of all the things he expected to find in the Bug world, Clive Feinstein sitting in the president's office was nowhere on the list.

"Frankly," Clive said as he leaned back and enjoyed his cigar, "I have no idea. One minute, I was in my office making tons of money then, bang, I'm in this sewer of a world."

"But this office?" Barney took in the room. It was the office of a major politician.

Clive could see the confusion in the other man and reveled in it.

"The first time I arrived I was dumped among a bunch of the scummiest people you ever saw. Actually, you did see them. You were with them. We were all running from these scary hover things."

Barney remembered that day. It was the first time the world of the giant bugs took on a real quality, a terrible real quality.

"You had some type of uniform on," Clive went on to explain. "You and that woman received special treatment. Lord love a duck, you should have seen and tasted the slop they fed us. Anyway, something interesting happened. We were sent to this refugee camp where one of the guards recognized me. I discovered that I was the duly-elected president of this dump."

"You!?"

"Go figure," said Clive. He motioned to a portrait of a dignified President Clive Feinstein on the wall. "Seems I'm very good at campaigning. Promise them everything, give them nothing, tell them it's someone else's fault and they will love you forever."

"But they tell me that the president has been giving humans over to the Bugs?" responded Barney with nothing but contempt for the other man.

It figured that Clive would be part of the government selling out the people they were supposed to be serving, helping. Self-serving regardless of the world he was in. Yet, there was still a worse problem. Clive may know that he was Clive but he also did not have a counterpart in this world.

Clive did not flinch, "You bet your life, I have. If I don't give them their monthly quota, they'll come for me. And I am not about to go into that hive thing."

"Clive, they eat humans!" Barney could not believe what he was hearing. "The Bugs eat human beings!"

Amazingly to Barney, Clive waved him off, "Big deal. Just as long as it's not me. Look, I'm not sure why I keep showing up in this poor excuse for a world. But until I learn how to stop it, I'm doing all I can to protect me."

Clive finished the cigar and stamped out the stub in the ashtray. Casually, he folded his hands on top of the desk and leaned forward, "Now, what can I do for you?"

"I want to speak to the Waspoid Queen," replied Barney. "I thought maybe I could negotiate a deal."

"Queen?" Clive thought about it. "They're led by some kind of queen? You mean like a real insect hive?"

Barney was stunned. "You're the president and you don't know who your enemy is?"

Clive remembered the first day after he was plucked from the refugee camp. He had a bath and decent food then a group of advisors joined him around a big table. That was when he discovered that his predecessor had tried fighting but the people tired of war so they had elected an appeaser, President Poisie, aka Clive Feinstein. They told him that he sent negotiators to meet with the Bugs. They never returned. So he sent more. Lost them as well. Eventually, third time was a charm; they were able to make contact with the insects and learned that they were alien beings from another planet. A spacecraft sent to populate the planet had collided with a human flying craft and crashed. The survivors included a queen who built a small hive to incubate her eggs. The few adult workers left alive cared for the hatchlings until they were able to construct a larger hive.

However, the Waspoids, as the human delegation had learned to call them, were cautious about sharing specifics about their specie. The negotiators tried to reach an agreement that would allow both species to live in peace but the Bugs were not interested. The best they would offer was to cease making war on the humans if the human government would provide a quota of slaves ostensibly to build their hive.

At this point, President Poisie realized that the Waspoids were on the planet to stay and the only hope to survive was to continue a policy of appeasement.

The president was visiting a collection point where people were rounded up to be sent to the harvesters when his entourage was attacked. Clive wondered out loud why he would do such a foolish thing and the answer was the Liberator. There were rumors of one whom the Waspoids feared. A human the insects believed would destroy them. The Bug buzz said that he was in the vicinity and Poisie/Clive wanted to find him before he caused trouble and eliminate the danger.

The appeasing president was content with the status quo and did not want the boat rocked for fear that he would come out on the wrong side of a conflict with the Bugs. It was bad enough that the Armed Resistance League was running around making trouble. He did not need some messiah uniting the people and resuming the all-out war that existed before President Poisie brought about peace.

What Clive pieced together was that an explosion had kick started his memory in this world. And he was nothing if not able to learn from his mistakes, even as President Poisie. The inspection of the collection point ruse had been a complete failure. Since then, Clive was content to remain in the security of the presidential palace and let others take the risks. But having seen Barney in the cave the day he became conscious in Bug land, instinct told him that the cost accountant would play some role in the politics of this world. That meant that their paths would cross sooner or later.

"Why haven't you learned the basic information about your enemy?" Barney repeated the question.

"Why do you want to talk to those pest things?" Clive demanded in response.

"To strike a bargain. I want to save this world. Make it livable."

Clive laughed. "Really? So Barney Berry, Cost Accountant is now Barney Berry, the peace maker?"

"You've heard about the Liberator?"

Warning, Clive's inner self-defense mechanism sounded. His pre-conscious self was concerned about this liberator so he should be as well.

He chose a flippant tone, light and unconcerned, "Oh, yeah. Some superhuman giant-killer who is going to save the world. Yep. He's a myth. A fake. No such creature exists."

But tell me what you know, Cost Accountant, he thought.

"The Bugs think I'm him."

Clive laughed. Of all the things Berry could have said to him, that was the least expected. "You!? You're the Liberator? Boy, are things desperate in the Resistance. Barney Berry, the Liberator."

His back to Barney, Clive poured two drinks. Into one he dropped a small pill and shook the glass until it dissolved. It was one of his little tricks when he wanted sex from a woman but wanted her lethargic. The drug broke down the individual's ability to resist. The helpless women who were subjected to Clive's advances knew what he was doing to them after the pill took effect. They just could not do anything to stop him.

He offered the doctored drink to Barney.

"Anyway, they believe it," remarked Barney, taking the glass and sipping the drink.

Strange, thought Clive, Berry did not believe that he was this liberator person. From what he knew about the Liberator, anyone who could prove to be such a person could write his own ticket among the humans. Berry apparently had no desire to be venerated.

"If I could talk to the Queen wasp creature," Barney said to fill the silence. "Maybe I could broker a better peace deal than... Well, stop them from using humans as..."

Taking his time with his beverage to buy time to allow Barney's drink to work, Clive considered his options. If the Bugs wanted the Liberator, he could give them their liberator as a bargaining chip in the big game called Clive Feinstein's survival. Yet, if he did, the people might revolt should they discover what he had done.

"Good luck, there, Buddy," Clive chattered on. "They have grown real fond of humans. From what I've learned, they prefer them over every other food sources. They think there's some kind of magic in eating human flesh."

"Magic?" Barney grabbed for the desk as the room momentarily swayed.

Clive pretended not to notice. "Who knows? Power. High performance. Whatever it is, they aren't interested in another type of food. That's why old Clive is out to protect himself. This guy isn't going to wind up having the life sucked out of him."

No, he thought, better to just be rid of the cost accountant quietly and be done with it. Clive reached under his desk and pressed a button. The other man was having trouble standing. Yep, the simplest plans are the best plans.

Staggering and woozy, Barney was nonetheless incredulous, "You can't mean that. I've seen what goes on inside that hive. It's terrible."

Clive paused. He momentarily regretted calling for the guards. If anyone else had claimed to have seen the inside of the hive he would have laughed in their face. But he had to believe that Barney Berry was different. It might be to his advantage to know what the cost accountant knew.

Instead he responded, "No one who has gone into the hive ever comes out."

But then the door burst open and Captain Waterly entered with a unit of soldiers.

"Pity," sighed Clive. He would never know what Berry knew of the hive. "Captain Waterly, arrest this man. He does not have an ID card."

"You can't do this, Clive." Barney tried to say but his speech was slurred and he was having difficulty standing.

Clive poured another drink and sipped it while the soldiers cuffed Barney's hands behind his back.

"You have a quota collection scheduled for tomorrow, do you not?" Clive asked.

"Yes, Mr. President," replied Waterly.

"This one will make one less of the quota to fill." Clive's voice was nonchalant. It sounded so casual he might have been ordering a drink from a bartender.

Waterly saluted, "Of course, Mr. President. You can count on me."

"Thank you, Captain. You're a true patriot."

But after the captain and his men left, Clive sat back in his chair, nursed his drink and brooded. It was a shame that he had not had more time to question Berry on the hive. The world was growing on him and he was contemplating plans that would allow him to stay here without the fear of becoming bug food. It was a shame.

Chapter 13

That night, Barney was left shackled in the back of a prison transport vehicle. He was given no food, water or means to stay warm.

The next day, the drug was still playing with his brain. Driven outside the city, he was taken from the truck and thrown into a line of people. His head hurt and his mind blurred. A baby cried and he turned his head toward the noise. There was a woman holding the crying baby sobbing. It was difficult to stand as the ground kept moving.

"Keep moving," someone yelled at him.

"Here?" Barney muttered. "How did I get here?"

A brute in what appeared to be a police uniform thrust his face into Barney's, "Are you deaf? I said, keep moving!"

"Barney looked around. He was in a line of people that shuffled toward an old bus in a dirt field filled with similar vehicles that had once been school buses according to their pealing yellow paint and fading lettering. Behind him, the weeping woman handed the crying baby to another woman. He stared in confusion at the man in the uniform.

His name was Kilroy, according to the patch on his uniform, and he was the lowest of slime bags. As a member of the local police force, his primary function was to find enough lawbreakers to fill the county's quota. They cited people at the slightest violation of the law and judges imposed maximum sentences on each and every offender. That gave the county officials justification to send them off to the collection points. They wore uniforms which made them feel powerful.

Kilroy pushed Barney, "Move your sorry butt, idiot. I don't want to spend all day with you scum."

Barney closed the gap with the person in front of him so the uniformed bully moved on to harass someone else. Barney leaned back to the women who had just given up her child.

"What's happening? Where are we going?" he asked.

Through the sobs, the woman managed to say, "A harvester. They're sending us to the harvester."

Harvesters were topics of great discussion in the ARL camp. Most in the resistance knew someone who was sent to one and never heard from again.

"All I did was try to feed my family," she wept on. "How can they give me to the Bugs for that?"

"Quiet in line," shouted Kilroy.

Barney took in a deep breath. His head was clearing.

A bus drove past and kicked up dust at the people in line. Many coughed and turned away. Barney caught a glance through the bus windows. Dejected, beaten faces stared out at him. Brutish Kilroy pushed him from behind and he stumbled. He was about to respond but saw the brute put his hand on his gun and did nothing. The officer stuck his sneering mouth near Barney's ear.

"Yeah! You want a piece of me but you know I can take you." He shoved Barney. "Move it, maggot!"

Another uniformed police officer named Grubber stood at the door to the bus with a clipboard. It contained the list of those scheduled to be shipped to the Bugs. He was careful to not every individual they prodded onto the vehicle and, once they arrived at the harvester, he would be sure to have the Bug leader stamp form acknowledging the exact number delivered. The best way to avoid being one of those given to the Bugs was to be precise in doing one's job.

"Identification?" Kilroy barked at Barney.

"Um, Barney Barry," he replied. His brain was still scrambled somewhat from the drug.

"Not your name, slime ball. What's your number?" Grubber asked angrily. These stupid idiots that were sent did everything they could to delay the inevitable.

Kilroy grabbed Barney's arm and pulled up his sleeve. "Where's your wrist band?" he demanded.

Captain Waterly and his men had cleverly avoided the extra paperwork associated with a person lacking ID by dropping the droopy Barney off without anyone noticing. They put him in a line waiting to be transported then drove away without anyone taking notice. The president did not want the disposal of the prisoner documented. The captain knew the truth, that people in the collection point would never be heard from again and those responsible for transporting them only cared that they had sufficient numbers to meet their quotas. Therefore, the officers working the site would fabricate whatever paperwork they needed. The prisoner's identity would disappear into a bureaucratic hole and his body would vanish in a harvester never to be heard from again.

Consequently, Barney did not have the wristband the other prisoners had listing their names and reason for being collected.

"I have no idea what you're talking about," he shrugged.

Kilroy grabbed the weeping woman's arm and showed Barney the band on her wrist.

"You're supposed to have one of these," he snapped.

"Sorry." The fog still befuddled Barney's brain.

The response so infuriated Kilroy that he considered drawing his weapon and shooting Mister Smart Man.

"Never mind, Kilroy," Grubber interrupted before the other officer took such a foolish action. "I'll make one up. No one checks these anyway."

Self-preservation motivated Grubber. His concern was that a dead "voluntary worker" might be fatal to him. It was not unusual for the collection supervisor to add a police officer to the list if they caused a short count. Fill the quota or become part of the quota was often whispered among those who worked the collection points but never joked about.

Grubber wrote a random number on his list. Who would check? It was one number among hundreds they would process during the day.

Kilroy's hand moved away from his gun and he sneered, "Bug food." Then he pushed Barney into the bus.

"Watch yourself, Kilroy," warned Grubber quietly. "Sheriff don't like to hear talk like that."

Officer Kilroy laughed. "What are you worried about, Grubber? It's not like we're ever going to see these losers again?"

Grubber could only shake his head. One of these days, the idiot was going to be part of those carted off to the Bugs, he thought of Kilroy.

Inside the bus, Barney stumbled down the aisle and sat near the front behind the weeping women. His mind was clearing. The last of the people were loaded onto the bus. Kilroy entered and took a seat in the middle while Grubber slid into the driver's seat.

Barney leaned forward and spoke to the woman, "Why did you come if you knew where they're taking you?"

Whop, Kilroy slapped him on the side of the head as he walked past. "No talking!"

Then the police officer settled back in his seat and lit a cigarette. Barney's mind was now sufficiently clear to understand how contemptible the act was. Smoking was a vice available to very few. Those who could afford tobacco did not worry about where their next meal was coming. The arrogance of Kilroy in doing so while sitting among these condemned people riled Barney.

The woman whispered without moving, "They take your family if you don't report when ordered. My children, I had to leave them with my sister."

Grubber fired up the bus engine and the old yellow bus lurched forward. Moments later, it drove through a collection of dilapidated buildings which were once a small town and headed out into the countryside. The road was falling apart and filled with potholes making the ride torture for the condemned inside. It was typical of the road systems outside of the cities and especially near the areas where the harvesters worked. The interior of

212

the bus was dirty, the seats worn and the engine smoke seeped in to foul the air.

Kilroy drops the butt of his cigarette, stepped on it then walked forward where he finally settled in behind Grubber. When the harvester came into view through the trees in the distance and grew closer in the windshield, tension descended over the passengers. The area looked as though a bomb had exploded. Trees were snapped off for a mile around the remnants of the road. There were holes everywhere. Barney felt the anxiety of his fellow prisoners. They were defeated people, bowed heads, faces somber. Meanwhile, the two officers were quietly taking as though on a casual outing. He stared into the back of Kilroy's head sitting behind Grubber. His eyes hardened.

Grubber shifted the gears down and slowed the bus. "Bugs are waiting for us."

"They make a mess of things," snorted Kilroy.

In the distance, tan worker Bugs swarmed over what had once been a farmhouse and its buildings. There were skeletons of a tractor and other farm machinery the insects were striping.

Outside the windshield, up ahead of the bus, a unit of five brown army Bugs waited in front of the harvester. The large machine of steel was stationary on its eight massive wheels. It was a newer model designed to protect itself with gun ports on each side and a laser torrent on the top. Around it were the tanned workers entering and exiting with machines for doing the work of collecting the materials to construct the hive.

Barney considered his options. With his head finally out of the fog, he realized that he needed a plan. When he shuffled his feet, the pebbles under them were annoying until an idea blossomed. Cautiously with an eye on the two policemen, he reached down and picked one up. He flung it at Kilroy and managed to hit the brute in the back of the head then quickly lowered his head and eyes, the epitome of innocence.

Kilroy leapt to his feet. "Who did that?" he shouted.

"What are you on about?" demanded Grubber. He was apprehensive. Getting this close to the Bugs always made him nervous. The sooner they could dump their cargo and leave the better.

"One of these scum hit me with a stone," growled Kilroy and before the other officer could stop him, he was headed down the aisle. "I'm going to find out who.

"Sit down, you idiot," Grubber snapped. "We're almost there. Let the Bugs take care of them."

But the other man had no intention of doing so. Kilroy stomped back to where Barney sat, grabbed him and pulled him to his feet.

"You! I know it was you."

But Barney motioned with his head toward a raggedy man across the aisle and whispered, "It was him, Sir. He did it."

Kilroy released Barney and turned on the surprised prisoner. But when his attention was on the poor man, Barney swiped his gun from the officer's holster and clubbed him on the back of the head. Kilroy crumbled to the floor. In the same motion, Barney swung the gun around and pointed it at Grubber.

214

"Stop the bus, right now," Barney ordered.

Grubber glanced over his shoulder confused. When he did not stop the bus, Barney fired. People screamed. The shot blew a large hole in the windshield. The bus lurched to an abrupt halt when the terrified driver stomped on the brakes. Everyone inside was thrown off balance and Barney tumbled onto the floor. Grubber lunged from his seat and tried to draw his weapon. Before he could aim, Barney managed to sit, grip the gun in both hands and fire twice. The first shot took Grubber low in the stomach; the second hit him in the chest and threw him backward.

"Thank you, Katelyn," Barney muttered, thinking back to the weapons training she had given him. Then he was on his feet. "Everyone out," he yelled.

No one moved so he fired two shots into the roof.

"Come on," he urged them. "Everyone out! Run for it!"

The prisoners reacted swiftly. In seconds, they fled the bus by way of the front and back doors. Barney was alone.

Through the shattered windshield, he saw the insect soldiers fluttering toward the vehicle. He snatched up Grubber's gun and slipped a spare clip from the officer's utility belt into his pocket. Aiming both pistols through the windshield at the approaching Bugs, he fired several rounds further blowing out the glass. One caught the lead insect in the body where the wing was attached and spun the creature around. The Bug kicked up dust and red slime when it smacked into the ground. The others ignored their fallen comrade and continued to advance only now with their weapons at the ready.

"I'm going to skin you alive!" shouted Kilroy behind Barney. He senses had returned and he was furious yet his stupidity was unrelenting. Not only did he announce himself but he was still too groggy which resulted in a stumbling attack. Whack, Barney delivered a roundhouse punch with one of the guns to the side of the officer's temple. Kilroy fell like a stone.

Barney was outside quickly. The four remaining Bug warriors were close, too close. He gave them a random burst with both weapons and ran without knowing if he had hit any of them. His goal was the tree line in the near distance. The pistol he had taken from Kilroy was empty. He was not sure how many bullets remained in the Grubber's but he was sure there were not enough to take out all four attackers.

Zap, a beam flew past him. He could hear the humming of their wings. This called for drastic action. Driving to the ground, he twisted around onto this back and dropped the empty gun.

Taken by surprise by the unexpected maneuver, the insects flew past. Barney was on his feet. He fired two shots and the trailing Bug exploded. He trained the gun on a second one and squeezed the trigger twice. The gun fired once then clicked on an empty chamber. The single shot hit its target. Instinctively, he flicked the release and the empty magazine dropped out. In an instant he slammed the spare from his pocket into the pistol, chambered a round and blew away the two remaining Bugs with a blast of brown body parts and red slime.

"Thank you, thank you, Katelyn," he whispered.

A beam zipped over his head. The alarm had been raised inside the harvester and reinforcements were fanning out in an attempt to round up the fleeing prisoners. It was time to leave.

Ducking into the cover of the tree line, he moved around to hide from the approaching giant insects. From his concealed position, Barney watched Waspoids herd a small group of recaptured humans toward the harvester.

Inside the bus, a disoriented Kilroy staggered over the body of Grubber and out the door.

"What happened?" he asked a Bug.

He assumed the thing was the commander of the unit. It was always hard for him to tell. The insects appeared to have a chain of command but it was not readily apparent to humans as there was nothing particularly different about their appearances.

"We captured some of them. Most escaped," replied the buzzing insect.

"No big deal. We'll just have to bring you some more." But Kilroy just wanted to leave. The creatures gave him the creeps.

"We do not accept failure." The Waspoid made a buzzing sound and motioned to his subordinates.

"I can understand that…" However, before Kilroy can finish, the Waspoid warriors seized him and drug him toward the harvester.

"No, wait," he screamed. "I'm one of you. I help you get humans!"

His desperate cries could be heard until he disappeared into the steel beast.

Eventually, the Waspoids gave up their search for Barney. The foliage made going into the dense woods difficult and they did not consider him worth the effort.

While Barney looked on, the tanned workers stripped the faded yellow bus and hauled its parts into the harvester along with the remaining prisoners they captured and the body of Grubber.

He was about to leave when a limousine and several armored troop carriers arrived. Federal Army troops under Captain Waterly's orders quickly surrounded the limousine as Clive exited it and spoke with one of the Waspoid soldiers. He immediately became agitated. Barney decided to risk discovery and wait around for a few minutes.

A hover craft approached and the General fluttered out with an escort.

"What is it you want, Human?" the insect general demanded.

For a second, Clive could not speak. He was stunned by the General's resemblance to Preston Unitus. His mind raced. Did Barney Berry know? He suspected he did since he claimed to have been inside the hive. It was unsettling but he managed to recover his composure when he considered that, if he could manipulate old Preston, he could certainly manipulate this mindless insect.

"I'm President Poisie," Clive announced, his confidence returning. "I'm told you just lost my present to the Queen."

Clive's people monitored the radio traffic of the Waspoids and he had changed his mind about quietly disposing of Berry. He was on his way to

218

personally inform the commander of the harvester when he heard that there was an incident.

Meanwhile, in the hive, the General also heard about the occurrence and decided to make an inspection of the situation. Experience combating the human species suggested that there was more to the attack than the commander of the harvester realized.

"What present?" the General demanded. An arrogant human was not uncommon, though he did not know what made the being so conceited.

Clive threw his hands into the air. "Idiots," he snapped. "The Liberator was in that bus and your insects let him escape."

He noted the confusion in the General's face. Unlike his counterpart in the other world, this beast did not know how to conceal his emotions. That was a good sign.

"The Liberator?" responded the Bug. "How do you know about that creature?"

The president suppressed a smile. These bug things would be easier to negotiate with than he thought. It was a calculated mistake for the old Poisie/Clive to allow others to negotiate on his behalf. But the new Poisie had the corporate experience of Clive Feinstein and would take charge personally. He was going to have these bugs for dinner.

"I want to see the Queen," Clive said in his best commanding voice.

The Queen received word that the creature who ruled the humans wanted an audience. She was preparing the next generation of Waspoids and did not appreciate the distraction. Yet, her instinct told her that this creature might prove useful to her goal and that instinct had served her well since the first days on this planet.

It was her destiny from the moment she was birthed out of the egg to rule a hive. Nevertheless, she aspired for more. She wanted an entire world. The planet of the Waspoids had grown crowded. Hives fought each other for the few remaining resources and the days of the planet seemed numbered. So the Queen decided to take a bold step. Instead of building a conventional hive, the Queen had her workers construct a spacecraft capable of finding another world to inhabit. She specifically birthed a Captain instead of a general and trained him in all that was known about traveling in space.

As the Waspoid specie was new to space travel, the voyage was filled with perils for which they were unprepared. Eventually the Captain located a suitable planet.

Unfortunately while descending to the surface, the spacecraft collided with a flying machine of the creatures already occupying the world and crashed. The few adult workers she had left alive managed to construct a small hive underground using the ruined spacecraft. The Queen laid her first set of eggs. They hatched and the new hive cared for the hatchlings until they were able to assume their duties. Among them was the General.

With her new generation, the hive grew in size and power.

It had the fortune to be located in a valley that was offered special protection as a reserve by the creatures who dominated the planet called humans. These humans set aside large sections of land as sanctuaries for the lower life forms. As such, the humans did not discover they hive for several generations as the Queen lead her colony to build bigger and stronger. When the humans finally did encounter the Waspoids, the Queen learned that her specie was technically more advanced than the humans. The General used it to his advantage as his Waspoid soldiers pushed the humans back. The Waspoid workers took what resources were needed for the colony and constructed an even more powerful hive. They also came to appreciate the taste of humans when properly processed into a sweet liquid pleasing to the Waspoid digestive system. It was far more satisfying than any of the other life forms on the planet.

If there was one mistake the Queen made, it was in the birthing of an Oracle.

On the Waspoid planet, each hive sought an advantage over the other hives. A queen who could hatch and develop an oracle had capacity of seeing into the future through her thereby giving that queen advanced warning of another hive's potential aggression. Therefore, the Queen naturally hatched the Oracle.

At first, using the Oracle's visions, the General crushed the human forces sent against him. Superior weapons, tactics and the Oracle's knowledge of the future gave the Waspoid warriors the sense of invincibility. Then there was the disturbing apparition.

One night in her vision, the Oracle saw a strange human moving among the other creatures. He first appeared as a shadowy figure, not part of the world but still in it. Concerned by him, she reached further, stretching her mind. She found the mysterious human in the future only he had become part of the world. She saw him growing in power among the humans even in his weakness. It was an antithesis to Waspoid thinking so when she tried to explain her visions to the Queen, her majesty could not comprehend their meaning. Power through strength, might crush the weak, that was the way of the Waspoids, the way of the Hive. The Queen felt she had no choice but to ignore the Oracle.

The difficulty for the Queen was that the General and his soldiers believed in the Oracle. They had the victories to prove her views into the future were accurate. Consequently, when rumors spread among the hive of her musings, the Queen's Waspoid subjects also believed in their eventual doom if the Liberator of the humans was not exterminated.

This was her world. She fought against her natural inclination to hatch another queen to start another hive. She had no plans of allowing another hive to compete against her creation. She was going to build a hive greater than anything any queen could dream of on her former planet. Five potential queen eggs had dropped from her nest since she started birthing new generations and she had cracked them all. And the Liberator, she was just as determined to capture this human and use the creature to nourish the largest generation any queen had created.

The message was relayed to the General to bring the human into her presence.

Then she settled back into what was the beginning of her nest. She considered the idea that it might be time to birth another oracle and dispose of the current one.

Meanwhile, the trip to the Hive was interesting. There were no seats on the hover craft as Clive was accustomed only pods that, though they seemed comfortable for the Bugs, were sheer torture for him. Once inside the hive, they walked down several winding corridors to the hallway outside of the Queen's nest. It irked him that he was kept waiting while the General went in to speak to the Queen.

Entering the darkened room and closely guarded, he moved cautiously to the light and the thing under it with the General at her side. This time, Clive was not surprised to find the image of Zelda Hampton's face on the Queen's body. He was beginning to understand this world and why Berry thought he could influence it. Chuckling at the thought, a cost accountant was no match for a man destined for a man of Clive's unique political skills.

"You are the humanoid who knows the identity of the Liberator?" asked the Queen in a booming voice that shook the workers around her and they fluttered away only to float back.

"Know him, why we're practically buddies," grinned Clive. Once again, the emotion on display by these buggy creatures was surprising. "I convinced him to come and see you, but your incompetent guards let him get away."

"I am not amused," the Queen spat. "I am close to bringing forth a new generation."

She motioned to the nursery workers constructing her nest. Her cycle was nearing and she wanted to nourish the new hatchlings as no other young had been before. Like the monuments these humans built to celebrate their victories, she wanted the life-force of this pretend liberator to feed the next generation of Waspoids hatched on their new home planet.

One worker lowered a bag of clear liquid with human body parts floating inside and Clive did not have to be told what the Queen intended for Barney Berry.

"That can be arranged...for a price," he said coolly.

Darkness had fallen. The presidential limousine and troop carriers waited even after another bus came, unloaded its pitiful cargo and left. Captain Waterly and his soldiers were visibly restless even more with the lack of light.

In the bushes, Barney leaned against a tree and wondered how long he should wait. Eventually, the hover craft returned and a happy Clive departed it. He climbed into the limousine like a man without a care in the world. The limo and escort vehicles rumbled off into the night.

There was suddenly a second hover craft but this one landed near to where Barney was hiding. The side opened, soldier Waspoids flew out and took up positions then four worker bugs carried out the Oracle on a platform using handles attached to each corner. Placing her on the ground close to where Barney was concealed, they retreated.

"He has betrayed you," the Oracle said to the bushes and Barney knew that she was aware of his presence. "He has traded your life for his. Stay and the Queen will take your life force from you."

Barney emerged from hiding. He knew as well that she would not permit the warriors to attack him. He sensed her fear and wondered which one of them was really the oracle.

"I did not choose this role," he spoke softly.

The creature who resembled Nikita strained to see him in the darkness. She struggled to speak human words, "You know that is not true. But you do risk death if you stay here. The Liberator will not survive the destruction of the hive. I have foreseen it."

"And you want me to believe you?" Barney asked wily.

"But you know that I have seen what I have seen."

"I cannot abandon the humans in this world," replied Barney and the words surprised him. When had anyone else in this world but Katelyn mattered to him?

"They are not your concern," said the Oracle breaking into his thoughts as though she wanted to distract him from them. "What matters only is that which gives your existence peace. So long as you persist in invading our world, the Queen will seek to hunt you down. She will take your life-force from you. Go back to your own world, Liberator. Live the life you have there and forget this world."

Barney moved closer to her. Her face had the appearance of being peaceful but the eyes hid a fire within her. The female insect may project the impression of a passive onlooker but Barney sensed a violent nature within her.

"Only the Hive is important," she buzzed.

Suddenly, a large stinger shot from the Oracle's mouth. Startled, Barney jumped back. For a split second, he knew real terror, real fear.

Chapter 14

That was very unexpected, Barney thought.

He stopped. Why was he walking and where was he going? Looking around, he was in Zelda Hampton's office. She stared out the window with her back to him and her hands behind her. Preston sat on the couch and picked imaginary lint from his trousers.

She spoke without turning, impatient, "So, Mr. Berry, you have a plan to deal with our issue?"

Before Barney can respond, Nikita was behind him, he could feel her probing eyes boring into the back of his head. Her soft, folksy demeanor was gone.

"Live the life you have here and forget that world," she buzzed menacingly.

Barney chose to ignore her and focused on Zelda. "The truth?" he asked after a moment of silence.

That provoked Zelda to turn to face him, which was exactly what he intended by the question. Her eyes blazed with anger, "My career is on the line and all you can ask me is if I want the truth?" Then sarcastically, "No, lie to me."

Apparently, Barney had been summoned to a meeting. He had no idea what day it was. He was carrying a file and opened it. There were notes inside in his handwriting. He remembered making some of them. Through the fog he recalled his initial strategy.

"We do the right thing," he said as he recalled the details. "We pay our clients and take the hit on profits for..."

He consulted his notes.

"...three to five years, depending on how aggressive we are with the payments, we should return to profitability."

Zelda exploded, "The right thing!? I can't go to the directors and stockholders with that...that... They would fire me. The company would tank."

She glared at Preston. That old fool had recommended this young fool as the one person who could get them out of this predicament. She considered taking the handgun from her desk and shooting them both. Justifiable homicide, as she saw it.

Agitated, she continued her rant, "I am Baxter Life. This company depends on my strength, my power. If I go down, the company goes down with me."

She started to pace, Preston closed his eyes as though in thought and Nikita slipped behind the potted plants.

"Nooo! Nooo!" Zelda elevated her voice even more. "I will not have a 45-year career flushed down the toilet by some lower-level malcontent. I will have a plan in place before the end of the month!" She twirled around and pointed directly at Barney's nose, "Understand?!"

Melodramatic witch, Preston Unitus thought. But what he spoke in an even tone, "That is one option. Is there another?"

There was second file in Barney's hand. He looked at it. Oh yes, he remembered this one. The sinister one he thought he would have to implement. He held it out tentatively."

"I did work up another plan..."

Zelda grabbed the file impatiently and read the summary page.

As Barney spoke, a small smile grew on her face, "It requires some unique shifting of funds to cover the payments. But we could spread the disbursements over several years. We would be dribbling out payments in most cases and there is a definite possibility that more than a few clients will die leaving their payments in legal limbo. It's not at all…legal or ethical. Some clients will take us to court and that will only add more time to the resolution of their claims. In essence, we will be running out the clock on some of the payments while stretching it out on the others."

"Now this is more like it," the CEO beamed. "Very good, Mr. Berry. Quite creative, indeed."

She handed the summary to Preston. He glanced at it and nodded his approval, a glint in his eyes said that he was impressed.

"It doesn't serve our clients' needs," Barney noted.

There was a whistling sound that caught everyone off guard, like a buzzing insect. Nikita had created it, waving her hand in the air as though swatting away that insect.

"Clients are of no concern," Nikita hissed while her face held a strange, distant expression. "Only Baxter Life is important."

It would have appeared as an odd reaction, thought Barney, if he had not encountered the Oracle.

"And my focus is making this company the largest insurance provider in the country! In the world!" Zelda proclaimed. "Around me the company flows and functions. I can boldly declare that there is none other like me."

Nikita slid up beside Zelda, the worker looking for a reward for the job well done. She whispered into the president's ear, "You are serving the greater good. And you have rescued the lost one from his spirit floating free. That is a job well done."

"There are also the incentives..." prodded Preston from the couch. He cast Zelda a knowing look.

"Oh, yes. Mr. Feinstein's position could be tentative," Zelda smiled at Barney.

The implication was so transparent that Barney could not believe these despicable people would try it. A last carrot to make sure he did his job correctly.

"You're offering me Clive's job for suggesting the company act in the same manner that got it into this mess in the first place?"

"This project's resolution could propel your career to new levels," said Preston.

Barney was momentarily tempted to believe them when another thought occurred to him. He turned to Zelda. Something she said struck a chord in his mind. The queen around whom the company flowed and functioned.

"You are the strength of the company?" he asked her.

Zelda looked up impatiently from studying Barney's file. "You have so much to learn about upper management. On the lower floors, employees are disposable, temporal. On the top floor, up where the direction of the company is managed, executives are not so expendable."

"You see yourself as essential to the life of the...company?

The president stuck her pompous nose into the air, "Critical, Mr. Berry. More than essential, I am critical."

Then she tossed the file at him and waved him away as she strutted to her desk. The problem was solved in her mind. Majestically, she sat at her desk. Her mind processed the information and her experience told her it was a sound means of handling the crisis. Oh, the man with the plan was finished. Barney Berry would receive a promotion, a new office and a nice salary. Then, when the details of the plan were well on the way to achieving their goal, whack, the man would be gone. He would never see it coming before it happened.

"See that the company is protected," Zelda Hampton ordered her underling. "Go with the plan that protects the company from the greater harm. Screw the clients."

Preston handed him back the summary page.

Barney realized his presence was no longer needed and meekly walked to the door. He passed Nikita and their eyes met. Then he hurried out. That toad of an assistant, Martin was waiting to close the door behind him. Barney had to admire the scum bag. He did always seem to know when his presence was required to do the bidding of his mistress.

Once Barney left, Zelda glanced up at the closed door with contempt. "And that little prick thinks he is management material. He couldn't lead

231

a bunch of fat men to a buffet. When this is over, I'll neuter him."

"That is a given," noted Preston.

"His spirit has surrendered," said Nikita. "Nothing can take him. He is ours, now. We have nothing to fear from him."

Riding down in the elevator, Barney's smart phone rang. He did not recognize the phone number.

"Mr. Berry," said an unfamiliar voice, "this is Theodore Newt. I am your wife's attorney."

Oh great!

But the lawyer did not allow him the opportunity to respond. "I have your wife with me and we need to set an appointment when we can discuss the terms of your divorce."

That was the last straw for Barney.

"I expect to be dead in a few days, maybe two weeks," Barney sniped back. "So why don't you and my wife just wait until then and you can pick over the remains of my dead, useless carcass, you blood sucking worm."

He ended the call before Theodore could answer back.

Across town, a stunned Theodore Newt stared at the phone in his hand. Across his desk sat Melissa McDay. Occasionally in the practice of family law he had the spouse who was not prepared to accept the inevitable. But the voice on the other end of the call was in a whole new and scary category; suicidal. In Theodore's opinion, the guy figured he had nothing to lose and was not going to be cooperative. As well, Barney Berry was a midlevel employee at a large insurance company with few assets, a pitiful salary and no apparent prospects of improving on either. The attorney was hoping for a quick settlement so he could bill the poor slob for his wife's expenses in the divorce and move on to better pickings.

He smiled for his client. "He apparently is under a bit of stress at the moment."

"Tell me something I don't know," moaned Melissa.

Before she knew what was happening, young Theodore was escorting her down the hallway and blowing cheap promises up her skirt about all that he was going to do for her. She was in the elevator and headed down when she realized that the lawyer had little interest in her case. The tears flowed. All the potential for a great life she saw in Barney was completely gone. She was living with her parents with her belongings in storage and enduring her mother's lectures on how poor her choices were, especially when it came to a husband.

She flagged down a taxicab. Traffic was heavy. Great, now she faced an hour in a stinking cab to get to her parent's Westside apartment. Then the pain started in her stomach. She must have eaten something at lunch that did not agree with her...

In his cubicle, Barney threw the files onto his desk. He was furious with himself for composing such a fowl, disgraceful strategy. He knew that the executives would not go for the truthful approach. However, he thought, rather he hoped they would find the other plan to deal with the crisis unacceptable.

He snatched up his coffee mug. He had hours and hours of tedious coding ahead of him to plug in payment schedules. Then there would be more monotonous hours checking each line for errors.

Jeffrey bounded out of the kitchen and nearly ran him over.

"Hey, Barney," chirped the younger man. "I haven't seen you come out of your office days. Burning all kinds of midnight oil, are we?"

"First of all," snapped Barney, it's not an office. It's a small, cramped and dreary cubicle. Secondly, I'm the one working the late hours. There is no we."

Jeffrey stumbled backward, knocked off balance by the reprimand.

Barney, though, brushed past him and into the kitchen. He pulled the coffee pot from the burner, there was a small quantity of what had once been coffee but was now burned sludge. He hated it when people left a small amount so that they did not feel obligated to make a new pot of coffee. What did it take, remove the old bag, insert the new one and switch on the brew cycle.

He wanted to scream; scream at the person who left the measly few drops to transform into mud, yell at Zelda Hampton and Preston Unitus because they were business demons and scold Melissa for not having faith in him and leaving him.

While he cursed the world, he made a new pot of fresh coffee. Outside the kitchen, others were leaving at the end of the workday. Barney, however, had a long night ahead of him.

He was walking from the kitchen when he suddenly doubled over in pain and staggered to the side into a large potted plant. Now he cursed himself for forgetting. He was not ready, he thought as his cup fell to the carpeted floor, bounced and...

Pain and a blur later, Barney crawled forward in full combat gear and an assault rifle. He peered over a fallen log where the Hive loomed. Shattner and Katelyn were already there with binoculars trained on the evil structure.

"What are we doing?" he whispered.

Shattner ignored him. He was studying the activities surrounding the entrance to the hive.

Katelyn leaned over and whispered back in his ear, "We're hitting the hive."

Around them, Resistance fighters also snuck quietly into position. Covered by camouflage, a team set up two large missiles. Behind them, a group of explosive experts were preparing their charges.

Barney tapped Commander Shattner on the shoulder. Reluctantly, the resistance leader lowered his binoculars. "This is monumentally stupid," Barney hissed.

"We're running out of time. We have to produce results and quickly," Shattner said back. "The president has put a bounty on your head. Soon, we will have the traitors who infiltrated the movement trying to take you out or capture you."

"What?"

It should not have been a surprise. Clive was not stupid enough to sit back and wait for Barney to make the next move. A good defense always included a good offense.

"Word went out yesterday, deliver the Liberator to the federal government or Poisie will start selecting whole towns to give over to the Bugs," said Katelyn.

"Not by coincidence, the ones mentioned are filled with family members of ARL fighters," added the commander.

"Blackmail!"

Shattner and Katelyn nodded in agreement.

"It won't take long for someone to cave and give you up," said Shattner. He turned to Katelyn, "Remember, Lieutenant, hold the breach long enough for the demo teams to do their jobs then get out of there."

Katelyn nodded and started to move when Barney held her back. "Wait! You're leading the attack?"

She smiled nervously, the first time he had seen that in her. "Someone has to."

"You could get killed!"

"So what?" she replied with a tint of angry sarcasm. "Isn't this just a dream world to you? You can dream me back to life the next time you're bored with...that other life."

The lower entrance to the hive was the only apparent part of the hive exposed to a direct attack. The large door used by the harvesters was a weak spot. Intelligence suggested it would be easy to blow it open but a terrible fight to move beyond and deep into the hive with a large contingent of Bugs that could be rushed to its defense. Shattner was counting on blunting the Waspoid counterattack responding to the initial attack then he would force as many troops as he could through the breach. After that, they would plant some very large explosives and hope for the best.

"We have to take the time to think this out," Barney insisted to Shattner.

But the commander was in no mood to listen. "Time for thinking has already passed. We need action and we need it now or the people who are counting on us to do the right thing will die."

"If I'm the Liberator," Barney said, "then you have to believe me when I say that this is not how it happens."

But he was too late. Shattner signaled and the rocket team fired. The two missiles arched into the night air one after the other and across the barren land around the hive. Ka-boom, the first hit the wall. It was designed to weaken the outer shell. Wham, the second punched a large hole in the door. Mortars landed at the base to create fighting holes.

Katelyn rose, "Let's go!"

Barney snatched Katelyn by the arm before she could advance. "You have to listen to me," he yelled at her over the battle cries of those rushing ahead.

But she pushed off his hand and ran on trying to get in front of her troops.

Barney swore. He could not just watch her die out there in this stupid attack. In a moment of passion, he dug in his feet and pushed off after her. If she was going to die, he was going to die with her.

Shattner ordered the mortar barrage. Shells loop over the first of the attackers to give them fighting holes and cover their advance.

The assault drew a heavy fire of blue beams kicking up dirt as well as wounding and killing attackers. Two of the demolition squad blew apart when the beams hit their charges.

Barney caught up to Katelyn at the breach in the door. Her platoon laid down cover fire while the demolition people where tossing as many explosives into the hole as possible. Two of them lost their lives setting the detonators when the Waspoids counterattacked.

The blue beam that almost took off Katelyn's head blew chunks from the wall and splattered her. She went down hard.

"Katelyn!" Barney screamed.

The demolition squad, what remained of them, and Katelyn's platoon were fighting their way to the fighting holes created earlier by the mortars. The second demolition squad raced forward with the larger explosives.

Barney jerked Katelyn to her feet, wrapped an arm around her and made for the nearest crater.

"Help me out, Katelyn," he yelled over the noise of the battle. "Come on, Lieutenant Sumner. Work with me."

"Who is Lieutenant Sumner?" Melissa asked.

She was dazed. "What happened to the cab? Where is the traffic jam?"

A blue beam came out of a big hole in a strange door and sprayed her with debris and smoke. She was knocked off her feet. Barney helped her back up. "Barney…?" There were more explosions. She and Barney were running for a hole in the ground. They dove into it then Barney was shooting a rife at some very big flying insects that blew into a million pieces.

"Barney? What am I doing here…?"

"Melissa?" The woman in the khakis with the trickle of blood from a head wound was Katelyn. The dark hair, the commanding tone to her voice, the eyes, they all belonged to Lieutenant Katelyn Sumner. But none of that mattered. Somehow he knew that this woman was Melissa McDay. "How...?"

Wham, the demolitions planted in the breach exploded and the ground shook.

Fighters passed Melissa to take the attack into the hive. She looked around desperately. She had lost her weapon. She located one on the edge of the crater beside a body. Ignoring the dead fighter, she snatched up his rifle, slammed home a new clip and raced after the soldiers pouring into the breach while a dumbfounded Barney looked on.

"Melissa!?" Barney called after her but she was intent on taking the lead in the attack. He had no choice but to follow her.

The second assault troops were right there with him.

The fight in the breach was vicious.

When Barney finally caught up to Melissa, they were inside the hive but traction was difficult with all the red slime covering everything. That part of Commander Shattner's plan had worked well. The Waspoids had counterattacked as expected. A large number of them were ripped apart by the explosion and the rest recoiled. The resistance follow-up attack pressed them back further.

It was time for the real work. The heavy demo squad fanned out and began setting their explosives.

Melissa along with Barney and the fighters around her were pouring fire everywhere but they had a limited amount of ammunition. The explosive engineers worked quickly then, their jobs completed, ran out. The lieutenant commanding the squad set the timers. But he was caught in the second Bug counterattack and killed.

"Time to leave," Melissa yelled.

They were losing people as the insect warriors fought to reclaim the breach. The time for fighting was over. Running was the new priority.

Not even half of those who made it to the breach managed to make the planned retreat back to the tree line where the attack originated. Melissa and Barney were the last to dive over the fallen log and join Commander Shattner.

There was a coordinated explosion inside the hive. Smoke and debris spewed out of the breach. The resistance soldiers waited. They were looking for secondary explosions and the hive to implode. Nothing happened. The smoke began to clear. Then a heavy barrage of blue beams started. Hover craft flew from the upper entrances. The Hive was very much still intact. There remained nothing else to do but retreat and regroup.

The rally point was a tree-covered hill two miles from the hive.

Barney, Shattner and Melissa watched the fighters stagger past. The count was not good. Nearly one third of the ARL forces had been lost.

"All those fighters and nothing," lamented the resistance commander.

Barney started to tell the commander that he had tried to warn him but Shattner's glare stopped him cold. Barney was certain that the other man might just kill him if he so much as spoke a single word.

"Barney, how did we get here?" Melissa asked. She was holding a temporary bandage over her head wound. "Why am I shooting disgusting buggy things?"

She looked at her clothing. "Good heavens, Barney, I'm wearing khakis. Khakis, Barney!"

Shattner was concerned, "Lieutenant, are you alright? Maybe we should get the medic."

"I can almost explain everything, Melissa?" Barney replied.

"Who is Melissa?" asked Shattner.

Chapter 15

In another world, another lifetime ago, there was a young woman named Melissa McDay. Her family was well-off but not filthy rich. Her parents wanted their daughter to have the best of everything so they sent her to exclusive schools. Pretty, personable, intelligent and talented, she could hold her own with any of her fellow students except when it came to money. She could not buy anything she wanted, any time she wanted and that placed her at a disadvantage. Her feminine classmates looked down on her and the males saw her matrimonially as a potential step down on the social ladder.

Melissa craved challenge and adventure. She was consistently at the top of her class academically, athletically she was a leader on the women's sports teams and easily likeable. Nevertheless, the issue of wealth always stifled her. While she excelled in so many areas, it exasperated her that those around her measured her worth by a monetary ruler.

Melissa determined to change that aspect of her life, and not by marrying into a social class. She would find a career-minded man as driven toward upward mobility as she then move up the social ladder by making money and career advancement.

Ambition blinded Melissa. In the city, the leading business was insurance. It was the capital of the industry. Its executives ruled from their top floor offices, expensive homes and attendance at every important social occasion. She saw inclusion in the upper echelons of the industry as an attainable goal.

One strange evening at a party that could not have been more tiresome, she met Barney Berry. He had a danger about him with talk of quitting his well-paying job for the unknown of running his own business as an artist. He spoke about cartooning, animating and blah, blah, blah. Oh yes, that part slipped into the background when he admitted that the financial rewards were sketchy at best. But when he told her about his job at Baxter Life and the potential for advancement given his skills and the limited number of people who could do what he did, albeit the boredom of the job.

Melissa was working for Treble and Associates real estate agency and demonstrated a talent for selling property. She calculated that the combined incomes and Barney's inroads into the insurance industry meant they could become big fish in the little pond.

In a painful blur of life and light, that Melissa McDay vanished.

Marching back to camp after the disastrous battle, Melissa reflected on how she had lost the person she wanted to be and created the shallow, self-centered woman she had become. She determined that she did not like Melissa McDay.

Then there were the memories she had of Katelyn Sumner. She commanded troops in combat, lived on the edge with excitement and adventure and risked her life for a good cause. She was not sure yet what she thought about Lieutenant Sumner.

The Armed Resistance League camp was a solemn and sad place. The fires were small and the conversations hushed, if any at all. Commander

Shattner stood in front of his tent but no one stopped to talk to him.

Barney returned from the field kitchen with two plastic plates of food and two plastic cups of a thin black liquid drink.

Melissa sat in front of a canvas sheet laid out with an assault rifle and cleaning kit. A bandage covered her head wound. She looked up at Barney in complete confusion.

"I've field stripped and assembled this four times," she said, choking back the emotion. "How do I know how to do this? Barney, how?"

She grabbed a handgun, ejected the clip then stripped it in a matter of seconds.

"I'm amazing, Barney. How did I become amazing?"

Sitting down beside her, Barney passed her a plate and cup.

"Do you know how to do this?" she asked as she tasted the food.

"You taught me."

Wincing at the food, she sat the plate aside and tried the drink. It was no better.

"How could I have liked this stuff?" she frowned. "Yuck."

Barney dug into the food. "Try to eat. We may be on the run for the next few days so rations will be sketchy."

One look at the food was all she could manage. After downing the drink, she disassembled the assault rifle again.

"What do you remember?" asked Barney with a mouthful. He knew hunger and he knew hunger on the march. Neither experience was pleasant.

Anyway, he had grown accustomed to the taste of army rations.

"All of it," she said as her hands worked. "It's like a flood of memories washing over me. A world with giant human-like wasps. I lead a platoon of fighters. Barney, I kicked you out of our apartment for going out with…me?

In record time, she completed assembling the weapon. "How did this all happen?"

"It's me," sighed Barney. "I somehow created this world to escape my life."

"Your dreams? These are the nightmares you've been having."

"Yeah, well they became real."

Melissa laid the rifle carefully on the canvas and grudgingly picked the plate back up. Part of her memories were eating this…stuff and she, too, knew what it was like to march on an empty stomach. She scooped a spoonful of brown goo into her mouth. What she could not remember was how she used to actually like this poor excuse for food.

"I remember that, as Lieutenant Katelyn Sumner, I love doing this," she motioned around with the spoon. "Living in a tent. Eating bad food. Dressing in khaki. Well, the bad food needs improving. But I kind of like how I look in the khakis."

"So do I," noted Barney with a twinkle in his eye.

She ignored the compliment and tugged on a lock of her hair. "When did I go black?"

"We need to go back to our real world."

Melissa shook her head definitely, "No way! They need us here."

That was not the response he had anticipated. In a flash, he had the answer to his dilemma of how to take Katelyn back with him. All he had to do was jump back and Katelyn or Melissa would be waiting for him. It would be over. Then they could discuss where their lives went from there. A bonus was that he did not think she would want their same old boring life back.

"Listen to me," he whispered. "You're here because you hate your life as much as I do mine. But if I go back, you'll have to return with me."

"Then don't go back."

"We'll die if we stay here. You saw the power of the hive. It kicked our butts. It's only a matter of time until it takes over this entire world."

She swallowed the last of the food and went to wash it down when she realized that she had an empty cup so she snatched his away from him. They were both shocked. The old Melissa would never think of drinking from another person's glass, shared body fluids and all.

"I don't want to go," she replied firmly. "I've never felt so alive as I did when we were fighting in the breach."

"This is a make-believe world, Melissa. It's not real."

"I don't care. I'm staying."

To punctuate her statement, she handed him an empty cup, took his sidearm from is holster and starting to fieldstrip it.

With a big sigh, Barney sat back and watched her. He regretted what must be done and how. But he had no doubt that the solution to his problem was both pleasurable and risky.

After patiently waiting for just the right moment, Barney nudged closer to Melissa. It was the moment he had anticipated since the first time he saw Katelyn. She had finished reassembling his sidearm and rifle. She smelled of gun oil and was expecting him to make the move. They kissed. It was light and gentle and unlike any they had ever shared. He led her to the tent.

Inside, they slowly stripped each other of their clothing while exploring one another's body as if for the first time. They were both desperate and passionate in their lovemaking. Finally, they collapsed together. They fell asleep in each other's arms, content.

Barney awoke. The office of Baxter Life buzzed around him, crap!

He stared into the mug of coffee. It continually amazed him how he could just arrive back in this dreadful world right in the middle of his life in motion. He remembered, he had a tedious job to finish. Turning from the coffee maker, he almost ran into Melissa. He would have smiled had he not noted the fury in her face. Where had she returned to consciousness, he wondered?

"You creep," she snapped in a very loud voice.

People all over the office were staring. Grabbing her by the elbow, he guided her to his dingy little cubicle and sat her in the chair while he dropped into his executive chair.

"I have…"

But she was not about to allow him to lie to her. "Don't play innocent with me." She wagged a finger in his face, "Don't forget that you told me about your ability to control your jumps. Or, rather, you told Lieutenant Sumner."

"I have this project that must be finished by the end of the week."

"Are you kidding me?" Her face went red with rage. "You can't possibly think that I'm going to believe that you want to do a good job for Baxter Life."

"Please keep your voice down."

"Why?" She stood so that her voice could project over the cubicle wall. "You hate this place…"

Quickly, he pulled her back into the chair and held her by her arms so that she could not escape.

"Please keep your voice down," he hissed.

"You're keeping us here," she whispered.

"It is important for both of us that I finish this job and do it right."

"Why? How could this job be anywhere near as important as destroying the Hive?"

"You used to want me to work hard and advance," he reminded her. "And if I don't get this project completed on time and right, Zelda and Preston will make sure I never get another job worth having for the rest of my life."

"I don't want this life anymore, Barney. It's boring. Tedious and boring." She leaned back in the chair with the air of one defeated by the circumstances. "I just closed on the Viper property. I hated every moment including when they handed me that big fat commission check."

Barney thought for a moment about the paradox. A few weeks ago, he would have been the one trying to appear pleased with her victory and she would have wanted to go out and celebrate.

"I've figured out how to handle a very tricky issue for Zelda. There's a promotion if I pull it off..."

"Promotion!? Are you hearing yourself? Promotion! What will that accomplish? Bigger salary? Larger office? You'll still be dying the same slow death."

"And don't you understand, death is very real in that other world," said Barney. "We can die." He hesitated, almost afraid to speak the words, then added, "I don't want to lose you now that I've found you."

"Which me? The me who dies a little every day in this life? Or the me who truly lives when she is leading her unit against the Bugs?" she demanded. "I want to go back and squish the hive into a pile of red slimy ooze."

"And the part about death being real?"

"I don't care. I would rather die while living than live while dying."

"I'm not sure the Liberator lives through the attack on the hive," Barney whispered. "The Oracle claimed I would not survive if I was successful."

Melissa was incredulous. "You've known all along."

"What I know..."

She rolled her eyes in disgust and her expression hurt him more than she could have imagined. He could see it. She thought that he was a coward, afraid for his own life. He wanted Katelyn, the Melissa of the Bug world in this world. Now that she was here, he regretted that she came with him. His soul ached.

When she finally expressed what was in her face, it wounded him even more. "You've known all along that you're the Liberator. You've just been playing dumb because you want out. You don't want to take the risk to free those people."

If she had just called him a coward, she could not have been plainer in her opinion of him. What did she know, he wanted to demand of her, to scold her? What did she know about courage? But Melissa had every memory of Katelyn Sumner and that woman was a hero, a leader of soldiers into battle.

He looked at the pile of papers on his desk. It was all there, all ready to enter. The solution he had created would pacify the Queen of Baxter Life and her General. The Oracle of the top floor would pronounce the hive as saved. And Barney Berry would be safe. Oh, he was not stupid. They would not keep him around for long, he knew too much. But with a new promotion, he could job hunt with it as a springboard. And Zelda and Preston would gladly but regretfully allow him to leave. Once gone, they could hide their tracks so that, if it blew up later, they would have a scapegoat. The Baxter Life hive would be safe and Barney Berry would be safe and the clients who would be slowly strangled by his actions, victims of the hive.

"Fine," Melissa said, resolutely. "If that's what you want, live your crappy little life. Go for your promotion. Update your resume. But I don't want any part of it."

He knew what she wanted. What he did not know was if he had the power to grant it to her.

"That world might not exist without me."

"If you love me, you won't force me to die a tedious death here with you. Figure out how to send me back."

"I need you."

"Why, Barney?"

A few short months ago, Barney did not love his wife. Melissa McDay was someone who sucked the life out of him along with this institutional hive of conformity and tedium for the sake of commerce. He wished he had married someone else or, better, never married at all. Now, across from him sat the most perfect woman he could imagine. He did need her to make his life complete. But could he reciprocate and make her life equally complete? That was the question and the answer possibly not to his liking.

He avoided her eyes and she did not need to be told why.

The silence became unbearable. Melissa stood, hesitated then left.

Chapter 16

Starting was always the hardest part. Once he did, Barney Berry fell into a rhythm. Part of his skill was the ability to create small programs that integrated large quantities of data into the Baxter Life system. Not trusting anyone else to input it, he dove into the job. His mind descended into a zone that filtered out the outside noises of his cubicle.

As such, he did not notice Walter until he was standing beside his desk. When he finally realized the man was there, he reflexively started to stand out of respect.

"Sit down, sit down, my boy," waved Walter in his old raspy voice as he sat in the chair previously occupied by his wife. "Dear me, but you look like you've lost your best friend."

Barney was not sure how to respond to that so he said nothing.

Walter struggled to get comfortable. "Old bones, old bones. Just can't do the things I used to."

"How are you, Walter?" Barney inquired halfheartedly.

"Cheer up, My Boy," said Walter with a pat on Barney's arm. "These are the best days of your life."

Barney rubbed his tired eyes. "I've been working some long hours."

"Yes. I heard that you were engaged in solving a difficult problem."

Suddenly, Barney was alert. Walter Higgins was a troubleshooter. He was called in by management when a department was having difficulties, solved the problem then moved on.

Usually it meant someone lost their job and the old man had no patience with incompetence. It made him a number of enemies up and down the corporate ladder which probably explained why Walter had a corner office on the floor below the top floor and was not expected to ever make his way up that last rung.

There was a reason Walter Higgins had traveled all the way down to the 10th. Barney chose his words carefully, "Any advice Baxter Life's senior employee can offer is most welcome."

Huff, Walter appeared to brush off the suggestion that he had anything to contribute, "Buff. Too much has been made of old Walter's tenure with the company. In my day, a young man expected to find a company with whom he could spend a lifetime. This new generation leaps from job to job at an alarming frequency. Breaks down the social fabric of our country. But mark my word, that is not the ticket to a contented life."

The older man was talking around the fringes. Barney suspected that Preston had sent Walter to casually check up on his progress. He had to be careful with what he said. It was annoying. He was so close to finishing the data entry. If Walter would just leave him alone, he could complete the job and get the nasty business done.

"You've been with Baxter a long time," Barney said.

"Oh, from the beginning. Even before it was Baxter Life," Walter's eyes glassed over in thought. "Changed names a couple of times, buy-outs and mergers. I started selling insurance door-to-door.

The secret is to keep at it. Plug away. Put in my time and gradually climbed my way up the ladder."

He leaned closer as through to share a secret and patted Barney on knee, "Listen, there's nothing like a life well lived."

"You must have had a thrilling life?"

Walter laughed drily, "Thrilling? Heavens, no. Hard work and complete dedication to one's job takes all a man has to give. But I look around here and see this company and I think, yes, I helped build this. Makes me proud."

He was not sure if it was the fatigue or just foolishness but, Barney opened his mouth and his thoughts spilled out. "You've never made it to the top floor."

Walter paused making Barney wonder if he had made a bad mistake. The old man frowned but there was no hint of anger in his voice. "Ah, well. There is that. Unfortunately, it will never happen. Circumstances being what they were."

"I don't..." Barney was searching for a discrete way of asking the man to leave. It was already late and he hoped to call Melissa when he was done and see if she might meet with him. Maybe he could mend a bridge or two. But that last sentence stuck in his mind and he could not shake it from his mind. "What circumstances?"

He realized that Walter might want to tell him something.

"I was mid-level management at the time," Walter began slowly. "Zelda was a VP in marketing and Preston was my department manager. There was a small problem. Mistakes were made.

254

Someone had to step up. Someone had to assume the responsibility for the sake of the company."

Barney was flabbergasted, "They sacrificed you?"

"The duty to Baxter Life was more important than my next career move," Walter said proudly. And Barney could tell that he was genuinely proud of what he had done. "I saved the company. It was a small price. No regrets. The company has provided me with a good living. Carolyn and I have lived very comfortable lives. Preston and Zelda, they went on and pushed this company to new heights."

"Preston and Zelda...? Even after...?"

Walter shook his head sadly, "It was not a duty they took lightly. Business is a war. And in every war there are casualties. I wear my wounds with honor."

There was no doubt in Barney's mind. Walter had sent Walter. Nothing happened at Baxter Life about which the old man did not know. He knew about Clive and his stupidity. He knew that the company was in trouble and that Barney Berry had been given the job of solving the problem. But more than that, Walter knew that, more than likely, Barney was going to take the fall regardless of how well he did his job. And Walter thought Barney should take the fall willingly, with pride.

In the opinion of Walter Higgins, he and Barney were kindred spirits. They were men destined to clean up the messes made by others with little reward for their loyalty.

Walter nodded toward the computer. "Is there anything I can do to assist you? Maybe this old mind can still be of some use to you young bucks."

255

"What?" Barney was temporarily lost in thought. "Oh, I think you just have, Sir. You have clarified my thinking. I believe I know what I must do."

That pleased the old man and he immediately struggled to his feet. In his mind he had checked another task off his list and it was time to move on. "Splendid, My Boy. Splendid. And, there's no need to thank me. Just knowing I could help a fellow spirit succeed is enough for me."

They shook hands and Walter shuffled out.

Walter would have lunch with Preston and slip a word of reassurance into the conversation. Neither man would directly address the situation but both would understand that the young man was prepared to fall on his sword should it become necessary.

Barney went back to the computer and scrolled through several lines. He thumbed through the printouts. Nevertheless, he could not refocus his mind on the project.

"This will not work," he whispered. "No, this will not be successful."

He switched his screen to his e-mail and typed in the message.

Then he went to work finishing the job.

Preston Unitus' corner office was not as impressive as Zelda's but it had dazzled a person or two. The most noticed was the wall of honor; framed photos of Preston with the movers and shakers of the country and the world. He knew people, met people. Preston was waiting behind a desk with a polished surface, completely devoid of papers, computers or anything associated with the desk of a busy executive. Paper trails were a bother

256

to him. Paper was for the minions under him performing tasks assigned by him. In front of his desk were the tools of his office, two chairs of no particular comfort, and behind was the other, a phone. He verbally gave instructions either in person or over the phone. Nothing physically linked him to anything happening at Baxter Live but he knew about and supervised every aspect of the company's operation.

Every morning his secretary gave him a single piece of paper with his daily appointments. Beyond that, those who did the work verbally updated him on their progress.

Barney entered and walked the length of the room. In his hand was his weapon, a file folder. Taking one of the chairs, he deliberately laid the folder on the shiny desk surface.

"I have all the data prepared," Barney said without waiting for Preston's permission. "I require authorization to download it into the system."

"Authorization?" asked Preston carefully.

That word implied that the young man wanted to cover his buttocks. Authorization from a superior would give him at least the appearance of following instruction as opposed to taking the initiative. These young people, old Walter Higgins would never suggest the need for this kind of formality.

"Well," said Barney, "I will have to release payments, defer others and reject some per my schedule. That necessitates computer access that I do not possess."

The computer was a grand invention for business. However, security required certain protocols to prevent illegal access to the system. In the old days, an executive could verbally order things to be done and they were done. Checks were signed by others with an oral command.

"Can't you just do it, Berry?" Preston foolishly demanded. And he regretted it immediately. It displayed a lack of knowledge, a naivety which he did not possess. He quickly waved off Barney's response. "What do you need to get the job done so we can get beyond this whole mess?"

Barney feigned innocence. "You mean me? I would need my computer profile changed so that I can…"

"Right, right, right."

Preston reached back and grabbed the phone on the credenza behind him. "Lois, get me Chandler down in IT."

He waited impatiently. When Chandler came on the line, Preston was short and to the point. "Chandler, give Barney Berry executive access to the computer."

Poor Chandler made the mistake of diplomatically suggesting that the order was not a good thing to do.

"I don't care if a level one profile makes sense to you," Preston snapped. "Just do it now and let Berry know when he can get the job I gave him done."

He was about to slam the phone back on the cradle then caught himself in mid motion. Carefully, he rested the receiver in place. Calm returned. Then, turning to Barney, he asked, "Is there anything else that is preventing you from accomplishing your task?"

Barney retrieved the file folder from the desk. "No Sir," he said timidly.

He walked from the room with the snug expression of the VP behind him. There would be no phone calls to Melissa. No attempts to mend the chasm that had grown so deep between them. Time was now an enemy. He had a long night's work ahead of him and at the end of it, he would have to live with the results of his actions.

The Baxter Life Building emptied then filled with the small smattering of people who worked to clean. Then they were gone as well. The first of the morning light entered the windows and crept across the cubicles when Barney Berry, Cost Accountant completed the task. He looked at the pile of papers with a myriad of his scribbles that represented all the work he had done. Up to this point, it was all an academic exercise. No action had taken place. Turning back was still an option.

It took all his willpower to type in the execute command. He felt sick to his stomach. The suffering he was about to cause could not be quantified. All he had to do was press the enter key and he would be liberated from the world of the Bugs. Barney let the emotional pain come and it doubled him over. Outside the walls of his cage his fellow employees were arriving for another day in the hive, buzz, buzz, buzz. His hand hovered over the enter key...

The elevator stopped on the 10th floor of Baxter Life. Jeffrey St. Clair bounced off and deposited his belonging in his cubicle before snatching up his favorite coffee mug. It was the one he purchased at the Grand Canyon. He had a donut in a bag just waiting to be eaten while checking his morning emails. First, though, he thought he would look in on Barney. Word around the office was that he had been tapped for a special project and the young Jeffrey thought he could get in on it and garner a little notice.

Jeffrey rounded the corner of Barney Berry's cubicle. The workspace was a mess. Strange, Barney was not there. Stranger still, Jeffrey was sure he had seen him at his desk mere minutes ago.

Chapter 17

Daylight, the sun drifted over the mountains but the Armed Resistance League camp had been active for hours. Resistant fighters were packing up their possessions or in groups engaged in quiet conversations. But all activity came to a halt when Barney marched determinately through the camp.

The Liberator had been absent since the defeat at the breach. Most took that as a sign that the war was over, lost to those winged creatures. Desertions followed. Even those with no place to go went. Only the most ardent supporters of the resistance movement remained.

Commander Shattner and his officers, including Melissa/Katelyn in khaki and black hair, gathered around a table. On it was the morning count and it was not good. They now had to figure out how to hold their force together and make enough of an impact as to slow down the Hive's advance. It was grim.

Barney approached and his eyes immediately met Melissa's. They said thank you to him.

It was all too confounding to him how she could be grateful. He had thrown her into a hornets' nest and the hornets were out for blood.

"Commander, what's going on?" he asked.

"The President is following through on enforcing his order against the Liberator," replied the commander. "The authorities started rounding up people this morning. A score of my fighters slipped out last night. They went home to protect their families. We could lose everything if we don't do something to stop it."

"Take out the president?" said Barney.

"We thought about that," acknowledged Shattner. "But he has locked himself in his office with a Bug guard, no less, and he issues orders from there."

"The Federal Army is afraid to disobey," added one of the officers. "Everyone is afraid that their families will be sent to the harvesters."

"We are looking at attacking the harvesters," said Melissa.

"But when we have done so in the past, it hasn't amounted to much," noted Shattner.

"They rebuild them as fast as we can destroy them," said another officer.

Barney picked up a paper with the daily count of fighters. "We will need more fighters, Commander."

"Tell me something that I don't know," responded Shattner.

He knew what had to be done. He had seen it in his dreams. Looking around, he realized that everyone was waiting for him, even Shattner. It was as if he were back in his cubicle with the execute command waiting to be entered. There was a glow in Melissa's face. It said he should enter the command.

"We're going to hit the hive with everything we have in two days," Barney said firmly. He looked the commander directly in the eyes and avoided the assorted responses by his officers, a few gasps but mostly giggles. "We're taking that sucker down," he declared definitely.

"They kicked the crap out of us last time," noted an officer.

But Melissa saw something in her husband, something new. She wanted nothing more than to believe in him, the Liberator.

"We'll have to do more than punch a couple of holes in it," she said.

"I have been blind, Commander," said Barney. "I thought the Hive was the monster but I was wrong. The Queen is the key. So stupid of me not to see it before. It's been right there in front of me all the time. Eliminate her and the Hive falls apart."

Shattner was not convinced. "She's just one Bug."

"Not so," Barney replied with a forced smile. He had a plan and it was a terrifying one. The words of the Oracle echoed in his brain. The Liberator would not survive the destruction of the Hive.

"It's all in the nature of the beast," he went on, the smirks and doubting faces were gone. The gathered officers heard the voice of the Liberator. "Or in this case, the insect. They're no different from any other winged pest. Without a queen they have no purpose. She dies, they die."

Melissa swallowed hard. "We have no idea where she is inside the hive."

She knew that they would need intelligence to locate her.

"We will in a day," said Barney with assurance. "Because I'm going inside."

"Don't be a fool," Shattner replied. But he was looking at the man's face and knew he was going to do what he said he would do. "You go inside; you become a meal for the Bugs."

"I'm going in and coming back out. Alive!"

Silence. The officers watched as the two men wrestle without speaking.

"It's time to put up or shut up, Commander," Barney finally challenged the commander. "Now are you going to have an army ready to do the job?"

"And who will lead this attack?" Shattner finally asked.

"The Liberator."

Their stares were locked together. Shattner did not believe, that was clear to Barney. He wished that he had the commander's lack of faith. But Barney Berry no longer had the luxury. There was nothing left for him but faith.

"The Liberator will have his army," said Shattner.

The camp left them to themselves.

They made love with a zest neither had ever experienced before. They hungered for each other, consumed each other and repeated it over again. The world did not exist around them. Their only reality was each other. At last, they were spent.

"Wow! Where did that passion come from?" Melissa was the first to break the silence. "You're a lover, Barney Berry."

"We who are about to die." Barney tried to sound flippant but knew she was not buying it.

"Going into the hive is crazy stupid. Even for the Liberator." She also tried to moderate her voice. There was no way he did not see beyond the lying mask.

"I've already been there and returned. I can do it again."

"Can you be so certain?"

She knew the answer. When he did not give it, she tried not to react. Death had become a real part of her experience in this world. Simon was fresh in her mind from Katelyn's memories. A tear trickled down her cheek which she attempted to hide by burying her face in his neck. It was a mistake. He felt the moisture.

"It is time for Barney Berry to live," he whispered. "No more cubicles. No more tedious reports or endless data streams. I'm going to live. To really live. One day, one week or one hundred years. I don't care how long; I intend to suck every ounce of life from every second that remains of my life."

Melissa wanted to tell him not to go. But then how could she when she bullied him into allowing her to return to her platoon. She knew the draw of the life on the edge of danger. The adrenalin charge when a battle was near. She could not deny him what she craved.

"Not to worry," he smiled, though she could not see his face. "I have a secret weapon. Anyway, I'll succeed. I've seen me do it."

She chuckled. She just could not help it. The tension was broken between them. When she did not know was that the anxiety for what must be done kept him in this world even after the ecstasy of their lovemaking.

"Infiltrating the hive won't be easy," she said.

"I guess I'll just have to convince the Bugs to escort me in." He kissed her and the urge for love stirred. "I'm going to need a telephone."

The nightclub was another one of those run by the gangsters, a different bunch located in an abandoned town near the capital. They were known for giving politicians free food, drink and personal entertainment.

Melissa had her best people inside and outside. She signaled to Barney, the other one was in place.

The goons at the door screening out the riffraff were hardly a problem. Barney had a new confidence about him that defied anyone challenging him. Had they done so, they would have found the weapon he concealed on his person. The real security was at the other entrances. They did not expect the direct approach through the front door.

The driving beat of dance music assaulted his senses when he entered. Lights flashed and a throng of partiers having a good time hindered his movements. So he made his way to the railing above the dance floor and circled around. His target was at a table beside the dance floor with several women. They laughed, drank and ate foods unavailable to anyone not filthy rich. There were more guards as expected.

Barney found his perfect spot and waited.

Clive Feinstein felt the effects of the drink. He had relaxed a bit since he heard about the attack on the hive. The ARL was weakened. He sent messages to the Bug queen looking for a deal. Clive would use Federal Army Forces troops to crush the resistance and the Waspoids would honor a neutral zone around certain populated areas. Then he was handed a gift.

He spotted that idiot Barney Berry on the balcony.

"You always were too cleaver for your own good, Berry you twit," he muttered.

The cost accountant wanted to talk but the president was not one to talk when action would suffice. The fool, Berry thought to deprive Clive of his Bug security escort by holding the meeting in a gangster establishment. Leaning back, he yelled a quiet word in the ear of his security chief. The trap was closing.

Barney descended the circular staircase to the bar. Clive was waiting for him with two drinks, on the house, and slid one over to him. The president sipped the other one.

Clive did not look up from his drink as he spoke, or rather he mocked, "So, planning to play the Liberator?"

"Still playing president?" Barney ignored the drink. He faced Clive while his eyes scanned the room.

Clive grinned over his glass but still refused to look at the other man. It was not that he was ashamed. He was playing a game he intended on winning, the game of politics.

"What happened to you, Clive?" asked Barney innocently. Naiveté was what Clive saw. "They just promoted you to Department Manager. The next step is VP? Maybe Preston's job? Why?"

Clive laughed. "Small peanuts compared to the potential here. I learned that power is as intoxicating as wine and as addictive as heroine. I want more. Just a little bit more."

And so he had. Clive loved ordering people around, making others do what he wanted. Oh, and the best part about power was how people were forced to grovel, beg and plead for him to throw them a crumb. For that was what was left over after the politicians raided the public coffers. Clive was smart enough to know that his life would not stand up to the scrutiny of voters in his world but somehow he had been handed this world where he was already president.

It did not bother him that the Bugs took away the occasional person for their own needs. He could govern a few million easier than a few hundred million. The insects would have to take a lot more people before it inconvenienced him.

"Why can't you accept what you have, become content with what success you've achieved at Baxter Life?" Barney asked.

As much as he despised Clive, he would not turn over his worst enemy to the Bugs. And that pretty much described Clive Feinstein.

"What can I say?" grinned Clive. "It's not like I'm going to change who I am. Eventually, I'll figure out how to stay here permanently."

A thought occurred to him.

"You wouldn't know anything about how we come and go, would you?"

But Barney ignored the question. He certainly was not ready to tell Clive that this world was his creation. Instead, he said, "If the Bugs take over completely, you might never be able to escape. They're not interested in stock options or big salaries. You could die here."

"They won't exterminate us," Clive replied. "They need humans for food."

Those he had sent to negotiate with the creepy insects returned to tell about how much the

Waspoids preferred humans over animals. The Bugs thought they were using Clive but he would beat them in their game of bug politics like he had beaten others. Then he would have it all. President? No, he was thinking, King Clive the First.

"How compassionate of you," said Barney sarcastically.

"Survival of the fittest, Barney, Old Boy. Then again, everyone has their price, even giant insects." Clive started to move away from the cost accountant. "I worked out a deal to solidify my position with them."

Barney fingered the glass but still did not drink from it. "A deal? Indeed."

His other hand slipped inside his clothing where the weapon was concealed.

People screamed as Waspoid warriors stormed into the bar. The unexpected intrusion caused patrons to scramble for safety. Clive edged even further from his victim.

"I've given them you," he stated. "They want to capture the Liberator. So, I offered them Barney Berry, Mister Liberator.

"Then, you believe I'm the Liberator?"

Clive backed totally out of the away as the Waspoids approach with their weapons at the ready. But the insect soldiers do not expect any difficulties. According to their briefing, the human patrons of the clubs were unarmed.

"Not a chance. You're nothing but a cost accountant and a glorified one at that. But, hey, I needed a sacrificial lamb." Clive was about to put more distance between himself and his victim as the Bugs closed in when another thought came to mind.

"Funny, you seem to fulfill that function here and at Baxter Life. Thanks for being there for me."

"You really deserve what's coming," Barney called after Clive.

A pistol appeared in Barney's hands. Two shots and two of the Bugs blew into pieces with red slime flying everywhere, including some of the club patrons. Then Barney rolled over the bar and behind it as the mirror, bottles and glasses shattered when the Waspoids opened fire with their beamed weapons. Crawling quickly for the other end of the bar, he was showered with shards of glass.

Barney came up firing, two more shots and another Bug exploded into slimy pieces. Fleeing patrons slipped and slid on the red goo covering the floor while Barney raced for the back door. A Bug was to block the exit but Barney was not the only one making for it. The warrior tried to aim in his direction. Too late, Barney got the first clear shot and a bullet tore off a shoulder. A second one finished the job and Barney was in the alley.

The streets of the old town had little traffic. Located on the edge of the Bug incursion, people had fled it for the capital and beyond. It resembled a place after a battle; some buildings still intact but most in various states of deterioration. It was quiet and the only noise was Barney's footsteps as he ran.

Then there was the distant hum he knew all too well, a hover craft. It swooped in and collided with several buildings sending debris everywhere but causing no damage to the hardened steel shell of the craft.

Barney fired a token shot at it, doing nothing to slow it down, then dove for cover. The flying vehicle sailed over him and he was up and running in the other direction. But the hover craft was back on his tail.

Standing in the center of the street, he assumed the ideal firing position and took careful aim. He emptied his weapon on the ship to no avail. It did not give him a chance to run again, a beam of yellow light thrust out at him. Barney was trapped in its grip. The world spun and the force of being carried up into the craft knocked him senseless.

His last thoughts were of Melissa. He hoped he was right for her sake. Then the blackness took him.

Barney regained consciousness in a small room strapped to a table. Near his head floated Waspoid workers. The door burst open and the Waspoid General entered flanked by two Bug soldiers. He had all of Preston's cool mannerisms. This was a cold and calculating creature, Barney thought.

The General winged over to him, "So, you are the Liberator? I have waited a long time to meet you."

"We've already met," said Barney.

The General's confusion amused him.

"It was…in another world," he explained to the insect warrior. "And you had another role. Though, not all that dissimilar to your job as the great Bug General."

The General's laugh sounded like a buzzing noise. At least, Barney took it for laughter. It occurred to him that he might be assuming anthropomorphic characteristics on these insect beings.

"Bug. I have always found that humorous," noted the General. "Humans, so predictable in your

271

attempts to insult those you war against. As though mere names will defeat your enemies.

"I have something else in mind," responded Barney.

The General buzzed in laughter again. "You appear in no position to make idle threats."

Barney leaned over, his voice a whisper. It was a secret for just the General, "I'm not dead yet. That's a victory, in itself. Anyway, I have a secret weapon."

"You are not dead because the Queen has willed it."

"Yeah, yeah. She wants my life-force to spawn a new generation, a more powerful generation." He made his voice more dramatic, "I shall die by her tongue." Then he pretended to laugh maniacally.

The General wisely felt the sting of the insult though he did not understand the sarcasm behind it. If it were in his power, he would have killed the human right there and then. But he was a soldier under orders and turned to his warriors. Barney listened to the high-pitched buzz the Bug commander assumed he could not understand. However, this was the human's terrifying world and Barney understood every buzzing word.

Then the General sneered a Waspoid sneer at Barney, "We shall…"

"Transport me to meet her immediately," Barney finished his sentence.

That did not please the Bug officer in the least. Either the human assumed he knew what orders the General had just issued or he actually understood them. More than ever the General wished he could kill this thing and have it done.

272

Instead, he was forced to put on a brave front for the pale creature, "Well, how would you humans put it? Tonight you dine in hell."

"Oh, there'll be a meal? Great." Barney smiled, "I'm starved."

The large hover craft passed through the opening in the walls and landed in the spaceport inside the Hive. The General flew out with his escort, two holding Barney between them, his feet just above the ground.

"Lord love a duck," Barney whispered.

The hive was so much larger than he had imagined. On the outside, it appeared to be a big skyscraper of a structure with a domed roof. But inside, it resembled a city, a very active city. The exterior walls were lined with assorted compartments to house the inhabitants. Worker and soldier Bugs fluttered everywhere in organized lines. Smaller hover crafts carrying cargo streamed about in their separate traffic patterns. There was symmetry to the activity, a choreographed dance. Light penetrated through the seemingly transparent ceiling.

The General saw him gazing about, the accidental tourist.

"We are orderly, each with his own task, each with his own purpose," buzzed the Waspoid officer with pride. "Not like the unfocused minds of a human."

Barney imagined Preston giving him a pep talk about the employee's responsibility to Baxter Life; live, work and die for the good of the company. He was as much a stranger in that hive as he was in this one.

Moving through an opening in the wall, Barney and his escort passed large rooms holding massive generators humming away. Barney noted their proximity to the exterior wall and the vibration they caused. Then they started down a ramped hallway. He started counting as they descended deeper. He made mental notes of each twist and turn of the tunnel, repeating to himself the route with each new change in direction or level.

It was a long way down and tedious work to remember. But that was Barney's gift, repetition of details until they were firmly in his mind.

They were twenty levels under the surface. Barney estimated it as a twenty to thirty minute sprint from the top. He recognized the level. No guards, though, this was a section where human slaves were not permitted and the Waspoids need not guard against themselves. He knew them by now, he had made so many dream visits to the hive, only once in this section, however. Anyway, he knew how they thought, robotic minds consumed with doing their tasks then going off to their nourishment and rest cycles. The General's short speech merely confirmed what he already knew. Each Waspoid knew his task and performed it. Order and function rule their lives.

They finally arrived at their destination and the General went through the door while Barney's captors held him outside. His feet were falling asleep, there was a slight tingle in them, and he feared he might fall if they released him.

The door opened and he was taken inside. The escort stopped just inside the door.

"Come," the Waspoid General ordered.

274

The soldier bugs dropped him but he managed to remain upright, a bit wobbly, but upright. With a show of courage, he casually strolled behind the General though the dim lighting. Two of the escort followed close at his back.

"Big room," he muttered.

The General and Barney emerged into a red light. The two soldiers stayed in the semi-darkness and Barney sensed that they were uneasy. They were warrior insects and fighting was their purpose. Being in the presence of the Queen had to be terrifying for them.

And there she was, the Queen rested on her nest above them and beneath the shower of a fire red light that bathed her. Workers all around her attended her needs. A large transparent pouch hung beside her with a feeding tube within reach of her mouth.

Barney cringed. He knew from the looks of it what was inside the bag.

Extending from a hole in the nest was a slide and the wall to which it connected was filled with cylinders.

The Queen saw his eyes taking it all in and laughed.

"Here is where I will birth the next generation, Liberator," she said with nothing but contempt in her voice.

Zelda Hampton in all her pompous arrogance, thought Barney, speaking down to him from her oversized desk of authority. She is the queen of all she surveyed and he was just a nothing, a nobody summoned to hear her pontificate.

"I am unimpressed," she continued, more than likely ignoring the disdain she saw in his face. But then, given her conceit, she might not have noticed. "This is the one I am to fear? He is but grub meat. Why should I fear this?"

Barney thought about answering her but the General replied instead before he had the chance.

"The Oracle has foreseen it. Her powers have never been in dispute." There was reverence in the General's tone.

"I dispute her visions!" spat the Queen. "This is my Hive. I found this world, built the Hive and populated it with my own hatchlings. She is one who would usurp my power through her vision, take control from her lowly station."

So much for order and function, thought Barney. Things in this hive were not exactly as orderly as they would seem.

"She is the Oracle not the Queen. She has never erred before…"

The Queen buzzed scornfully. "Nothing in the Universe is made perfect. Even you, General, are capable of mistakes."

Barney thought he saw the General's expression one of defiance for just a moment, "Perhaps the error is yours?"

"Be very careful, General," she warned. "You can be replaced. I could easily have no further need of your services."

The Waspoid warrior's insubordination was immediately gone. "I beg forgiveness, Majesty. My words were without merit."

276

With a little more courage than he really possessed, Barney said, "You know, if I'm in the way, here, I can come back another time."

This could still go seriously wrong, he thought. A bunch of things could go very wrong; including killing him on the spot for smarting off. The two soldiers reminded him of his predicament with a flutter of their wings. Involuntarily, he flinched and regretted the reaction.

"Do you know before whom you stand?" roared the Queen. "My power and authority are unquestioned."

"I know you," said Barney. "I know your type, oh Queen-of-the-Top-Floor."

He mockingly bowed.

"Do you see, General? Humans, you are such an undisciplined specie." Then she turned back to Barney, "Is it no wonder you have been so easily crushed? You allow choice. Many perform tasks for which they are unsuited. How pathetic!"

"And you think you have a better system?" asked Barney.

Well, she had not yet killed him. He just might live long enough to work his plan.

The Queen flapped her wings; their high-pitched whine irritated his hearing.

"I breed my young for the task they shall perform in life," she bragged. "Each lives to service my needs. My general, here, was bred as the ultimate warrior. He knows how to obey orders and when to die for my hive."

Barney could not help shooting a barb at the General, "how sweet."

277

With the exception of the flutter of her wings, the Queen Waspoid had not moved. She turned her head and a Bug worker brought the tube of the feeding pouch to her mouth.

The Queen continued speaking but Barney's attention was elsewhere, "The Hive is everything. A Waspoid lives to serve the greater good of the Hive. Without the Hive there is no purpose for their existence."

She was bigger, he thought. The last time he saw her in a dream she seemed trimmer. He knew that the Oracle could not fly. However, the Queen had been mobile. She did not look terribly mobile now. The eggs forming in her body made her vulnerable.

"Humans believe in freedom," said Barney. But he was just keeping the conversation going while he let his eyes wander.

"Really? Is that what you believe?" sneered the Bug Queen. Then she laughed in that irritating way Bugs had, all buzzing in that high-pitched fashion. "I like your little planet. Your specie shall serve my needs; become the source of subsidence for my hive. In time, I will breed you as a crop. Carefully controlled for your nutritional value. We shall grow in numbers and strength. I shall have the greatest hive in the universe."

That made Barney chuckle. It was the exact same speech Zelda gave him with the same haughty self-confidence his human boss exhibited.

"You find me humorous, human?"

Barney shrugged. He was getting pretty good at casual bravado. "I've heard this speech before from another queen," he said. "Grow larger, be bigger than the other hives. That queen will fall, too."

The Queen had run out of patience with him. "Take him to a cell," she ordered gruffly. "When my time is right, I shall birth my eggs. His life-force will be the seed of a great new generation."

Whew, Barney was relieved. It would have been tricky to jump under pressure but everything had worked out as he had hoped. He was not going to die right away and make Melissa angry with him.

"Boy, now I'll be looking forward to that," he said with a genuine smile.

The General hesitated. He spoke in the language of the Waspoids even though he suspected his prisoner could understand, "Majesty, is it wise to allow him to live? His kind will most certainly attempt to free him."

"I will tolerate no further questioning of my commands, General!" growled the Queen in her buzz-laced Waspoid voice. She was unaware of the human's skill with their language. "He is completely under my control. His specie neither possesses the force nor the technology to infiltrate my Hive. Carry out my orders."

Then she leaned forward, the most motion Barney had seen from her since they had entered her nesting area. He was actually concerned that she might roll off the nest and fall on him. But her menacing comments were aimed at the General, "See to it."

Realizing that he had pushed his queen too far, the General bowed submissively, "The word of the Queen is the law of the Hive."

His statement was intended for his soldiers. It would not do to have his warriors talk of their commander being at odds with the queen of the hive. He motioned for his warriors to pick the human up and they started for the distant door through the semi-darkness.

Barney called over his shoulder, "I will see you again, Your Queenness. Though, at our next encounter I shall not be so pleasant."

The Queen's high-pitched buzzing laughter followed them and caused Barney to cringe.

"I will use your blood to make a swarm more powerful than any my specie has ever known," retorted the Queen. "Think upon that while you wait my pleasure, Liberator." She laughed all the harder. "Think on that."

The camp of the Armed Resistance League was unusually quiet. Extra sentries were posted and everyone was on the alert.

Gerald was a spy for the ARL and the most dangerous of all the spies Shattner had because he appeared to collaborate with the Bugs and the federal government. Only the commander knew he was a spy and not a collaborator.

It protected Gerald as much as it put him at risk. Since Shattner alone knew he was a spy, there was a reduced chance that he would be betrayed and exposed. However, if he was ever captured by those loyal to the Resistance, he could face death as he had no means of proving that he was a spy.

The advantage was that Gerald had access to information no other human did.

The spy slipped into camp in disguise. He was waiting in the commander's tent when Shattner returned from the field kitchen.

"They have him," Gerald said simply. "He's still alive. Kept in a cell. The Queen has a special use for him."

Commander Shattner nodded. He would never question the authenticity of Gerald's intelligence or question the spy further. Gerald did not play games. He always spoke directly and gave everything he knew. Shattner left the tent. He knew that the spy would be gone before he returned and no one would suspect that he had even been there in the first place.

Melissa sat in front of her tent where she field stripped and cleaned a weapon, a focused robotic machine as Shattner approached. She could not stop her hands from working or her mind from thinking. It was the fourth weapon she had disassembled and reassembled. They were on cold field rations and her empty containers sat beside her.

She could not cease to be amazed that she knew how to perform maintenance on the weapons and that she had regained an appreciation for the food. What was even more astounding was how good she thought she looked in khakis.

In frustration, she had volunteered her platoon for a patrol in an area where the Bugs were very active. She really wanted to punish Barney for placing himself in danger by also putting herself in harm's way. As expected, they encountered a bug foraging party resulting in a firefight.

She loved every frightening moment of it.

How that was possible, she had no idea. One thing she thought she knew for certain was that, when and if Barney went back to their real world, she would go with him. And she knew that she would hate every moment of it.

The light of the campfire was partially blocked. Her commander was standing over her.

"The Bugs have him," he said simply. "They took him inside the Hive."

"He'll be back."

"Once a true believer, always a believer?" Surprisingly, there was not the usual cynicism in the commander's voice. He had no idea he was speaking to Melissa McDay and not Katelyn Sumner. Yet, she knew he was just as different as was she.

"To the end," she replied.

Shattner hesitated. He knew the entire camp was watching them or would know the two had talked before he arrived back at his tent. He wished he could say more. The relationship between his officer and the cost accountant had taken a strange turn which the commander did not understand. They had become like two people who knew every intimate detail of each other's lives. How that was possible in such a short period of time that they had known each other, he could not say. The lieutenant continued to work on her weapon though her eyes had lost their focus. She was worried, he thought. Nevertheless, he had no comfort to give her. So, he headed back to his tent and the loneliness of command.

In the Hive, Barney hit the floor of the cold cell and rolled.

"Ouch."

His Bug escorts had tossed him unceremoniously into the cell and he had a couple of floor burns.

The General floated into the doorway and gave Barney what passed for a sneer, "Such a shame we shall not meet in combat, Liberator. For I sense in you the power of a warrior."

Barney drug himself into a sitting position with his back against the wall. "I have yet to hear the fat lady sing."

The General laughed. "Even in defeat, you humans maintain your humor. It is a curiosity of mine, how you are made."

All right, Barney had reached that point where he was tired of the condescending attitude. "What do you know of us, Bug?" he snapped.

The General regarded the human for a moment. They were such weak creatures. He could not help but enjoy the nourishment the workers had learned to create from them. Nevertheless, if it were his decision to make, he would destroy all the humans on the planet. There was sufficient wildlife in the form of other creatures to provide them sustenance. The insect commander considered the continual existence of the human species as a danger to the Hive. It was the Queen who considered the energy value of humans superior to all those other creatures.

"I study those I will conquer," the General finally responded. "The Queen errs on one point. Humans are not so different from Waspoids. You have your hives. Yet you have no pleasure in their construction. Your hives once covered this planet.

283

Dreary places. Weakly built. They were the first to fall."

"I'm going to destroy your precious hive," said Barney.

This human's confidence momentarily caught the Waspoid general by surprise. His only real experiences with the creatures were either at a distance or on his computer through his studies of them. He never thought to soil himself by having personal contact with them. They were weak willed and shallow beings, easily dominated. They could be turned on their own simply hinting that they could save themselves from destruction by doing so. He sensed a difference in this one and it worried him.

"The Hive will stand forever, human," said the General, attempting to bolster his own confidence. "I am ready to die to make that so."

"Then prepare to die," responded Barney.

The General regarded the thing on the floor a minute, laughed then motioned for the guard to close the door. But then he flew several paces before he abruptly stopped to think. It did not make sense. It had all been too easy. He knew of the Queen's lack of faith in the Oracle but he believed in her powers to see into the future.

Meanwhile inside the cell, Barney sat in the corner with only the red beam from an observation hole in the door for light. His eyes closed and his mind focused. He smiled to himself as he remembered. That first night flooded back when he met Melissa at the party, sitting beside the plant while the party went on without them. He fell in love with her and he knew one thing for sure...

His head falls back as his breathing increased.

"I love you, Melissa," he whispered.

He laughed as the sensation he remembered from that night consumed him. "I love you, Melissa," Barney shouted.

Outside the heavy door and down the corridor, the Waspoid General heard the laughter, heard the human cry out. He understood neither. Rushing back, he ordered the guard to open the door again. He was afraid of what he would find inside. He stepped into the doorway. The empty cell greeted him, mocked him.

Chapter 18

Someone was entering the apartment. Barney glanced around the empty bedroom from where he sat in the corner, blinked and stood. He walked down the hallway to where three people stood who were not expecting him.

"Excuse me, who are you?"

Barney knew the woman. Lilly Cramer was a partner at the real estate office of Treble and Associates where Melissa worked. He met the abrasive woman a few times but he was insignificant to her which was why she did not recognize him. Lilly was everything Melissa had hoped to become; successful, wealthy, a socialite and well connected.

"The owner," he said simply.

It hardly seemed possible but, Lilly Cramer became colder toward Barney. "Melissa assured me that the apartment was vacant."

"You will find that is not exactly true," Barney sniped back.

How true it was. Melissa had taken everything but the furniture and art supplies in Barney's office. He could not stand the idea of living in the other rooms he had once shared with his wife so, he pulled an old sleeping bag from the closet, a remnant of his single days when he would go to the state park on overnight camping trips to escape the tedium of Baxter Life. Given the conditions of the ARL camp he had endured every time he jumped into the Waspoid world, sleeping on a padded carpeted floor was almost luxury.

"Where is my wife?"

"You will excuse me, Mr. McDay," Lilly said with her nose firmly in the air. "I have clients who want to view the apartment and do not have time for dealing with other people's marital problems."

Lilly led the couple into the kitchen.

Barney opened his mouth to correct her. He was not Mr. McDay but Mr. Berry. But instead, he clamped it closed and let the anger build. These were the type of people with whom Melissa wanted to associate? Self-absorbed snobs. Clutching his fist, he looked at the ceiling and screamed.

Lilly Cramer raced back into the empty room, furious at the low-class idiot her associate had married and ready to give him a piece of her mind. But the room was empty.

"Idiot," she muttered then returned to her clients. She expected a quick sale and nice commission. Business before all else.

Across town, Melissa woke in her bed. She was living with her parents until she sorted out her affairs. Her father offered her a large loan to pay for a condo on the south side where she could set up a new life as a single, successful woman. Late twenties, early thirties single women were so common these days that they were quickly becoming the norm not the exception. But that was before she came alive in the fantasy world she was convinced that Barney had created.

How she hated these trips back since the awakening. She heard her parents stirring on the lower level and wondered if she should go down. Glancing at the clock, she saw that it was early morning. They were having breakfast. Her mother would want to discuss Melissa's new life and make plans for Melissa. It seemed she had given the older woman a new lease on life. Her mother's new goal in life was to manage her daughter's single life.

The trouble was that Melissa McDay did not want a life as a single woman and she did not want her mother's vision of what that life would look like; even though a few days ago she did. Instead, she longed to have a weapon in her hand, on patrol and a canopy of trees overhead. Danger, she wanted the sense of danger and adventure that made Katelyn Sumner come alive.

Striping off her nightgown, she went into the bathroom and the therapy of the shower. But the warm water did not sooth her confused mind. She had treated Barney so poorly, stifled her husband's life. It was because of her that he had created the bizarre world of giant bugs.

She wept, her tears mixed with the water streaming down her face. She grabbed for her stomach.

Tina McDay, Melissa's mother knocked on the bedroom door then finally opened it when her daughter did not respond. The girl had been in the shower way too long and Tina was concerned that Melissa had fallen or otherwise harmed herself. Tina entered the bathroom, pulled back the shower curtain and turned off the water. Strange, Melissa was gone. She shook her head; the girl had completely lost it.

Well, once the girl came back, Tina planned to have a mother/daughter talk with her.

A blurred world away, the first thing Melissa did was check to be sure that she was completely clothed. Whew, she was. If she crawled out of her tent naked, Lieutenant Katelyn Sumner would not hear the last of it.

The camp was alive. Something was happening and the news swept from group to group.

Melissa hurried over to Commander Shattner's tent where all the officers had already gathered.

The rank and file soldiers also came together. This was the day the Liberator promised the hive would fall. About the time a murmur began to circulate about where he might be, the assembly parted and Barney strolled casually toward Shattner. The fighters were fearful and amazed. The Liberator had returned, they whispered. He had gone into the Hive and come out again. No one had ever done that before.

Melissa could not hold back her emotion and raced into his arms.

"You're back!" she whispered into his ear.

He kissed her on the cheek and that sent a ripple of approval through the ranks of the ARL.

"Told you," Barney replied softly.

Commander Shattner stepped away from his officers and toward the couple. Silence. Everyone strained to hear. Melissa released Barney so that he could face the commander. The two men stood face-to-face.

"So, you are the Liberator," Shattner said, his tone light, noncommittal.

Barney suppressed a smile. "You seem unimpressed, Commander."

The ARL commander shrugged, "The Hive still stands."

There was a long moment of quiet.

When Barney spoke, his voice was confident but even. "Then, let's go knock it down."

The assembly cheered.

In his presidential office, Clive Feinstein sat behind his presidential desk and smoked his expensive presidential cigar. He was really beginning to hate the jumps back to his life at Baxter Life. In the safe he had installed in his apartment were documents pointing fingers at Zelda Hampton and Preston Unitus for the crisis Clive had created in the process of earning his promotion.

He shook his head. Those two old fools had not questioned him as he manipulated his accounts to produce above average profits for his division. Clive easily outperformed the other managers with Zelda and Preston accepting his results because it improved the bottom line for Baxter Life. The two executives did not verify that Clive had played by the rule and not circumvented the safety protocols put in place to avoid illegal actions by employees of the insurance company.

Once the auditors discovered Clive's malfeasants and reported it to Zelda and Preston, they called Clive in to fire him only to find out that he had signed letters from them authorizing his actions. They were documents Clive had slipped into a pile of other documents they signed when they were too busy to read what they were signing.

Clive was using the papers to blackmail the executives for an office on the top floor. Zelda guaranteed him a position but he had grown tired of working, even though he had others like Barney Berry to do most of it. Being an executive in an insurance company was overrated.

Looking around the office of the president, Clive nodded contentedly. But being the president of a country, now that was easy living. Want something accomplished; appoint a special advisor to get it done.

He had to figure out how he was moving from world to world. He thought that Berry knew but the cost accountant was history, probably already dead in the hive so Clive had to come up with another plan for learning how to stay in this world. He had jumped back to his office in Baxter Life then back again.

Savoring the cigar, he considered what to do.

Bam, the door to the president's office shattered. In an instant, Waspoid warriors burst in and grabbed him.

Clive protested loudly. He had a deal with the Queen. These brain-dead creatures did not know what they were doing.

Nothing he said made any difference. The Bugs flew past the terrified staff, out of the presidential palace with him trapped between two of them and into a waiting hover craft. His attempts to reason with his insect captors fell on deaf...whatever passed for ears on the bugs.

They hauled him out of the presidential palace with petrified staff hiding from view and dead Federal Army soldiers lying dead everywhere. The front of the palace was littered with the remains of a small battle. The president was thrown into the waiting hover craft which was immediately airborne.

The bug craft landed inside the Hive and Clive was drug down winding corridors into the bowels of the dreadful place. The Waspoid soldiers unceremoniously tossed him onto the floor in front of the queen's nest. He was relieved. His worst fear was that they would send him to the labor gangs building the Hive. They needed him, he kept repeating in his mind.

Clive shaded his eyes from the red glow over the Queen which seemed to bounce off of her body and reflect across the room. The Waspoid Queen sat on her nest surrounded by her workers. She sucked from the tube of the large clear bag of human body parts floating in liquid hanging beside her. Wisely, he remained on his knees and waited. In his experience with executives, it was always best to let them start the conversation.

At last, the Queen spit the tube from her mouth and a worker had to rush to stop the flow but not before some of it spewed onto Clive. He had to fight back the impulse to vomit.

"The Liberator has escaped," the Queen said.

Ah, well Clive had no idea where Berry was or how he could have gotten away from his insect captors. He stood and wiped off some of the human liquid sludge.

"What does that have to do with me?" he demanded. "It's not my fault..."

But the Queen did not let him finish. "Silence," she bellowed. "Our agreement was that you would give him to me."

Clive studied the Queen for a moment. What he saw was not good. She had lost her air of arrogance and invincibility. The last thing he wanted was a weak ally, especially when he had created so many enemies and was counting on the protection of the Waspoids.

He shook his finger at the insect queen, "You're afraid of him. The Liberator scares you."

"Enough," she shouted back.

Wham, one of the guards behind him knocked Clive back down to his knees. Clive whimpered. He tried to convince himself that he was wrong.

"My time approaches and I require a strong life-force to nourish my hatchlings," continued the Queen.

"Of course," replied Clive. It was more a plea because he had the sick feeling that he knew where this was going.

"You could not give me the Liberator…"

"I tried," Clive responded quickly. "I gave him over to you, I really, really did."

"But that was not sufficient, was it?"

"It wasn't my fault!"

Two of the queen's workers swooped down, grabbed Clive by the arms and lifted him up to the Queen. He was inches from her face, the terror filled every part of him.

"You, of all the humans, must understand what is to come next."

The stinger shot from her mouth and into his. His screams were cut short as it drove into his chest and slowed his heart. Eventually, his body ceased twitching. Clive was completely paralyzed, conscious but unable to move or speak. The Bug workers carried his limp body to where it would better serve the hive.

Half a world away, far more comfortable, Barney held Melissa. They were snuggled up inside her sleeping bag.

"You're sure about this?" she asked.

"Very," he replied. "Contentment in this world sends me back to…our world."

"I had begun to think of this as our world."

"It isn't. It is merely my creation, my hiding place when I can no longer tolerate my own life." He saw the disappointment in her face. "But since I have found what I came for, it is time to leave it forever."

She hesitates to ask. "What did you find?"

"Love."

"Awe!" She pulls him closer, he kissed her neck and she felt his need for her growing.

"What happens," she teased, "if we don't finish before you go?"

"Maybe we should hurry just in case."

"No, please," she said with her hands exploring him. "Make it last."

Their passion built. They hungered after each other. She gasped as he brought her pleasure then she cried out…

The tent swirled around as though in a windstorm.

Barney took a deep staggered breath, the pleasure of their love still fresh in his mind. He signed and looked around, Baxter Life. He was near the kitchen so he got a coffee using one of the community mugs. It was just for appearance. As a practice, he never drank from any mug but his own. Then he strolled through the cubicles with the fresh smell of coffee while he tried to act natural. At

294

Jeffrey's cubicle, he glanced in, saw the younger man and drifted within the drab walls. Jeffrey looked up and scowled.

"Where have you been?" Jeffery demanded. "I've had to handle your calls all morning."

Barney shrugged nonchalantly, or what he hoped appeared nonchalant, "I'm dealing with an insect infestation. Anyway, you haven't seen Clive lately, have you?"

He sat down and sat his coffee mug on the desk.

Jeffery already had a snide response to whatever excuse Barney had to offer. Word had it that Barney Berry was on his way out as Clive Feinstein was expected to rise even further. Young Jeffery saw his opportunity to slip into Clive's new position. But he was caught off guard by Barney's flippant response and even more so by the question.

"Clive?" The younger man thought for a moment, "Can't say I have. Is he missing?"

"When was the last time you saw him?" Barney asked.

Jeffery glanced at the pile of reports on his desk that Clive had given him saying something about Barney was cleaning up a mess of his own making so he was unable to keep up with his regular jobs. He thought that he had no other choice but to tackle the extra work if he was to prove he deserved promotion. For the additional work alone Jeffery was mad at Barney. "What? Are you the hall monitor?" he snapped.

"What happened to Mister Positive?"

"Do you see this?" Jeffery motioned to those reports. "Your work. Clive dumped it on me. I'm tired of it. I mean, who died and suddenly made him God?"

"Maybe you'll get lucky and some big insects will swoop down and eat him," said Barney lightly.

Jeffrey laughed dryly then returned to his work in what Barney took as a snub and hint that he should leave. He gave Jeffery one final sympathetic smile and went out but left the coffee mug behind. By the time Jeffery noticed it when he bumped it with his elbow, Barney was in his cubicle.

Jeffery glared at the small spill, "Great, another Barney Berry mess I have to clean up."

Meanwhile, Barney settled into his swivel chair, signed onto his computer and checked his email. There were several from Zelda and Preston demanding an update on the solution to the crisis. He deleted them. Taking a piece of plain paper, he sketched different angles of the hive as he remembered it. It was a curse and a gift, a perfect memory for details. He marked a spot on the exterior wall with an X. On another paper, he wrote the route to the queen's nest.

While tapping the paper with the eraser end of the pencil, his other hand touched the file folder tucked away in his stack of trays. He opened it and flipped through the pages of handwritten notes. He liked to write out his thoughts before starting a project. It helped to focus his mind. The solution was there…the solutions were there.

His computer beeped, another message from Preston demanding a meeting for an update on the project.

Yes, he let the anger at those two arrogant people sitting up there in their throne room build.

They would construct their company on the shattered lives of the clients they were supposed to be serving. However, stopping them would be risky. His head was on the block. Oh, he had no illusions; Zelda would sacrifice him without a second thought. No, that was wrong. She was going to sacrifice him to save her own miserable career.

He slammed closed the file and tossed it back in the tray. They had only to read the file and they would know what he had planned to solve their wretched problem. But they would never think to look for a few scrawled notes. They expected to find a well-crafted report with diagrams and charts and a fancy program created in the system. And that was their mistake. He seethed.

Jeffery finally lost control of his restraint. The coffee mug mocked him. So he scooped it up and marched over to Barney's cubicle. He was going to ream Barney Berry a new one. However, he stopped dead in the opening. It was empty. He spun around looking for the missing cost accountant. "Barney, where are you...?"

"Here we go," said Barney from behind the commander.

The delegation arrived at the camp the following morning, all the president's men. ARL spies had brought the news earlier so Commander Shattner was aware and prepared. The commander waited with his officers and Barney. Apparently, Interior Secretary Tuttle was nominated as the spokesman.

"The president was called to meet with the Queen of the Waspoids," Tuttle began. He was nervous. All of the members of the cabinet were fearful. "He has not returned. We believe…"

They needed President Poisie to protect them from the Bugs. Without him, they had little power and could easily find themselves prisoners of the Hive.

One of the junior officers laughed and Shattner had to cast him a scolding glance, even though he was fighting the same response.

"What do you anticipate that we can do about it?" Commander Shattner asked.

It was a fair question. It was not like the Armed Resistance League had a working relationship with the Bugs.

"We need a working government," stammered Tuttle.

"Why?"

The question threw Tuttle and the rest of the cabinet members off guard.

Shattner continued, "What has this current government done but betrayed the people it was supposed to serve? You sold their futures to those insects to protect your own personal power and wealth. The planet is better off without your precious President Poisie and, I dare say, all of you."

"Um, well, we came here today to offer you the office of the president," Tuttle said.

The toads around him eagerly nodded.

For his part, Commander Shattner thought he could die today and that would be fine with him. Hearing these cretins cower so low as to plead for him to rescue them was more than he could have dreamed.

"There will be a special election, of course," added Tuttle when the commander did not respond. "You'll win, naturally since there will only be a token candidate. You know, to make it all official."

Tuttle and the herd of toads smiled. What followed was a period of uncomfortable silence.

Shattner maintained his calm and nodded.

"I will let you know my answer in a day or so," he said casually.

Tuttle was dumbfounded. "We need an immediate reply."

"I'm not prepared to give you one," said Shattner. "I'll contact the presidential palace when I make a decision."

The cabinet members were dismissed. But they were not anxious to go.

"If there is nothing else?" prompted the ARL commander.

With no other choice, the cabinet members started to leave when Tuttle abruptly rushed back to Shattner.

"The Federal Army Forces, we think they are planning a coup," Tuttle blurted out, close to tears.

Secretary Tuttle had a wife, children and a mistress. He supported two homes and a luxurious lifestyle by selling protection. It was a lucrative business.

Commander Shattner remained unmoved.

With a sigh and his head down in despair, Tuttle rejoined the other cabinet members and they hurried from the camp. They had preparations to make.

"Rats leaving a sinking ship," spat an officer. "I hope they drown."

"Captain, rats and cockroaches are the last to die," said Shattner contemptuously. "That group has a better chance of surviving than we do." Then he turned to Barney. "What do you know about our illustrious president?"

"Bug food," Barney said bluntly.

He wanted to care about Clive but just could not find the compassion.

"So what now?"

Barney produced a drawing similar to the one he made in his cubicle in that other world. It did not take him long to explain the plan. It was not all that complicated.

"Logistics will be the key," Barney summed up at the end.

The officers gathered around the table looked toward their commander. It was all in his hands now. As for him, Shattner knew that every one of them wanted to go with the plan. Not because it was a great plan but because it was the Liberator's plan. He could say no. But did he dare?

"Are you're sure about this?" he managed to ask with an even voice devoid of doubt.

"Where's your faith?" smiled Barney. It was settled. The two men were in agreement. "Assemble your people."

Shattner issued orders. Mentally he was calculating the odds, the force he would need and his estimation of casualties. The latter was not pleasant. He dismissed the officers to organize their units.

"The unit going in…?" Shattner looked from Barney to Lieutenant Sumner.

"My people," she said before Barney could speak. "I'll need a unit of demolition experts. The best we have but volunteers. There are no guarantees."

"You'll have them, Lieutenant."

Then he left them. He knew from experience when to retreat.

Melissa immediately raised a finger that she stuck directly into Barney's face. "Don't even think of leaving me behind."

"I jumped back to the office," said Barney softly. "Clive is AWOL. Seems he hasn't been seen for at least a whole day. He should have gone back with me, just like you did but I don't think we'll ever see him again. Death in this world is death in the real world."

"What's your point?" she demanded and there was fire in her eyes. "That we might die here? I've told you, I don't care. Better to die young for a great cause than to live forever in a bland life."

He loved that fire in her. This was the dangerous Melissa McDay he thought he saw that night they met at the party hidden behind a fern. He loved it and he loved her.

"I'm in," she said firmly.

"There's a limit to what I've seen through my dreams. It's all risk, no guarantees."

She kissed him, "If this is our fate, then we live or die together."

He swallowed hard and choked back the words he knew would be spoken in vain. He knew that look.

"I love you," he whispered.

"I know."

301

Had anyone paid any attention to the scene, it would have appeared strange. There they were, two people in love's embrace among soldiers preparing for war.

Chapter 19

A majority of the camp moved with the approach of darkness. They went in small groups to avoid the Bugs detecting a large-scale redeployment of troops. Two larger units were sent and attacked two separate harvesters as decoys to attract the Hive's attention.

However in the Hive, the Oracle jerked awake. Her flimsy wings fluttered uselessly.

One of her workers floated over. "Oracle, how may I serve you?"

"Serve me?"

The Oracle did not know whether to laugh or cry. She had witnessed the end of the Hive in her dream. For a moment, she considered summoning the General or sending a message to the Queen. The General would come but before she could issue the warning, it would be too late. The Queen was birthing and most likely would not receive the message. Even if she believed the Oracle, which she probably would not, it would again be too late to take action.

She cursed her gift. To know but have no power to act was a terrible state to be in. She could not help but admire the Liberator. He could act.

"We are dead," the Oracle said softly. "There is nothing the dead require."

The worker fluttered back to her station and waited in ignorance of what the Oracle meant.

With the darkness waning, Barney and Melissa watched from their concealed positions near the Hive as several squadrons of attack hover crafts flew overhead on their way to support the harvesters that were being assailed and possibly counterattack the ARL soldiers. The open doorway was the signal.

Whoosh, a rocket arched up from the tree line, sailed over their heads and dropped between the closing doors and exploded. It was a perfect shot. Barney's fire support unit had shoulder-fired missiles. They would be unable to make a dent in the thick wall of the Hive but that was not the point. Each entrance was protected by beam cannons. They would be a problem for assault troops running across the open ground and had to be taken out. The doors for the hover crafts were incapacitated, now the rocket teams concentrated on the gun ports. This was not the main entrance so there would be other attack ships flying from other openings.

The sun peaked over the morning horizon.

Barney stood and surveyed the ground they would have to cover to reach the Hive. He wore khaki green camouflage, a bush-style hat barely on his head and a pistol belt around his waist. The .45 felt natural in his hand. The knapsack straps pulled against his shoulders. Everyone in the attack unit had to carry his or her share of the load, even the Liberator.

Wham, an explosion threw up dirt, smoke and potential death around Barney. He flinched then reprimanded himself for showing weakness. His soldiers needed strength, his strength if the next hour was to be successful.

Quickly, he surveyed the battlefield. His mind was clear. He knew what had to be done. The end of the long road was near, in sight.

Boom, boom, incoming landed on his left and behind and showered the area with debris. This time

304

he didn't react. Unfortunately, one of the rounds found at least one member in his unit. He could hear his muffled cries. Putting the suffering soldier out of his mind, it was time to move. It was what a good commander did in battle, tune out suffering and focus on the mission. His concentration was on the Hive.

He scanned the terrain and checked his watch. Three, two, one...the earth shook in conjunction with the massive blast. He was so predictable, his enemy, the General. The Bug commander thought they knew Barney's mind, understood his tactics. Wrong again, Barney muttered.

At the front of the Hive, two large rockets flew into the main entrance. They were timed to explode sequentially, the first to weaken the door and the second to pierce it. Shattner had started his part of the operation. A third rocket was launched. It fell at the base of the shattered door and finished the job. The breach was a large one. The Waspoid General had seen this strategy before and knew it could succeed in allowing human fighters to penetrate the hive.

Barney could not see around the hive so he was only able to imagine that Shattner's soldiers now advancing.

The Bug General would think Barney's smaller assault was the decoy and Shattner's force was the main point of the attack. The orderly insect mind of the Waspoids would be his undoing, Barney hoped. No, he was the Liberator, he knew.

A few rounds fell on his position but they were tokens from the few remaining blaster cannons still operational around the side hover craft entrance.

The enemy fire had already shifted to the breach; the insect battery crews were on their own to repair their weapons and fend off the decoy units. Barney tried not to think about how many Shattner would lose, a sacrifice to maintain the illusion. His ability to win hinged on allowing such thoughts little consideration. Too many were counting on his clarity of thought to betray them with those things for which he had no control.

He raised his hand. "You know what has to be done," he called to those around him. Then he muttered to himself, "Today you live."

Melissa and the others stood and passed him as they charged on the hive.

A succession of beams tore up the earth and they were forced into a foxhole while a soldier with a shoulder-held rocket took aim. A beam took him out but a second fighter fired her weapon and the cannon went silent.

Barney looked over at Melissa, "Have I ever told you that I like your hair?"

They both scrambled from the hole together.

She reached the wall of the hive first. But Barney knew where they were going and jogged parallel to it with the platoon trailing after. He touched the cold surface then stopped. He felt the generators and motioned for the demolition fighters indicating exactly where to attach the charges.

"How do you know this is the spot?" asked Melissa over the noise of the battle.

"When the Bugs brought me in, I felt the distinct vibration of the generators as we passed them. That sensation faded as we descended."

306

Barney tapped the wall. "There's a generator behind this wall."

The charges set; everyone pressed up against the hive and protected their faces.

In the trees facing the main entrance, Shattner trained his binoculars on the edge of the hive where the Liberator should be at the wall. He could not see around the rounded surface but he did not need to. He was looking for just one thing.

There was a muffled explosion and a puff of smoke. That was from the shape charges blowing a hole in the wall of the hive.

Shattner returned to the breach his forces had blown in the door. His troops were fighting their way into it. He wondered how long they could hold their ground before the superior numbers of the Bugs forced them to retreat. For a moment, he considered joining the attack. However, the Liberator had forbid him. It was the only firm order the Liberator had given.

"There must be at least one of us who survives the attack," the Liberator had said.

Shattner understood the implications and stayed put.

Meanwhile on the other part of the hive, Melissa peered through the smoke into the hole created by the charges. Several soldiers pushed past her to check for the enemy and take up positions.

"You were right. We've tapped into one of their maintenance tunnels," she said to Barney.

On the other side of the hole was a large room closed off to the rest of the hive. Unless a generator was damaged and in need of repair, there was little chance that anyone but a stray a worker would enter the room.

"Say that again," he teased.

"What?"

"The part about me being right."

Shaking her head in mock disgust, she stepped into the hole.

An explosion overhead drew Barney's attention. In the sky, a large ship belched smoke and lost altitude. It tore up the ground when it crashed.

"The commander took out a big one," remarked a fighter on his way past Barney and into the hole.

Another hover craft sailed over them without stopping. Reinforcements headed to the front door to take on the attack.

Inside the hive, the General arrived in time to see humans fighting their way through the hole in the main ground entrance. The hover doors above it were disabled. The duty officer was dead, killed in the initial attack. His replacement had managed to blunt the advance of the humans and organized a counterattack that was just underway. The General was late because he had first started for the decoy attack on the side door but when the rockets were reported on the main entrances, he knew it had been a trick to draw his forces away. Fortunately, the insect commander was smarter than the humans and redirected all the support units immediately.

The General ordered everything they had into repelling at the breach. Then they would press an attack on those forces supporting the assault and follow them back to their camp. In his mind, he saw the perfect opportunity to destroy the human resistance army for good. He started calculating his enemy's strength and formulating his plan.

He shook his head and buzzed, "What are you doing, Liberator? This will accomplish nothing. Humans are so foolish."

What the General did not realize was that what he took as a blunted attack was planned. The human attackers were establishing defensive positions at the breach and not trying to penetrate further.

Around the hive at the hole, Barney, Melissa and her unit started down the corridor. A rear guard stayed back to secure the hole as best they could. For those descending into the bowels of the hive, it was their only way out again. But most did not expect to return.

Barney took the lead. Within minutes, they were in a maze of corridors where he had to rely on his memory to take the right twist and correct turn. His mind for detail took over.

For the most part, the tunnels were empty of warrior Bugs. They encountered a few Waspoid workers continuing their tasks and blew them away. The red slime splattered everywhere made running tricky as it clung to their boots.

Then they rounded a corner and Barney recognized it just before he was pushed aside by Melissa. A squad of soldier Bugs were guarding the door and a short firefight ensued. One of the human fighters was killed amid a shower of slime and insect body parts.

The explosive experts then planted charges around the door while the fighters took up defensive positions.

"We've won," Barney announced. "Whether or not we live a minute longer, these charges are more than enough to destroy the tunnel and the nest on the other side of this door."

The resistance soldiers nodded tensely.

Outside, Captain Vernon raced thought the trees until he found Commander Shattner. He had one major responsibility during the battle and only one. The commander had picked him specifically because he wanted someone who could obey orders under any circumstances. While the fighting raged on, the captain was carefully protected in a foxhole dug to assure the inhabitant's survival from any bombardment except a direct hit. He watched as the Liberator led Lieutenant Sumner and her unit to the wall of the hive, punched a hole in it then disappeared inside. He saw the rear guard take up positions then emerged from his protected hole in the ground and ran.

Vernon dove into the foxhole where Shattner observed the fight for the breach.

"They're in, Commander," he said then waited. The commander did not budge. "Shall we pull back, now?"

Shattner scanned the battlefield. Humans and Waspoids were engaged in a fierce fight over the rubble of the breach. Explosions shook the ground. Hover crafts were relentlessly attacking the reinforcements trying to support those holding onto the entrance.

"What's our status?" he yelled into his comlink.

"We're taking casualties but, holding," came the reply from the lieutenant commanding the defenses in the breach. The young woman was now the highest ranking officer still alive.

Through his binoculars, Commander Shattner saw several new units make it to the breach.

"We stay, Vernon. The longer we hold the Bugs, the longer the Liberator has to do his job," he said finally. Then into his comlink, "Hold the attack as long as you can."

He was so focused on the battle that he did not notice Vernon slip away. The captain's task finished, he was intent on joining the attack.

"Make it happen, Liberator. For the sake of the lives we'll lose today, make it happen," Shattner whispered, his binoculars trained on the breach.

Outside of the Queen's nest, Melissa shot away the door's control panel and it slid open. She and five of her fighters raced in before Barney could enter.

The chamber was soundproof so the Queen had no idea that a war was raging around her precious hive. Suddenly, a bunch of humans burst into her sacred room. They sprayed her workers with automatic fire. Red insect pieces and slime splattered the walls and covered the floor. While the workers instinctively back away from their queen, they did not attempt to escape. It was not in their nature to do so. Consequently, they made easy targets for the humans.

The red light bathing the Queen had softened since the last time that Barney had been in her presence. Through the haze, he saw Clive hanging weakly with a tube extending from his body to the queen bug as she sucked the life from him. The former manager of Baxter Life and president of the

Waspoid world was close to death and beyond caring.

Barney had his .45 trained on the Queen but she did not move. From the hole in the side of the nest, a glowing, almost florescent yellow egg tumbled out and slowly slipped down the slide. But no red torso worker waited to gently catch it and carry the insect larva over to the wall where other yellow glowing eggs rested in their places. Therefore, the egg fell onto the floor and cracked open. A yellowish slime oozed out.

The eyes of the Queen flared with anger and Barney stared back at her.

"Poor creepy Clive," Melissa remarked.

He switched his attention to the wretched man. "Sorry I can't fix your mess this time, Clive. Good news though, it will all be over for you in a few minutes."

But he could not keep his eyes from the fuming, furious ones belonging to the Queen.

Then Melissa realized that Barney and the Queen had locked eyes. "She's not moving."

Barney chuckled dryly, "Can't, it's her reproductive season. She's helpless. Apparently can't speak either."

"How do you know all of this?"

Barney broke contact with the Queen long enough to give Melissa his most ironic glance.

"Right," she acknowledged, "your dreams."

"Yep. I've been here before."

He returned to staring at the bug queen and she motioned for her soldiers to place the remaining charges. They would be set to explode at the same time as the charges previously put around the door.

Then she ordered the squad out. It was just her, Barney and the Queen.

Barney slowly approached the nest, his eyes glued on the Queen. Another egg slid down a tube on the side and joined the other one on the floor. He carefully positioned his explosive at the base and switched on the detonator. For a moment, he could not bring himself to leave. How many times had he seen this evil creature in his dreams? Watch her torture innocent and kill innocent people to build her hive, her power base?

"All the charges are now primed and ready," Melissa said softly. "We have 20 minutes."

"She's not so tough, now," he said unconsciously.

"What?"

It was as though he were in a trance. "She tried to own me. Tried to take away my life. I almost let her."

Then he sneered, "Zelda..."

Melissa nudged him. "The timers, Barney! Time is not on our side."

"She is a monster who consumes human lives to breed more monsters. Perhaps I owe her gratitude for giving me a second chance at life."

He looked over at Melissa and saw her tense smile.

"It will be a short one, 19.5 minutes..."

Looking at the woman he loved, Barney suddenly realized what she was telling him. "Right. Let's go. We need to hurry."

"Got that right," she replied as she pulled him toward the door.

Then the Queen managed a hideous screech of a sound.

Barney stopped and shook his fist at the Queen.

"You sucked the life from people and tried to eat me. Do you think I'm going to be terrified of your pitiful little noises?"

He aimed his weapon but instead of shooting her, he shot the food pouch hanging near her head. The liquid poured onto the floor. He looked back into the cold red eyes and laughed. Then he and Melissa were out the door.

Barney led the team in a sprint through the maze of tunnels. They blew away the occasional bug worker on the run. There was no time to stop for a firefight and, anyway, the workers were unarmed and had no defensive instincts.

"You sure this is the way out?" asked Melissa when he hesitated.

"As sure as I can be," he glanced around then chose a ramped corridor headed upward. "At least, if I'm wrong we'll never know. The blast will tear us to pieces."

They were off and running again.

"That's reassuring," mumbled Melissa.

In the breach, the lieutenant was hit by a beam and the remains of the defenders were feeling the pressure of another counterattack. The wounded officer considered her options; die gallantly but unable to achieve any meaningful advantage for the Liberator's unit the hive or withdraw and draw the Bugs into thinking they were winning the battle. Wisely, she ordered the retreat.

The General saw his plans working to perfection. The humans were in retreat and he was prepared to harass them all the way back to their camp where he intended on killing or capturing every last one of the creatures. Then the messenger arrived with news that the decoy attack had continued and the leader of the Waspoid army knew he had made a terrible mistake. Quickly, he flew away before the messenger finished and abandoned his command post.

At the breach, the warrior Waspoids charged through the shattered opening in the door, but were premature. The retreating humans had left behind explosives on timers that detonated as the bulk of the counterattack reached them. The attack stunted, the human fighters managed to reach the ARL defensive positions.

Deep within the Hive, the Queen sat on her nest. Two more yellow glowing eggs had rolled to their demise. Helplessly, she watched the explosives. She could see human characters in what was a countdown but she had no idea how to read human writing so when the timer reached zero, she was unprepared for the blast that killed her.

Several stories above, the General was directing his troops when he felt the ominous rumble. He could not know that he had seconds to live.

The fighters holding the hole heard their comrades coming and started running. Not far behind them ran Barney, Melissa and the other fighters.

Barney was not sure if they heard the explosives go off or just knew it was time. In any event, they all dove for the nearest cover just as the sound of the explosion shot from the hole along with a cloud of dark gas.

The ground shook. Several secondary blasts ensured. The gaseous air and confined spaces of the Hive's nest magnified the effect. The earth rocked then flames blew from every opening and the fortress hive was engulfed in smoke and fire.

"Everyone up," yelled Barney. "Run for it."

A unit of Bug soldiers was not far behind. Realizing his mistake far too late, the General gathered warriors on his way to the generator room where the last reports indicated the humans had somehow penetrated. The Bug officer thought he had the decoy unit caught out in the open and he personally led his warriors out of the hold in the wall.

Wham, wham, the rockets slammed into the bug counterattack.

Commander Shattner had changed the plan. Instead of retreating once the attack on the front door could no longer be maintained, he led a quickly assembled group on a covering maneuver for the Liberator's unit as it withdrew. They arrived in time to find Barney, Melissa and their fighters out in the open when the Bugs emerged. The commander's few remaining rockets and heavy small arms fire made quick work of the General and his counterattack. The Bug General died when the first missile blew him to pieces. The rest of his small force perished with him.

Once in the trees, Barney and his resistance fighters turned to look.

The loss of the General brought the counterattack to a halt. Confused without their leader, the bug soldiers did not know what to do. They swarmed around the hive without purpose.

316

Within the hive, many of the workers stopped receiving their instructions. With the death of the Queen, the chain of command for the workforce began to breakdown. Confusion flowed across the ranks of every aspect of the hive.

Shattner ordered his forces back into the trees. Smoke eased from holes in the massive structure, the giant insects buzzed around seemingly without purpose and there was almost an eerie quiet slowly falling over everything.

Melissa flew into Barney's arms. He had never felt such a monumental accomplishment.

"We did it!" she exclaimed.

They kissed.

"We did it," he repeated. Then he realized the implications. "Yeah, we did it," he repeated. "It's over."

Melissa's smile vanished. "This world," she said, "they don't need us anymore, do they?"

Arm-in-arm, Barney and Melissa turned to watch the hive in its death throes.

Wham, secondary explosions erupted from inside the hive as its well-ordered systems began to fail. They flinched.

Chapter 20

A door closed somewhere in the Baxter Life building on the 10th floor which jolted Barney from his thoughts as he watched the morning break through the window and sipped cold coffee. The previous night was a blur. Okay, he did not remember the previous night just knew that he had been in the building all night working. The tedious job did not seem as bad when he considered those he had liberated. And he had liberated more than just a bunch of people whom he did not know.

He was wearing khakis and boots. Most inappropriate attire for the office.

There was a reflection in the window. He did not turn around when Nikita approached from behind, a frown on her face.

"The Queen is all that matters. Without her, the collective is nothing," Nikita moaned softly.

Barney took a long drink of the cold coffee. Below, the world was waking. It was a beautiful world full of potential and possibilities. Without turning, he said, "You're wrong. The humans out there, they're the ones we should protect. I'm liberating them."

"I had a dream last night," Nikita spoke softly. She was reliving the horror of it. "I saw the hive tumble down. It imploded in on itself and there was nothing that I could do to prevent it."

Barney stood and faced her. Nikita recoiled from the expression of confidence she saw in the cost accountant. There should be a passive acceptance of what must be done for the sake of the…company but it was not there.

"I told her that you would not fail," she lamented.

Barney smiled. "I have to tell you, I don't think you have a knack for being an oracle or intuitionist. Perhaps you might consider a career change."

Then he walked away.

She looked at the world awakening beyond the windows of the Baxter Life Building for a long time then turned and quickly walked toward the elevators.

Nikita did not have an office. There was not a workspace that she called her own. So it was that when she step out onto the sidewalk any signs that the intuitionist had ever been in the offices of Baxter Life went with her. The morning commuters swallowed her up and she vanished among them.

At the same time, Barney dumped his cold coffee and refilled his mug with a fresh brew.

The elevator dinged to announce the first of the employees to arrive.

He strolled to his cubicle and examined the computer screen. His program was running smoothly. The email messages were flowing into inboxes of clients far and wide and the banks were receiving their instructions for electronic transfers.

He propped his feet on the desk and leaned back to savor the flavor of the coffee. He could not remember the last time was when he actually enjoyed the fact that Baxter Life could afford to hire the best coffee service company possible. Yum, a hint of chocolate greeted his taste buds.

Jeffery rounded the corner, saw his casual posture and fumed. In one breath, he spewed out, "Have you seen Clive? I decided last night that I've had enough. I'm going to make sure that you take back all this BS work that has been piled on me."

"Clive has been terminated," Barney said softly. Raising his mug with a smile, he added, "Have you ever tried the Hint of Chocolate feature on the coffee machine?"

"Ter...ter...ter...?"

"I believe that's the correct phraseology."

"You twit." Zelda's voice could be heard across the entire 10th floor as she stepped off of the executive elevator. "You sniveling little twit."

Poor already shaken Jeffery diplomatically slipped away to hide in his cubicle. Discretion was for him the better part of valor.

Zelda Hampton stormed across the room as the startled, confused and newly-arrived employees scrambled to move out of the way of her wrath. Preston Unitus trailed closely behind her. She marched directly to Barney's cubicle and waved a computer printout in his face.

"Is there something wrong?" Barney asked innocently. He took another sip of coffee and glowed with delight.

The office had lapsed into inactivity. There was an eerie quiet.

"You know full well there is, you little slime bag," Zelda screamed. "You authorized every claim to be paid in full." She waved the report and screamed, "In full!"

"Zelda, please," begged Preston. "Your voice is carrying."

"Just wait until I shoot him," she retorted angrily. Her face was so red that Barney thought she might blow a few blood vessels.

The vice-president tried a more tactical approach, "This is unacceptable, Barney. Your instructions were to protect the company's profitability."

"What can I tell you?" sighed Barney. "I had it all entered in the system. I made this nice little program to do all the work for me. Just could not press the enter key. Instead, I chose doing the right thing for the client over saving the hive."

"The hive…?" questioned Preston.

Zelda missed the reference and shouted back, "Well, you just go back to work and implement the plan we agreed on!"

"Sorry. No can do. Remember you gave me the power? Preston gave me the authority. I made the choice and acted on it."

"Unacceptable," screamed Zelda.

"Let's deal with this as reasonable men," said Preston. "We'll agree that it was an unfortunate course of action. The next step is to reverse everything and…"

"That's not going to work," replied Barney before the VP could finish. Preston was annoyed by it. The man was not in the habit of people interrupting him.

"And why not?" he asked curtly.

"Well," said Barney. "Call it a bit of a bomb. Boom, set the whole thing in motion last night. You can try to stop it, of course, but not without some very embarrassing questions. The electronic transfers started going out this morning."

Zelda shouted in the direction of Clive's office. "Clive Feinstein, get out here!?"

"Ah. Um, he's suffering from a nasty insect bite. I don't expect him back."

Now completely beside herself, Zelda shook her fist under Barney's nose. "Your career is dead. I'm going to make sure you never work again, ever."

Ding, in the quiet the elevator arrived with another batch of unsuspecting employees who would be disappointed to know what they missed. Among them was Melissa dressed in khakis with a backpack, her blonde hair trimmed short and sunglasses hid her eyes. She walked nonchalantly over to the cubicle and kissed Barney on the cheek. Zelda glared at her, unhappy with the interruption.

"Who are you?" Zelda demanded.

"Wife, girlfriend, lover and a whole lot more," she replied. "But you can call me Melissa Berry." Turning to Barney, she asked, "Ready?"

"You will find my resignation in your inbox," said Barney.

Reaching under his desk, he retrieved his own backpack, hat and sunglasses. He slung the pack over his shoulder, flipped on the hat and adjusted the sunglasses.

"Listen, Queenie," he said finally, "I suggest you work on your resume. You may need it when the quarterly profit statements come out. Boom."

Together, Barney and Melissa walked toward the elevator with every eye watching them. They pass the stunned, silent employees frozen where they stood.

"What do you think? Southern California? New Mexico?" Melissa asked.

Barney considered the question. "They say there are places in Alaska so remote you don't even have flush toilets or cell phone signals."

"Do you think they have big insects?"

Barney laughed as they entered the elevator, "Not to worry. I brought bug spray."

With everyone on the 10th floor watching, Barney and Melissa pivoted to face the opening. Helplessly Preston and Zelda watch in disbelief as the doors closed and Barney and Melissa disappeared.

For the very first time in the company's history since moving into the Baxter Life Building, the hive was silent, fearfully, horribly quiet.

THE END

THE END